Praise for *Her Heart's Desire*

"Gray skillfully sketches a sympathetic cast of characters who will endear themselves to readers."

Publishers Weekly

"Focused on the values of friendship and forgiveness, it is a lighthearted read that takes on real-world challenges such as loneliness, sacrificing dreams, and knowing one's worth."

Booklist

"This series is off to a great start! Five stars, hands down!"

Interviews & Reviews

"Shelley Shepard Gray's stories are always so refreshing, and *Her Heart's Desire* is no exception! The warm writing voice, the engaging characters, and two sweet romances will leave readers light of heart and smiling too."

Reading Is My Superpower

"What a fun story! While an enjoyable read, it also featured some valuable lessons concerning forgiveness, especially when it is difficult to do so after you've been hurt."

Write-Read-Life

Books by Shelley Shepard Gray

A SEASON IN PINECRAFT

Her Heart's Desire

Her Only Wish

Her Secret Hope

A SEASON IN PINECRAFT • 3

Her Secret Hope

SHELLEY SHEPARD GRAY

Revell

a division of Baker Publishing Group
Grand Rapids, Michigan

Published by Revell
a division of Baker Publishing Group
Grand Rapids, Michigan
RevellBooks.com

Printed in the United States of America

Library of Congress Cataloging-in-Publication Data
Names: Gray, Shelley Shepard, author.
Title: Her secret hope / Shelley Shepard Gray.
Description: Grand Rapids, Michigan : Revell, a division of Baker Publishing
    Group, [2023] | Series: A Season in Pinecraft ; 3
Identifiers: LCCN 2023010517 | ISBN 9780800741693 (paperback) | ISBN
    9780800745097 (casebound) | ISBN 9781493443529 (ebook)
Subjects: LCSH: Amish—Fiction. | LCGFT: Christian fiction. | Romance fiction. |
    Novels.
Classification: LCC PS3607.R3966 H47 2023 | DDC 813/.6—dc23/eng/20230310
LC record available at https://lccn.loc.gov/2023010517

Scripture quotations are from the Holy Bible, New Living Translation, copyright © 1996, 2004, 2015 by Tyndale House Foundation. Used by permission of Tyndale House Publishers, Inc., Carol Stream, Illinois 60188. All rights reserved.

The author is represented by The Seymour Agency.

This book is a work of fiction. Names, characters, places, and incidents are the product of the author's imagination or are used fictitiously. Any resemblance to actual events, locales, or persons, living or dead, is coincidental.

Baker Publishing Group publications use paper produced from sustainable forestry practices and post-consumer waste whenever possible.

23 24 25 26 27 28 29   7 6 5 4 3 2 1

Let us think of ways to motivate one another to acts of love and good works.

Hebrews 10:24

Never look down on someone unless you're helping them up.

Amish proverb

1

OCTOBER

PINECRAFT, FLORIDA

Even though Lilly Kurtz had stayed at the Marigold Inn before, she'd never realized that there was a small shed marked "office" nestled in between two blooming flower beds in the backyard. Oh, she'd noticed the cute little building before. Painted a light green with matching trim, it almost blended in with the grass and the many trees and shrubs that surrounded it. The window boxes were a lovely touch too and were currently filled with geraniums and pansies.

The structure looked friendly and welcoming. Honestly, the place was all so perfect, it looked like something out of a children's storybook. Her mother would've called it charming.

Lilly frowned and gave her head a stern little shake. This was not the time to think about her parents, the home she recently left, or her past. She needed to focus on the present.

She had an important interview to get through.

Which meant, of course, that she had to leave the main part of the inn, walk through the backyard, and knock on the door of that cute little building. It was only a few steps away, but she felt as if it was going to change everything about her life.

Lilly ran her sweaty palms down the skirt of her pale blue dress. She hoped she didn't get flustered and forget all the talking points she'd practiced.

What was she going to do if she messed up?

"Lilly, are you okay?" Esther asked.

Though she inwardly jumped, Lilly smiled at her friend. She'd first met Esther Hershberger two years ago. Esther, along with Mary Margaret and Betsy, had been planning to stay at the Marigold at the same time Lilly had taken a leap of faith and traveled to Pinecraft by herself. The Lord must have known that the four of them needed each other because they'd all become thick as thieves.

It was still something of a shock, especially since none of them had been all that popular in their respective hometowns.

Boy, she sure didn't want to go back home.

"Lilly?" Esther sounded worried now.

Turning to her friend, she pasted a smile on her face. "I'm sorry. Yes. I'm fine. Just overthinking a bit."

Esther's expression eased. "I know you're nervous, but try not to be. I'm rooting for you, and I feel like the Lord brought you here too."

"Thank you for that. I'm sure everything will happen the way it's meant to, right? All I can do is my best."

"There you go!"

Lilly smiled weakly as she turned back to stare at the building yet again. Everything Esther had said made a lot of sense . . . but honestly, how could she not be nervous? She needed this job. If Nancy White turned her down, Lilly was going to have to find not only a place to work but a place to live too.

She doubted that any other inn or hotel was going to allow her to live on the property.

Looking even more sympathetic, Esther said, "I came to tell you that Nancy is ready for you."

"Now?"

"I'm afraid so." She gestured to the little cottage. "Just go on out, take the path, and then walk right inside. There's no need to knock or anything. That's what everyone does."

Lilly ran her hands down the front of her dress yet again. "Danke. Do you have any advice on what to say?"

Esther chuckled, then seemed to realize Lilly was serious. "You know you have nothing to worry about, jah? Nancy is the nicest woman. Plus, you know her and she knows you! You even have experience cleaning hotel rooms. Everything will be fine."

But what if it wasn't? "Sometimes I don't do too well in interviews."

"She hired me and promoted me, and I didn't have near the experience you do." Esther reached for Lilly's hand and squeezed it gently. "Please don't worry so much."

"You're right. I better go on out there before Nancy starts to wonder where I am."

Esther opened the door and motioned her through. "I'll say a prayer, Lilly. You've got this!"

Lilly wasn't so sure about that, but it was time to at least appear confident. She shot Esther a smile before heading down the stone walkway toward the small building. When she got to the door, Lilly hesitated. What to do? Esther had told her to go on in.

Too nervous to rely on Esther's word, she knocked.

"Come in!"

Opening the door, she was treated to a view of the most darling space. It looked like a combination dollhouse and high-class, modern hotel. A plush, inviting sofa took center stage. Two embroidered pillows rested on top. One of them said "Marigold Inn" in gold block letters while the other said "Stay Awhile" in green cursive. A white Lucite coffee table rested in front of it. In the back of the room was a little desk, computer, and chair. All of it was arranged on a gleaming hardwood floor.

"Hi. I heard you were ready for me?"

"I sure am." Nancy strode forward. "Welcome back to Pine-craft, Lilly."

"Danke." She held out her hand.

"Don't be silly. Of course I'm going to hug you. We're friends now."

Lilly barely had time to agree before she was engulfed in the woman's cushy body. Nancy was likely in her fifties, at least six inches taller and likely sixty or seventy pounds heavier than herself. She was English, bright and cheerful and pretty. She also gave great hugs.

Lilly hadn't realized how much she'd needed a hug until she'd received it.

"Have a seat and tell me all about your trip down. Did you take the Pioneer Trails bus again?"

She shook her head and sat down. "Not this time. I had too much to bring down. My parents looked into the prices and determined that it would be less for me to purchase a train ticket than for me to take the bus and ship the rest of my belongings down." Of course, now that she'd just shared all of that, she second-guessed herself. Maybe she sounded presumptuous?

But Nancy didn't look put off by her words. She clasped her hands together like she was imagining taking the journey herself. "I've heard the train is great fun. Did you enjoy your journey south?"

Lilly nodded. "I did. I got a little roomette so I was able to get some sleep. And everyone on the train was very friendly. Some of the passengers were even Amish like me."

Looking wistful, Nancy sighed. "One day I want to hop on a train. I want to sit and read books and knit while someone else takes me places."

"I hope you'll be able to do that one day."

"Me too." Nancy snapped her fingers. "It just takes the right time and a little bit of determination, right?"

"Right." It took those things, and enough money to pay for the train ticket too. But she supposed that was obvious.

It had also taken a lot of prayer. It was a bit of a miracle that she'd made the move at all, because nothing about the preparations had been easy. It had been difficult to convince her parents that it was time for her to leave the nest. Her mother had been hurt, saying that Lilly was abandoning them, while her father had asked her dozens of questions.

Returning to the present, Lilly sat a little straighter. "I'm very happy that I made my decision to move to Pinecraft and thankful for the Lord's help."

"Indeed." After staring at her another moment, Nancy stood up. "I suppose we'd better get to the reason you're here." She picked up a floral file folder and placed it on the table in front of Lilly. "This is your employment contract. Read it over tonight. If you don't have any questions, sign and date it and then we'll get you on the schedule."

Realizing that Nancy wasn't about to ask her a dozen hard questions, Lilly stared at the folder. "That's it?"

Nancy sat back down. "I'm sorry, did you want to talk about

the job some more? I'm afraid the pay will still be the same that I quoted you when we talked on the phone. And the hours. Forty hours a week and two days off, usually not together. Breakfast is included."

"The terms are fine. I just expected you to have a lot of questions." Plus, there were all those talking points she'd been ready to share!

"Lilly, we already know each other. Plus, you mailed me the nicest references. When I called your former boss, Teresa, she couldn't sing your praises loud enough."

"Oh." A thousand things seemed to be racing through her head, but she was still too nervous to put any of it into words.

As Nancy stared at her intently, a line formed between her brows. "You poor thing. I'm sure you're exhausted. When you go in, ask Esther to take you to her old room. We tried to get it all set up for you. Unpack, rest, and go find yourself something to eat. I'm sure you'll feel better after all that."

Glad that she was going to be able to take some time for herself, she nodded. "What time should I start tomorrow?"

Nancy looked aghast. "Of course you're not going to start on Saturday! Take the weekend off and rest and see your friends. Enjoy Pinecraft! You may start at seven on Monday morning."

"Are you sure about me staying here without working? I don't—"

"I'm sure," Nancy interrupted in a firm tone. "I know you're going to want to see Mary Margaret and Betsy. And spend time with Esther and Michael too." She clasped her hands together. "Sometimes I can hardly believe all that has happened to you girls. Why, three of you are married already."

"You're right. There have been a great many changes. I'm really excited to see them."

"Of course you are. You're going to have a lovely time catching up." She walked to the door and opened it. "Go enjoy the day, Lilly. It's a good one."

Holding the folder in her hands, Lilly turned to Nancy. "Thank you again. I was so hoping I could work here."

"You're welcome. See you tomorrow at breakfast. We'll be having pancakes, so come hungry."

Walking back down the stone path, Lilly shook her head. Why had she gotten so nervous? Esther had been right. Everything was going to be just fine.

Maybe even better than fine.

2

Lilly took her time returning to the main building. Since the gardens were empty, she walked along the aggregate paths, admiring the way everything had been arranged. The vibrant flower beds had been designed in such a way that they were neatly arranged but just a little bit chaotic too. The overall effect was very pleasing to the eye.

In addition, there were two birdbaths and a modern-looking stone and metal fountain. The trickling water tempted one to sit on one of the bright blue benches scattered around and simply relax and listen.

Honestly, the longer she was out in the gardens, the more she was tempted to do just that. So much so that she sat down on a bench, kicked out her feet, and relaxed. At last.

"This is what you need to do more of, Lilly," she murmured to herself. "You need to take more time to enjoy your surroundings and just *be*."

Of course, the problem was that she had no experience doing that. By nature she liked to be busy, and she'd been brought up learning the value of a hard day's work. Not relaxing and enjoying fountains, chirping birds, or pretty flower beds.

Deciding she'd done enough daydreaming, Lilly stood up. As she headed toward the back doors, she was disappointed not to see Esther nearby but understood. Esther was probably cleaning. Just like she would be on Monday.

She had a job! Happiness and a true feeling of satisfaction bubbled inside her. All of her plans and hopes might work out after all. If that was the case, she would be so happy. Happy and shocked too.

"Excuse me? Miss?"

She turned to find an Amish woman in a black dress and white kapp hurrying toward her. Well, as much as one could hurry when using a cane. "Yes?"

"I was wondering if you could tell me where I could get a glass of water?"

"Of course." Noticing that the woman looked tired, she added, "Are you all right?"

"I think so. It's just been a long morning. My grandson has a lot more energy than these old bones."

"Let's take this path back inside." Lilly made sure to walk beside the woman just in case she lost her footing. It took a minute, but eventually they went through another set of French doors.

Listening for signs of a little boy, Lilly heard nothing but silence. Imagining a rambunctious child climbing on furniture in the dining room, she said, "Where is your grandson? Do you know? I mean, do you need him?"

"I don't need him, dear. He's in the bathroom. Besides, I'm just fine. I reckon he'll be out shortly."

Still worried about leaving a young boy on his own, she asked, "Would you like to wait for him or go to the dining room? That's where the beverage station is."

"I'd like to go there now." Seeing Lilly scan the empty hallway again, she added, "Don't worry about Eddie. He'll come along sooner or later. He always does."

Lilly still didn't think they should leave the child alone, but she wasn't an official employee yet and she didn't know this woman or her grandson. There was always a chance that he was more responsible and mature than Lilly was giving him credit for.

"In that case, let's walk into the dining room. You can sit down there."

"Danke. That sounds perfect."

As they slowly walked down the hallway, the woman's cane making a soft tap with every step, Lilly asked, "So, when did you two arrive?"

"Last night."

"I arrived recently, as well. Were you on the train or did you take the bus to Pinecraft?"

The lady grinned. "Guess what? We did neither of those things. We were at Disney World. We hired a driver to take us here last night."

"You went to Disney World?" Lilly was taken aback until she remembered that she knew more than a couple of Amish girls who'd gotten the chance to visit the famous theme park over the years. This woman was giving her grandson a vacation of a lifetime.

Lilly couldn't help but be a little bit jealous. She couldn't imagine a child being so blessed to have not only such a doting grandmother but one who wanted to enjoy things like Disney World. Hating the selfish bit of hurt that threatened to overtake her, she pushed it aside. "Was it wonderful-gut?"

"It surely was." Her smile widened. "It was everything I had hoped it would be. Eddie said he had a ball too."

"I canna imagine he wouldn't."

Walking into the dining room, Lilly gasped. "Oh, but this is lovely." The last time she'd been in the dining room, the colors had been muted shades of green. Together with the light brown woodwork, it had been relaxing and felt faintly tropical. Now the walls were painted a light violet and the curtains were dark purple with butter cream yellow accents. It was busy and bright. Happy looking.

The woman frowned at her. "I thought you knew your way around. Oh my stars! You're not an employee?"

"Not exactly." She smiled to show that there really were no hard feelings. "I've stayed here before, but I haven't been here in over a year. Nancy, the owner, has redecorated."

Eyeing the beautiful drapes, the lady said, "It doesn't look all that plain and simple, does it?"

Lilly grinned. "Not at all. But I like it. What about you?" She pulled out a chair for the woman to sit down.

"I like it too." She sat down with a sigh and rested her cane on the chair next to her. "Honestly, it makes me feel like I'm on vacation. I like that."

"Me too. Now, do you care for water, iced tea, or lemonade?"

"Water, please."

"Coming right up." She picked up a glass and filled it half full before setting it down in front of the woman. "Here you go."

"Thank you. Now, I'm just realizing that I never got your name."

"It's Lilly."

"Lilly, it's nice to meet you. I'm November."

The name was so unusual, she couldn't help but comment on it. "Did I understand you correctly? Did you say your name was November? Like the month?"

She chuckled. "It's actually Mary, but back when I was small, practically every other girl was named Mary. My mamm got tired of getting three girls every time she called for one. So, she asked me what I would like to be called instead. It happened to be my favorite month, November. So I said that."

"And she was fine with that?"

"Oh, jah. She said she knew of a woman named May and another named April, but she'd always thought that other months might be feeling left out. November it was."

"Your mother sounds like a wonderful woman."

"She was, at that. Though, to be fair, I have a feeling that she was thinking that my November name would get bothersome eventually and I'd want something else."

"I like November." It was memorable. Like this woman.

"Danke, dear. I like it too. Thank you for helping me. I appreciate it."

"It was no trouble."

A deep voice rang down the hallway. "Mommi, there you are! I've been looking all over for you."

They turned to find a man about her age heading their way. He had dark hair and bright blue eyes. The same eyes as November.

He was about as far from the little boy she'd been imagining as could possibly be.

November winced. "I'm sorry, child. I guess I should've told you where I was headed. I was thirsty." She held up her glass as evidence.

"There's nothing to apologize about. If you were thirsty, I'm glad you got something to drink. But you know I worry about you."

"I know you do, and I'm grateful for your care and concern.

18

But right at this moment, there's no need. I wanted something to drink so this very nice girl was kind enough to get it for me. Eddie, please meet Lilly. Lilly, this is my grandson."

"Hello, Eddie." Unable to help herself, Lilly chuckled. "November, you sure had me fooled. I thought your grandson was a little boy."

November smiled. "Well, he was little once."

"Mommi, don't start reminiscing with strangers."

"All I was going to do was tell the story about when you got lost at the mud sale. Why, remember—"

"Nope. We're not going there."

November sighed. "Fine."

Lilly grinned at his discomfort, though it was easy to see he wasn't all that upset with his grandmother.

She could see his point, though. This man was not anything approaching a little boy. He was tall and well-built and handsome. He was blessed with really broad shoulders too. And . . . she was now looking at him far too much.

He turned to Lilly. "Lilly, it's nice to meet you. Thank you for taking care of my grandmother."

His expression was so warm and caring. Even meeting his gaze made her feel as if she was receiving a hug. "It was my pleasure," she replied. "Your grandmother and I have been having a good conversation."

"It sounded that way. I caught the tail end of your chat." Smiling at his grandmother fondly, he said, "Mommi has a real good story about her name."

Intrigued, Lilly asked, "Does Eddie have a good story too?"

He chuckled. "Not especially."

"Edward was my son's best friend," November said. "Hank named Eddie here after him."

"Ah. It seems your name has a story after all," Lilly said.

"What about you?" Eddie asked. "Do you have a story behind Lilly?"

She shook her head. "No, I'm just Lilly." Her birth mother had named her, but she had no idea why she'd chosen the name.

November clucked her tongue. "I'm sure there's a reason you were named after a lovely flower. One day you'll have to ask your mother why she chose your name. Everything has a story, dear."

Since it would do no good to explain that she was likely never going to meet her birth mother, she smiled politely. "I think you're right. I will."

That wasn't exactly the truth, though. While November was right, that everything did have its own story, Lilly made sure not to think about her own story much.

She'd realized the hard way that dwelling on it wasn't a good thing. It wasn't a happy story.

3

Though it wasn't polite to stare, Eddie couldn't help but watch Lilly walk down the hall until she was out of sight. She was so pretty, and she had a kindness that seemed to emanate from her. It made him want to spend more time with her, just to be the recipient of that kindness.

He knew his grandmother thought the same thing. She wouldn't have asked Lilly for help if she hadn't.

He was so glad Lilly had been there for Mommi. He didn't think too many women her age would stop what they were doing in order to escort a stranger to the dining room to get a drink of water. Most were simply too consumed by their own lives to do something like that.

Even after he'd arrived and she'd known his grandmother was taken care of, Lilly had lingered. She acted as if she didn't have anything else to do besides chat with an old woman. Though he believed that his grandmother was a great person and fun to converse with, she was also a stranger to Lilly. There was no reason for the young woman to give her so much of her time.

But she had.

He wondered what her story was. Did she do things like

that all the time? Or had she stopped to chat because she had nothing else to do? If that was the case, why? And where was her man? Surely a woman like that was already snapped up.

He was so curious about her.

No, it was more than that. He hoped he'd get the opportunity to see her again.

"That girl was a looker, Eddie," Mommi blurted.

He turned to face her. Maybe he should be embarrassed that his grandmother had been watching him watch Lilly, but he wasn't. "You think so?"

Putting her glass down on the table, she raised her eyebrows. "For sure and for certain. Don't you?"

He absolutely did think she was attractive, but that wasn't what had fascinated him. That said, no way was he going to sound too interested. His grandmother would start matchmaking, and as his brother James and two sisters could attest, that could be a disaster. His grandmother's good intentions didn't always come into play in the best ways.

So, he took care to be honest but not too effusive in his praise. "I think she's very pretty."

"Hmm. Pretty is as pretty does. That Lilly sure seems something more than that. She's unique." Folding her arms over her chest, she harrumphed. "I reckon she's a fair sight prettier than Hanna, ain't so?"

Hanna. His former fiancée. Every time he thought of her, he got a bad taste in his mouth. Mommi might as well have poured dishwater over his good spirits. "I don't want to discuss Hanna."

"Eddie, lots of time has passed. Surely there's nothing wrong with bringing up your former fiancée in conversation. Just as there isn't anything wrong with speaking her name."

"You're right. There isn't. Except for the fact that I really, *really* don't want to talk about her." When his grandmother looked like she was about to argue, he cut her off. "Mommi, I mean it. I told you two years ago that I was done talking about Hanna. What's done is done. You need to respect my feelings."

Her lips pinched. "I respect the fact that you canna seem to get Hanna out of your system." Before he could fire back a response, she added, "You need to let her go, son."

Eddie could practically feel his blood pressure rise. He loved his grandmother dearly and would do most anything for her—except discuss Hanna Conway. "Mommi, please don't make me say anything more about this."

"All right. Fine. Let's talk about something else."

"Danke." He glanced at the clock on the wall. "It'll be five o'clock soon. Where would you like to go out for supper?" He thought of all their favorite spots to eat whenever they visited. "How about Yoder's? It'll be just like old times."

"Thank you, but I've decided to eat here."

Yet again, she was changing her mind. That was something his grandmother seemed to do an awful lot these days. Whether it was about grocery lists or travel plans or supper, Mommi thought nothing of changing her mind on a whim. Or expecting him to somehow make her new wants a reality. "They don't serve dinner here at the inn, Mommi. Don't you remember our conversation about that?"

"Good grief, Eddie. I haven't lost my marbles. Not yet."

"Are you sure about that?"

She disregarded his sarcastic comment with a wave of her hand. "Edward, what I'm trying to tell ya is that I already spoke to Nancy and explained to her about my condition. She's found someone who will help me order food from various restaurants

23

and have it delivered every evening." Looking pleased, she smiled like a Cheshire cat. "Isn't that wonderful news? This is a full-service inn, ain't so?"

"Jah. I mean . . . nee." He shook his head as if doing that could make him understand what she was saying.

"Nee?" Her tone turned more direct. "What is it that you don't understand?"

"How about none of it?"

"Honestly, Edward. Instead of worrying about me understanding things, you should maybe consider worrying about yourself a bit. I'm going to eat supper here. My meals are taken care of so you don't need to worry."

November Byler could be absolutely maddening! "What I'm trying to say is that these plans of yours are news to me."

"Obviously. I didn't tell you about them until now."

"Mommi, we're here to spend time together. I'm happy to make sure you get to all the restaurants easily." He waved a hand. "I can call for a car to take us. Or even push you in a wheelchair."

She rolled her eyes. "Like I'm going to want to parade around Pinecraft in a private car or wheelchair. What will my friends think if they hear about me doing such things? They'll say I've started putting on airs."

She was plucking his last nerve. It was no wonder his parents had looked so delighted when they dropped the two of them off in Berlin to catch the Pioneer Trails bus. "Mommi, you are being unreasonable."

"I could say the same about you." Softening her tone, she added, "Eddie, I want to spend time with you, but I don't want to be by your side 24/7. Now that we got to visit Disney World, I want to relax. I get tired and like to sit in the evenings."

"That's fine."

"No, it is not. You, sir, need to go out and do things. Meet new people." Her eyes sparkled. "Kick up your heels."

Oh, for heaven's sake. "I don't need to kick up anything."

"That's your opinion, not mine."

"Furthermore, I don't need to make new friends. I have plenty of friends back home."

"Your friends live on farms outside of Middlefield, Ohio. They aren't here."

"I realize that."

"If you do, then you must have remembered that you came to Pinecraft to see the beach and have some fun, remember?"

He'd actually come to Pinecraft to take his grandmother on a vacation.

But before he could point that out, she added, "And, just so you know that I know what I'm talking about, I know what you do all day. You, Eddie, spend the majority of your days working in a field, not around people."

"Plants don't grow themselves, Mommi."

"They also don't talk," she blurted. "Child, even a devoted farmer like you needs a break from the soil every now and then."

She'd played him. She'd already had this all figured before they'd gotten in last night. No doubt she'd mentally practiced her responses when they were sitting on the bus.

His grandmother was something else.

Trying a new tack, he said, "Listen, how about this? I'll find something and bring it back, then join you." He patted the table. "We could eat right here."

"Nee. We will not be dining together. I am going to eat supper by myself every evening in the comfort of my room."

"But . . ."

She yawned. "I'm tired of this conversation. I'm going to go relax in my room for a spell." Giving him a pointed look, she got to her feet and added, "That means I want to be by myself. Without you, Edward."

Taken aback and a little irritated with her efforts to push him to do things on his own, Eddie leaned against the wall and watched his grandmother toddle down the hall to her room. She had painful knees, a generous girth, and had recently finished a series of radiation treatments for cancer. Even so, an air of happiness and peace surrounded her.

She was a handful, for sure and for certain. But she was also a mighty good woman.

Love for her tugged at his heart. November Byler was the best person he'd ever met. She was everything he aspired to be, and he'd searched for many of her qualities when he was looking for a wife.

He'd thought he'd found them in Hanna, but he couldn't have been more wrong.

Feeling at a loss for what to do, Eddie pulled his sunglasses out of his pants pocket and decided to take a walk. Just as he reached the door, he almost ran into a man about his age coming in with a shopping bag in one hand. He moved to the side just in time.

"Ack! Sorry," the guy said.

"No harm done. I wasn't paying attention to who was on the other side of the door."

"Michael, here I am," a sweet voice called out.

The guy—Michael—paused and looked toward the stairs, and then his entire posture changed. He stood a little taller, seemed a little more alert. Honestly, it was like he'd been only half alive until the woman had called out to him.

"Esther. There you are."

Eddie turned to see a pretty blond hurrying toward Michael. He stepped out of the way. Michael set the bag on the ground and reached for her hands. Eddie was pretty sure that if they'd been alone, their reunion would've been far more demonstrative.

Another wave of sadness engulfed him. Not just because of his broken engagement but because it was scenes like this that made him realize that he and Hanna had never been so completely enamored of each other. He couldn't think of a single instance when she'd run to his side.

Or when he'd had to hold himself back from pulling Hanna into his arms. Boy, he wished he hadn't wasted so much time on her.

He sighed.

Which, unfortunately, seemed to capture Esther's attention.

Dropping her man's hands, she turned to him. "I'm sorry. Have we met?"

"No. I'm staying here. I, uh, just about ran into your guy when he walked through the door."

"Ah."

Feeling more embarrassed, Eddie added, "Sorry, I didn't mean to stare at you two. I was just wondering where to go for supper and I guess I zoned out."

Esther's eyes lit with humor. "You hear that, Michael? You're my guy."

"I'd prefer you call me your husband." Stepping toward Eddie, Michael held out a hand. "I'm Michael Hershberger."

"Eddie Byler. It's good to meet you." He smiled at Esther. "Both of you."

"Welcome to Pinecraft," Esther said.

"Danke."

"Where are you from?" Michael asked.

"Ohio."

"I'm from Ohio too," Esther said. "What part?"

"Middlefield."

"I'm from Trail. That's not too far."

"You're right. It's not." Not wanting to take up any more of the couple's time, he shoved his hands in his pockets. "Well, I hope you two have a good evening."

Esther stepped forward. "Wait, are you staying on your own?"

"I'm here with my grandmother. But she wanted to eat supper in her room. Someone is going to deliver it."

"I think that was me." Picking up a large, insulated bag, Michael added, "I'm an assistant manager at the Boardwalk. Nancy asked me to bring this by for a lady staying here."

"I'd pay you, but my independent-minded grandmother would be insulted. She's currently very pleased to be handling everything on her own."

Michael grinned. "I'd say she's doing a gut job of it, since everything's already been paid for." Softening his voice, he said, "Esther, I'm going to give this to Nancy and I'll be right back."

"I'll wait for you here." Esther turned to Eddie. "We were just about to go out for pizza. Would you like to join us?"

He would, if only so he wouldn't have his thoughts and regrets for company. But good manners forced him to be more circumspect. "Danke, but I wouldn't want to impose."

"You wouldn't be. It's nearby. We each order a couple of slices and sit outside at the tables. It's nothing fancy."

"The pizza's delicious, though," Michael added.

Thinking again of his grandmother's words and how he wasn't eager to dine alone, Eddie made a decision. "If you're sure you wouldn't mind, I'd like to take you up on that."

"You're going to be glad you did," Michael said. "Give me a moment to deliver this meal to Nancy. Then we can go."

As he walked off, Eddie said, "I guess I should have offered to take it to my grandmother myself."

"Is your grandmother staying in room 1?"

"Yes."

Esther smiled. "Nancy told me that she was going to be bringing in a television and a set of DVDs for the guest there."

"My grandmother's going to watch TV?" He was shocked.

Esther pressed a finger to her lips. "Shh! I heard that we're supposed to keep that a secret. Rumor has it that the woman in room 1 has a grandson who's kind of a stickler for rules."

That would be him. Realizing that he had sounded rather outraged, which was ridiculous, he said, "I'm not a stickler. I mean, not exactly. It's just . . ."

"That she's older and Amish?"

"Yes."

Esther's eyes danced. "You're soon going to learn people do things a little differently in Pinecraft."

"Like watch movies in their rooms?"

"Yes." She winked. "I used to think it was only young people at the end of their rumspringa who enjoyed a little bit of extra freedom. Now that I live here, I realize that everyone enjoys a small break from their daily lives. After all, who can blame them? We're all only human."

Esther made some good points, though he wasn't sure he agreed with everything she said 100 percent. "I had no idea."

Her lips twitched. "Eddie Byler, forgive me, but I'm starting

29

to understand why your grandmother is sneaking around. You are easily shocked."

He opened his mouth to protest, then closed it again. Esther might have a point. He was acting like his grandmother watching a movie while on vacation was scandalous.

He decided right then and there to try to relax. He was starting to think that if he didn't at least try to have some fun, he was going to be the only person in the town who wasn't. Not only would that be a real shame but he was pretty sure it was going to be a lonely existence too.

4

Looking around at Mary Margaret's house, with toys stacked in the corners, unfinished sewing projects tossed in wicker baskets, and more than one surface in need of a good dusting, Lilly decided the surroundings were exactly what she'd been needing. Nothing was perfect or pristine. And it was clear she wasn't expected to be that way, either. Though Nancy hadn't made her feel that way during the interview, Lilly knew that she'd put those expectations on herself.

Adding to her sense of comfort was the happy laughter drifting through the screened windows. Mary Margaret's toddler, Tricia, was playing outside with her daddy. Mary's husband, Jayson, was obviously having as much fun playing the game as Tricia. It was some kind of hide-and-seek game, mainly consisting of Tricia covering her head with her arms and then saying boo and Jayson pretending to act surprised. It was silly and adorable. For some reason, watching the two play was the last element she'd needed in order to finally feel at peace.

Curled up on the chair across from her, Mary was sipping peppermint tea and half-heartedly working on a prayer shawl for church. "You've been kind of quiet this afternoon. Is everything all right?"

"It's better than that. Everything is great." Stretching her arms out in front of her, Lilly added, "It's taken a while, but I think I've relaxed at last. Coming here was exactly what I needed to be at ease."

Mary frowned. "I'm surprised to hear you say that. This haus is a mess. Jayson always tells me not to clean every minute that Tricia is napping, but I probably should be doing more than I do." Running a finger along a table, she frowned at the dust. "I'd be so embarrassed if my mother saw the state of everything."

"I have a feeling your mother would only care about Tricia if she was here."

"I suppose so . . ."

"Mary. Seriously. I'm glad you didn't clean up for me. I'm not a guest, remember? I'm a friend. I'd be upset if you ran around cleaning before I came over."

The worry that had appeared in Mary's eyes eased. "I appreciate that. With Tricia being so busy now and another on the way, I'm afraid putting everything neatly away is the last thing on my list."

"I still can't believe you didn't write to tell me your news. I couldn't believe it when you came to the door."

Mary chuckled. "I would've written you if you hadn't been about to move here. Some things are better shared in person, don't you think?"

"Absolutely. Now, let's stop talking about the state of your house. I don't think it looks as bad as you think it does. Besides, I told you that I would be happy to help you clean from time to time."

"You're going to be working as a maid at the Marigold.

There's no way I'm going to ask you to clean a single thing on your time off."

"I wouldn't mind. I'm good at cleaning. Besides, you worry too much about me working. I'll be fine."

"Maybe."

"I know I will. Esther has been doing just fine at the Marigold."

"She only works thirty hours a week. Not a full forty."

Esther was also married to the handsome Michael, who doted on her like she was the sun and the moon in one perfect package. Lilly had a feeling that he would voluntarily work extra hours if Esther didn't want to work even that much. Esther did, however. They were saving for the down payment on a house. Every time Esther talked about their plans, her voice sounded so dreamy and cute.

Lilly's circumstances, on the other hand, were far different. She'd moved without much of a support system and now she was on her own. "I need the money. Having a job is a blessing."

After Mary studied her a moment, the line in between her brows eased. "You always put a positive spin on things."

"I don't. But in this instance, there's nothing to put a spin on. I'm finally here in Pinecraft with you and Betsy!" When the three of them had bonded after being forced to sleep in a rundown motel room during an ice storm in Georgia, Lilly's life had changed for the better. By the time she'd fallen asleep that night, she'd instinctively known that she had two best friends. One of the things they'd done during that first trip was promise each other that they'd find a way to stay in touch. They'd done one better—now the three of them lived in the same town! Esther's appearance was an added bonus.

"When I saw Betsy last week, she was giddy with excitement,"

Mary said. "Of course she wants to throw you a welcome to Pinecraft party."

"Which I already told her I did not want."

"Did she listen?"

"I doubt it." Betsy was . . . Betsy. She was impulsive and busy and constantly making plans. She was practically the opposite of Lilly, who always had to overthink every decision.

Mary chuckled. "I wish she could've come over tonight."

"They had plans with August's aunt and uncle. She offered to see if just August could go, but I asked her not to do that. I'm going to be here for a while."

"For a while or permanently?"

"I'm not sure." She knew that she wanted to live here permanently, but she also knew that dreams and wishes didn't always come true.

"Really? What's your plan?"

"First, live at the Marigold and work. Then, in a year I'll rent an apartment and eventually one day maybe find a house to live in."

"Not a bit of that involves falling in love and getting married."

Lilly knew that. But if she hadn't fallen in love yet, she was pretty sure that it wasn't going to happen. She was slowly coming to accept that too. The Lord must have a plan for her to do something besides getting married and having children. "You sound like my sister. She's sure that I'll be happiest when I'm married and settled. She tried to bet me a dollar that I'd be back home in three months."

Mary raised her eyebrows. "I want you to be happy but not move away. Why does your sister think you'll return? Does she really think you won't be able to handle things on your own here in Florida?"

34

Lilly shrugged. "I don't know."

"Come on. Talk to me."

"Mary, we are talking."

"You know what I mean. Don't be flip." When their eyes met, she knew that Mary Margaret was about to press her for more information. Mary loved to organize and "fix" things.

But that didn't mean Lilly had to always follow her lead.

"Mary, I love you, but I don't want to talk about my family right now. I don't like to talk about home."

"Were things really that bad after you returned from Betsy's wedding?"

"Nee." That was true too. Things were never "bad" at home. They just weren't very comfortable.

"Please talk to me." There was a plaintive sound in Mary's voice now. She was worried, and Lilly keeping her feelings secret wasn't making either of them feel better.

"There's not that much to say, Mary. My parents are lovely people and I love them. Katie and John were annoying, but they were good siblings." When Mary continued to stare at her, Lilly allowed herself to share a little bit more. "But, it wasn't exactly an easy life," she explained. "I was adopted when I was two."

"I know that. It was a blessing, yes?"

"It absolutely was." During her rumspringa, against her parents' wishes, she'd visited the children's home where she'd lived the first two years of her life. She hadn't been looking for answers, exactly, just more of an understanding about her birth mother's circumstances.

Before she'd met with the administrator and the woman who'd been assigned her case—and who was miraculously still working there—she'd received a lot of information she hadn't even realized she'd needed.

Instead of having a pair of uninterested English parents like she'd always imagined, she'd learned that her birth father was in prison and her mother had given birth to her as a teenager and hadn't been in the best of health. She'd had some kind of kidney disease and was going to need dialysis and maybe even a kidney transplant one day. Because of that, the young woman had given Lilly up for adoption. She and her parents and even the birth father had feared that keeping this unexpected baby was simply too much of a burden when her future was already uncertain.

The social worker had no idea what happened to her birth mother. After much prayer, Lilly had realized that she didn't need to know. Yes, she'd been given up, but it wasn't exactly for selfish and terrible reasons. Her birth parents and their extended families had thought it was for the best.

Lilly couldn't blame them for that.

Besides, her adoptive parents had been just fine. It felt selfish to wish that they would've forgotten the origins of her birth and thought of her as simply their child.

She bit her lip, hating to seem ungrateful. But there was a slim part of her that was tired of always being grateful.

She wished there was something in between.

"Mary, I've always known that I was adopted."

"There's nothing wrong with that, is there?"

"Nee. But that knowledge created a bit of a barrier for me." Momentarily forgetting that her girlfriend was avidly listening, Lilly pushed herself to analyze her feelings once again.

She sipped her tea as memories and her actions swirled in her head. "Sometimes I wonder, though, if not every wall was built by other people. Maybe I erected them myself."

"I was teased for years about something stupid I did as a child. You can't foist all the blame on yourself."

Well aware of Mary's past of being bullied, Lilly nodded. She didn't want to disagree with her friend, but in this case, she didn't think that her friend's assessment was exactly true, either. "I'm not, but I think it's time I took some responsibility."

"Lilly . . ."

"No, I mean it. Maybe all this time I've been carrying around a bit of a chip on my shoulder. Or, at the very least, made those walls so impenetrable that it was nearly impossible for anyone to ever be strong enough or tall enough to break or scale them." Frustrated with her words, she waved a hand. "I don't know. All I do know is that I always believed that the wall was there and that I was different than my siblings."

"I wish you wouldn't put all the blame on yourself."

"I'm not. I'm only trying to explain that I always felt a little bit different from my parents and my brother and sister. Even my looks were different. My hair is almost blond, and my eyes are light blue. Everyone else in the family has dark brown hair and matching eyes. Even our skin tones are a little different. My sister could be out in the garden all day and end up with only a tan. I would freckle and burn."

Mary Margaret frowned. "You're acting as if you aren't pretty. You are. You're lovely, Lilly."

"I'm not trying to get a compliment. I . . ." She swallowed. "Let's talk about something else, okay? All this dwelling on myself is becoming boring."

"Nee. It is not. And listen, please. I'm not just saying something to make you feel better. There is nothing wrong with your figure or your looks."

This sure wasn't going the way she'd planned. "Listen, I'm not saying the Lord didn't do fine by me. I just mean . . . everyone always knew I was adopted. Sometimes when my parents met someone new, they would introduce us as Katie and John and then Lilly, their adopted daughter. I always had that title."

"That's not very nice."

The comment, spoken so vehemently, made Lilly giggle. "You're right. It wasn't very nice at all." She shrugged. "It wasn't a Cinderella situation or anything. Katie and John had chores too. It's just that . . . I don't know . . . I always felt that I was supposed to be grateful. And I am." She lowered her voice. "But every once in a while, I wanted to shout to everyone that being given up for adoption wasn't my fault. Why do I have to continually be thankful and good because of something my birth parents did? I was just a baby."

"I agree. And I can see your point of view. It's not wrong for you to feel that way."

"Do you really think so? Every time I voice my thoughts, I think they sound ungrateful."

"I think it makes you sound human. You don't need to be perfect in order to be grateful."

Mary's words sounded so earnest, Lilly felt the tension inside her ease. "Thanks for saying that."

"I'm only speaking the truth," Mary replied. Looking thoughtful, she added, "Well, the truth as I see it, anyway."

"It's appreciated."

"So, moving on, Katie thought you'd probably be back home soon. What did your parents say when you told them you were going to move?"

"They acted confused, but they didn't forbid me to go." Realizing how uncaring she made them sound, she added, "They wished me well." Well, they kind of did.

"Did they give you some money to help pay for the trip?"

She knew both Betsy's and Mary Margaret's families had helped them get settled. Though both women had earned most of the money to pay for the bus fares, their families had helped finance other things.

It was only because she valued their friendship so much that she didn't scoff at Mary's question. "Did they volunteer to help finance my moving away from them, maybe even moving across the country for good? Nee, they did not. They might not be perfect, but they do love me, and they were hurt."

"You wanting to move wasn't about them, though."

"I agree, but that doesn't mean it doesn't hurt. It's all right. I'm fine and I'm here right now."

"This is true." Mary's expression lit up. "Now all we have to do is find you a husband."

"Like your Jayson?"

"Nee. Jayson is amazing and unique. We want a man who is perfect for you."

"I don't know about that."

"Come on, Lilly. You need to be more positive. After all, I found Jayson almost immediately."

"I realize that. But don't you remember the discussion that the three of us had in that hotel room in Georgia?"

"Of course I do."

"Then you'll remember that the three of us vowed to be friends."

"And we've done that."

"We have," Lilly continued. "But we also said that we didn't need men to make our lives complete."

"That is true, but I can't help but think that my life is pretty wonderful with Jayson in it. His love makes me happy, Lilly. And now that we've started our family, everything feels even better."

"I understand. I just don't think that future is for me."

"It could be, though," her friend countered. "All you have to do is open your heart and mind to the possibility. God will take care of the rest."

"We'll see." Lilly didn't think that was going to happen. She didn't think it had anything to do with God, either. No, the problem was all her. She overthought things and second-guessed herself far too much. Neither of those qualities made it easy to jump into a relationship. Plus, what were the chances of all three of them falling in love and settling down in Pinecraft? Slim to none!

Mary Margaret reached for her hand. "Lilly, you're right. We're focusing on all the wrong things. We should be spending our time giving thanks and making plans to get together again soon."

"Thank you. I put enough pressure on myself. I really don't want to start dwelling on the things that I don't have."

"You're right. Exactly right. I think we should make plans to do something fun and interesting soon."

"Just for the record, I do not have a life list like Betsy. I do *not* want to take up golf."

"I completely agree. But we could do something else fun. Maybe not just go to the beach but to the community pool too. Do you like to swim?"

"Sorry again. The last time I went to the pool with Betsy and you, I could barely walk the next day. You two swam so many laps, I could hardly keep up."

"How about if I make Betsy promise that we'll just relax? We could just enjoy being together." She drummed her fingers on her chair's armrest. "Hmm. Or maybe we could take the SCAT to different places and explore."

"I would enjoy that."

"I would too. And it would allow me to bring Tricia sometimes too."

"You have to bring that little sweetheart. I want to get to know her."

"So, will you try to relax a bit more and worry about the future a bit less?"

As much as she felt overwhelmed, Lilly was also struck by how incredibly blessed she was to have such good friends. "I will, but let's not make firm plans just yet, okay? I need to get through this first week of work. One step at a time, right?"

"Right." Standing up, Mary said, "Now, let's go have some pie before Jayson eats it all and Tricia gets cranky." Suddenly looking worried, she asked, "You do still eat pie, right?"

"Now that's a silly question. I might be attempting to reinvent myself but that has nothing to do with pie."

"Thank heavens for that. For a moment there, I thought you really had changed."

"Never that much," she joked. Glad for the break, she stood up. "I'll carry the cups, you lead the way, Mary."

She had a feeling their laughter could be heard down the street.

5

By the time she'd worked four full days, Lilly decided that cleaning rooms at the Marigold Inn was a whole different experience than cleaning the modest motel rooms back home. Different in many good ways.

First of all, Nancy employed a whole assortment of people who seemed to work only twenty to thirty hours a week. That meant everyone breezed in, chatted happily, did their work, and then promised to return in a day or two. Or three. Some of the girls almost acted as if the job was part of their social calendar. Oh, they worked hard, but they also caught up on each other's lives, offered advice, joked around . . . and had the most amazing coffee breaks Lilly had ever seen. Every day seemed to bring an entirely new assortment of fruit, cookies, pies, and tiny sandwiches too. People brought in treats, and whatever they didn't bring in, Phillip, the inn's cook, made. He always seemed to make more than was needed and had out a plate or two on the island in the kitchen just in case someone got hungry.

When she'd asked Nancy how she organized it all, she'd laughed, saying that it was a potluck situation. People brought what they could. And before Lilly could apologize for not bringing anything to share, she'd told her not to do a thing. Esther had even said that if Lilly went out and bought treats, most everyone would be offended since she was so new. It seemed the bounty was meant to be shared.

Nancy had put together a wide assortment of employees. Phillip, the cook, was in his fifties. Gavin, the full-time gardener, was in his early forties with four teenagers at home. Amber was just sixteen. Though she usually worked in the kitchen, she liked cleaning rooms just as much.

Esther, like herself, was in her midtwenties. Penelope, who usually worked in the kitchen with Phillip, was around thirty years old and was a "dog mom" of three golden retrievers. Wayne rounded out the group. He was both the funniest member and the oldest at near seventy. He only worked one day a week, supposedly in order to keep in shape. He helped to weed flower beds, ran small errands, and swept patios and porches.

Not only were their ages all over the place, but so were their backgrounds. Some were Amish while others were English.

As each day passed and she began to be more familiar with the rhythm of the inn, Lilly was surprised that they all seemed to enjoy working with each other and appreciated one another's unique outlook. It had been her experience that people were often suspicious of those who were different.

But maybe that had just been her experience? She wasn't sure. All she knew was that she was coming to think of this group as not just friends but an extended family. Each person seemed determined to look out for her and make sure she was happy.

After taking a short break to eat one of Penelope's amazing raspberry white chocolate scones, Lilly got to work on the rooms near the back hallway on the second floor. These were new rooms for her. Before, Esther and Amber had taken the second floor while she'd worked on the rooms on the main floor.

As she rolled her cart into the hallway, Lilly made sure that each room's door was locked. Then she picked up her clipboard and marked that the room was clean and ready for a new guest.

She'd just done that when Nancy appeared. "Lilly, just the person I was hoping to find."

Caught off guard, she practically stood at attention. "Did you need me someplace else?" Before Nancy could answer, she rattled off another question. "Is everything okay?"

"So far, so good. All of our guests seem like they are doing well and enjoying themselves." Scanning Lilly's face, she smiled. "Don't look so scared, dear. I only wanted to see how you were doing. Have you had any problems?"

"Not at all. Esther left the cart in good order and also told me where to find all the supplies if I needed to restock." When Nancy still continued to look at her intently, she shrugged. "I just finished cleaning my last guest room for the day. It's ready."

Nancy looked at room 5's closed door. "This one?"

"Jah."

"Would you mind if we walked through it together?"

She swallowed. "Nee." Just as she reached into her apron for the master key, Nancy opened the door with her own.

It was silly, but Lilly experienced a moment of panic, like maybe the room had somehow fallen into disarray in the five minutes since she'd cleaned. She stepped just inside the door and waited to see what Nancy thought.

Obviously unaware of how nervous Lilly was, Nancy looked around the space. "Everything looks good," she said as she opened drawers and the small closet and inspected the glasses in the beverage area. "Did you switch out the glasses with fresh ones?"

"Yes, I did."

She opened the silver ice bucket resting on a sturdy black melamine tray. Peering into the insulated space, she nodded. "This looks good too. It's obvious that you wiped the outside as well as added fresh ice cubes."

"Esther reminded me to make sure to go over everything that guests could have touched." Now, if she could have also warned Lilly to be prepared to have her work checked by the owner herself, that would've been very helpful.

"Mmm. Well, let's go see how the bathroom looks."

Her stomach now in knots, Lilly followed Nancy but stayed in the doorway as Nancy's eagle eyes studied the counters, toilet, bathtub, and floor. Then she checked the complimentary lotion, soap, shampoo, and conditioner. "Everything looks to be in good order. The tile is clean too." Her smile widened. "I'd even call it sparkling."

"Thank you. I tried my best."

"Esther told me that she cleaned two rooms with you the first morning and you had no problems."

"I canna do a great many things, but I have a lot of experience cleaning guest rooms." Of course, the moment she heard her tone, she wished that she could take her words back. She sounded defensive and almost too proud.

But instead of looking upset, Nancy gentled her tone. "I'm sure you can do a great many things, dear. I hope you didn't mind me double-checking your work."

"Of course not. This is your bed and breakfast."

Nancy smiled, but it was obvious that Lilly had struck a nerve. "That is true, but I want all of my employees to feel the same sense of pride that I do about this place. When you put on that gray dress uniform, you become a part of the Marigold Inn."

"I understand. I want to be a part of the team."

"Dear, you already are." Leading the way out of the room, Nancy added, "But you're more than simply part of a team, right? Not only are you on staff, I also want you to feel like you're part of the family."

And . . . the lump that had settled in her throat returned. "Thank you."

Nancy gestured for her to lock the door, which she did.

"Now, I already heard from Phillip that everyone has been treating you to all their homemade goodies."

"They sure have."

"The food gives a whole new meaning to coffee break, doesn't it?"

Lilly couldn't help but smile. "Oh yes. It's all very good. And there's so much of it too."

"I've learned over the years not to indulge too much. But from time to time, I love to try the treats or bring something from my own kitchen." Her cheeks bloomed. "Whenever Phillip doesn't mind me making a coffee cake, I bring that."

"Phillip told me not to worry about bringing anything."

"Good. You shouldn't. It's not an expectation, dear. Besides, you just started and you're living on the property. Even if you wanted to cook, you'd have to convince Phillip to let you use his oven!" She patted Lilly's arm. "Don't go worrying about things that aren't problems, okay?"

Lilly released a lungful of air she hadn't even realized she'd been holding. "Okay."

"Good. I'm hoping that everyone has been helpful as well?"

"Yes. Very much so."

"That's what I wanted to hear." She glanced at her watch. "It's just about time for you to call it a day, right?"

"I was going to go back to the dining room and make sure there was water and such in the containers."

"There's no need. I believe that Penelope already took care of that before she left for the day."

"Oh. Well, I'll just do a quick walk through the halls." Guests left coffee cups and water glasses in all sorts of places.

"Lilly, what I'm trying to tell you is that no one expects you to do more than your fair share. Especially not me. Amber is on until seven this evening. She'll roam the halls. I promise."

"I didn't mean she wouldn't . . ."

"I know, honey. Now, after you put up the cart, why don't you go enjoy the rest of your day? Take off your uniform, put on something cheerful, and enjoy the sun. It's a shame to waste it, yes?"

"All right."

"Good." Nancy smiled again before walking down the hallway.

Lilly watched her disappear, thinking all the while that things so far had been very different than she expected. Though Nancy did keep tabs on her, she also encouraged her to take time off and relax too. That had been a nice surprise.

Still thinking about Nancy and her free afternoon, she walked down the hallway.

And almost ran into Eddie as he pushed open his door.

"Sorry," he said. "Oh, hi."

"Hi." She could practically feel him taking everything in, from her gray dress to the cart she was pushing. It was obvious that he was surprised that she was a maid. She probably should've told him that when they'd first met, but what did it really matter? "How are you today?"

"I'm well. And you?"

"Fine." Deciding to attempt to ease the awkwardness, she smiled. "Just cleaning guest rooms."

"Yes. I just noticed you were wearing a uniform."

"I don't mind it. These gray dresses are comfortable and keep my regular clothes clean."

He stuffed his hands in his pockets. "Sorry, you took me by surprise. I mean, I didn't know you were a maid."

She hadn't been trying to make him think she was anything but that . . . but it was a disappointment to realize that her occupation meant something to him.

Something that obviously wasn't all that good.

But what could she do? "Well, I am." She smiled again, but the air between them felt even more awkward. "Which means I should get going. Have a nice afternoon."

"Yeah. You too."

He stepped to one side so she could continue to wheel her cart down the hall.

As she passed, Lilly could practically feel him watch her walk by. Though, she was probably imagining things. Old habits kicked in, and she looked down at her hands on the cart's handle.

She wasn't embarrassed to be a maid. She was grateful to have a job.

But she supposed she was still a little too prideful. For some reason, even knowing that she had a good job and that working was nothing to be ashamed about, she still felt embarrassed.

Just once, she ached to be a woman whom a man looked at with longing. Or admiration. Like he wasn't concerned about her job or that she'd been adopted or that she was a little too tentative and shy.

One day, she wanted to be thought of as just Lilly, like that was enough.

Maybe that would never happen, but maybe, with God's help, it would. If it did, that would be so wonderful and amazing.

It just wasn't going to happen today.

6

Nancy had stopped trying to be everyone's mother long ago. She'd learned the hard way that not every employee at the Marigold Inn was in need of a concerned guardian. But there was something about Lilly Kurtz that pulled on her heartstrings. The girl was such a contradiction of tentativeness and tenacity. And she seemed lonely.

How could a pretty young girl who seemed so on the ball also seem so alone? What had happened to her?

Standing in the back hallway just a few feet from the French doors leading out to her she-shed office, she looked down the hall. The janitorial closet was there. No doubt Lilly had not only put the cart neatly away but also restocked it and taken a few more minutes to reorganize and restock the supply closet too. Everyone on staff was learning that Lilly didn't just go the extra mile, she carefully swept it and planted flowers and shrubs on the perimeter too. She also never complained and always said everything was good.

Nancy didn't know if she went above and beyond because it was her way or if she felt like it was necessary to earn her keep. Nancy had been tempted more than once to call her in to her office to attempt to reassure her, but she didn't want to make her even more nervous.

But maybe she could mention something to Esther? They were good friends . . . maybe Esther would be able to find a way to encourage Lilly to relax a bit.

But then would Lilly be upset because Nancy had been talking about her?

Ugh. Problems like this had never been mentioned in her online hospitality classes.

"You're looking a little worried there, Nancy."

She smiled at Phillip—and tried to pretend that her pulse hadn't just sped up. Why, why did he have to be so gorgeous? He had a unique heritage; his mother was Mexican and his father Italian. She thought she remembered that one of his grandparents had emigrated from Ireland too. The combination blended together into striking looks. Dark eyes, salt and pepper hair cut short, a perfect jaw. Full lips.

She really hated that she noticed his lips.

Or how attractive he was.

That was hard enough to ignore. Unfortunately, his good looks paled in comparison to his personality, which was full of charm and vigor. He also had a way of looking at things (and her) that made every nerve ending feel frayed.

She really needed to stop being so flustered around him. If she didn't, one day he was going to realize that his boss—who just happened to be four years older—had a serious crush on him. He'd probably start looking for a new job. Then, she would not only be mortified and feel even more like a lonely widow than she already was but she'd also be without one of the best chefs in the area.

She needed to remember that.

Oblivious to everything that was going through her mind, Phillip stepped closer, bringing with him the faint scent of aftershave. Why did he have to smell so good? It really wasn't fair.

"Nance? Did you hear me?"

She pressed a hand to her chest. "I did. Sorry, my mind was drifting."

"Yeah?" He eyed her more closely. "What's going on? Is everything all right?"

"Everything's just fine. I mean, no." She felt like slapping her forehead with the palm of her hand. She needed to get it together and fast.

Oblivious to her mushy mind, Phillip was still obviously trying to make sense of her words. "No?"

Why couldn't she ever seem to speak coherently around him? It was like she turned into a bumbling teenager with a huge crush on the star quarterback.

Okay, she'd never been interested in the quarterbacks—she'd been more into the artsy types of guys—but whatever. It was the same difference. She had a too-big crush on her chef. She signed his paychecks!

Swallowing hard, she told herself to get a grip. Fast. Pulling herself together, she smiled. "You're right. I am a little worried. But, um, it's okay."

"It's not if you're worried about something. What's going on?"

"Um."

His expression turned more guarded. "I'm sorry. Am I overstepping? Is it personal? I mean, with a relationship or something?"

"No. I mean, it's work. Not a personal relationship. I mean, I'm not in a relationship. It's work."

"Ah."

She was almost sure she noticed that something in his expression shifted. "So, no worries."

"Who's giving you trouble?"

"No one. It's something else." Why had she mentioned a thing? "I . . . well, I was just worried about someone."

"Who?"

She met his perfect brown eyes, allowed herself to get lost in them for a quick second before pulling herself together. "I'm sorry, but I can't talk about it. I mean, not here. It's too public."

"Then let's go to your little house." Without waiting for her to comment, Phillip opened one of the French doors and gestured for her to step outside.

She walked through the doorway before she thought better of it.

As they walked the short distance, she scanned the area. Force of habit led her to survey the area, checking for trash, dead flowers, guests who looked disgruntled or unhappy. To her relief, everything was in good shape and the only guests who were sitting outside were a trio of ladies in their late twenties who were staring at their phones and laughing.

They didn't even look toward Nancy and Phillip.

When they reached her office, she flipped the decorative brass plate to the right to reveal a keypad. She'd elected to have that so she wouldn't always have to have a key on her person and so other people could get into her office if she wasn't available.

Phillip stood to one side while she punched in the numbers and opened the door. Then he followed her inside and sat down on the small loveseat.

What to do? If she sat down at her desk like she'd intended, it would seem too formal. However, if she sat down near where he was, she'd have to join him on the loveseat.

She should really have thought about this seating arrangement better and maybe added at least one chair next to the couch.

"Nancy?"

"Sorry." Deciding to stop acting like such a ninny, she sat down next to him. Yes, they were just a few inches apart now, but he probably couldn't care less. She needed to remember that and pretend she didn't notice, either. "I don't know what's wrong with me."

"I do."

"Oh?" *Please don't let him know my feelings.*

"Someone has you rattled." Studying her face, he said, "Hmm, is it Penelope?"

"Penelope? Not at all."

"That's a relief."

"Why do you say that?" Nancy knew that Penelope helped Phillip in the kitchen from time to time but thought they got along well. "Did something happen with her in the kitchen?"

"Not lately. We've finally gotten into a good groove. I spoke to her two days ago and told her to be more careful when she was cutting fruit, but that's probably my fault. Breakfast service was crazy, and I was barking orders."

"You were ordering everyone around in the kitchen?" she teased.

Looking embarrassed, he said, "I know. I can be difficult. I apologized to everyone, though." Studying her again, he added, "So, if Penelope isn't worrying you, is it Amber? I know she's young, but she seems to take direction well. I thought she was doing great."

That was Phillip. He fussed and worried, but he also cared about people. He didn't try to hide his emotions, either. She loved that about him. "It's Lilly."

He frowned. "Really? What's wrong with her? Everyone thinks she's great."

"You're right. She is."

He continued to sing the girl's praises. "She's super-efficient and always goes the extra mile."

"I know. I've noticed that too."

Worry lines appeared on his brow. "What's going on, then? Uh-oh. Is she unhappy?" His voice deepened. "Is someone giving her a hard time?"

"No. I mean, not that I'm aware of." Now she was starting to feel like she'd been making a big deal out of nothing. "I guess I just feel for her. She's such a sweet girl and she seems so alone."

"I thought she was friends with Esther."

"She is. And I know she has other friends in town too. But . . ." She paused, debating about the best way to share her concern, then decided to simply just share her thoughts. "We've had a lot of employees here over the years. Some are young like Amber, others are older or more experienced or whatever. Some need a lot of coaching; others need a good amount of supervision or even redirection."

"True."

She chuckled. "And some just don't work out."

"And some just don't want to work."

She knew he was referring to an assistant he'd had two years ago who would never show up on time but would lie about it. "Yes. But I don't know, maybe I'm reading too much into her actions, but sometimes I feel like she's almost desperate to do a good job. Like she's afraid that I'm looking for a way to fire her."

"Hmm."

She scanned his expression. "What are you thinking?"

He shrugged. "Nothing."

"Come on. I didn't tell you all this just for you to keep your opinion to yourself. Am I being silly?"

"No."

"But . . ."

"I'm not sure if you want me being completely honest about what I'm thinking."

"Now you really have me curious. Be honest."

"It's only that you're a caring person, Nancy. I'm not surprised that you're worried about her. It's one of your best qualities."

Phillip thought she had good qualities? "What do you think I should do?"

"Wait."

"That's it?"

He nodded. "You're her boss. Sorry, but anything you say will put her on edge."

"I guess that's true." She stood up, needing to put some space between them before she completely embarrassed them both. "I'm glad we talked. Thank you."

He blinked. "That's it?"

She folded her hands together. "Yes. I don't want to take up any more of your time."

He stood up too. Then he stepped closer. Close enough that she had to lift her chin to look into his eyes. "You know you aren't. I like talking with you. You know that, right?"

"Phillip. Of course I know that."

"I hope so." He motioned between the two of them. "Nancy, come on. What we have is not just professional, right? It's personal."

Personal sounded good. "Right. I mean, yes, I know we're friends."

His voice softened. "We're a lot of things, Nancy, but we're not just friends."

And just like that, her mouth got dry . . . because she had just realized that her lips had parted. "What are we?"

He shook his head and smiled. "Honey, I think you already know the answer to that."

Then he turned and walked out the door.

And when the door closed again, even though she was now completely alone, the space suddenly felt too small. Too confining.

Too much a symbol of what she was, at least when work was done and most of the employees went home: alone.

7

Eddie had a lot on his mind. His brother James had sent him a letter full of worries about the farm. He'd started off by talking about how a couple of cows had been acting peculiar, moved on to the increased price of grain, and finished the message with the news that their father had seemed especially tired last night.

As soon as he'd read the note, guilt hit him hard. Yes, he was in Florida to look after his grandmother, but it was evident that she didn't need too much looking after. So instead of doing something selfless—like look out for their eighty-year-old relative—he'd had a lot of time on his hands.

That extra time allowed him to dwell on the fact that James sounded overwhelmed. And how could he not be? He had a wife and a baby depending on him. In addition, they didn't even live on the farm. James and Sally lived near her parents' homestead about four miles away.

Four miles was not a problem when Eddie was there to keep a constant eye on things. But now that he was in Florida, it was a different story. Though he knew there wasn't much he could do from so far away, Eddie wished he could.

When he'd called home, no one had answered. It made sense, of course. No one at the farm had the time or the inclination to sit near the phone shanty and wait for an incoming call. But it was still disappointing. He was tempted to call his parents, who had a phone in the kitchen since they were New Order, but after much debate, he refrained. If his mother answered, she would have a dozen questions about the trip, which he didn't want to answer at the moment. If his father answered, he'd ask if James had reached out to him . . . which would lead to an uncomfortable conversation about the state of their father's health and his older brother's inclination to exaggerate problems.

Eddie had been stewing so much, he'd knocked on his grandmother's door and encouraged her to come out with him. However, she'd declared that all she wanted to do was sit on the front porch and read one of the four books she'd brought with her. She'd also stated that she did not want him to sit with her while she read.

All of that meant he had a lot on his mind, too much time on his hands, and no idea what to do.

Which was how he found himself thinking about Lilly Kurtz. There was something about her that kept him wondering, and that was a fact. Every time he'd had the opportunity to speak with her, he'd been charmed. She was so sweet and shy. Maybe a little bit hesitant too. Honestly, it was a bit surprising how tentative she seemed to be about most everything. She was a beautiful woman, and his experience with beauties was that they expected everyone to cater to them.

But maybe that was simply Hanna.

He frowned, thinking about how hurt he'd been when she'd broken up with him. He'd been even more upset when he discovered that she was seeing someone else. Even though everyone in his family said he was better off without her, his heart was still broken.

Until now.

To his surprise, he hadn't thought about her in days. It seemed that his belief that he'd always be hurt and despondent about Hanna's betrayal hadn't been true after all. Time really did heal wounds, and the Lord really was so good. Here in Pinecraft, he was learning that life was full of surprises. He just had to open his eyes and his heart to them.

Of course, what that had to do with his feelings about Lilly, he had no idea. Should he pursue her because she'd struck his fancy or play it safe because nothing was likely going to happen between them since they lived in different parts of the country?

He didn't know what to do.

"James would say to spend more time with Lilly, just to be sure," he murmured. "But Daed would tell ya to stop being so hesitant and trust the Lord's will."

Both points had merit, but he had no idea what he should do. He felt at a loss.

"That's because you aren't used to having any time at all," he murmured to himself. That was the truth too. He spent most of his time on the farm. He was tending to either the fields, the barn, the animals, or his family.

When Hanna was in his life, he'd often had to force himself to get away, and then usually sat or walked by her side while she shared her burdens with him.

In fact, the only reason he'd convinced himself to take a vacation was because he hadn't planned on doing anything but look after his grandmother. He'd had these visions of him being at her beck and call.

Which, now that he thought about it, was a little embarrassing. His grandmother didn't need a lot of assistance doing anything. In addition, she'd never been especially eager to be entertained. She was actually a lot more fun that he was. She was outgoing and chatty, often visiting with strangers or the variety of people in her life whom she'd developed friendships with over the years.

When a young couple eyed him curiously as they walked down the front steps, he sat down on one of the rocking chairs. Perhaps he should go to the inn's library and check out one of the novels on the shelves? There had to be at least a couple hundred books to choose from. He could probably find some book to spark his interest.

When the front door opened again, Lilly appeared as if he'd conjured her up.

She looked as pretty as ever. She'd changed out of her gray uniform and was now wearing a bright yellow dress and flip-flops. The color suited her. It made the gold highlights in her hair shine and her pale blue eyes appear even more striking.

When their eyes met, Lilly hesitated. After seeming to make up her mind, she stopped in front of him. "Hi again," she said politely.

"Hi, Lilly. How are you? I guess you're done for the day?"

She smiled. "I am."

"Are you on your way home now? Do you live nearby?"

That pretty smile deepened. "I'd say so. I live at the inn."

"I didn't know there was room for employees. Do you like it?"

She lifted a shoulder. "Well enough. I like having a place to live. And there's something to be said for being able to sleep in a little bit." Her lips curved slightly, as if she had a secret joke. Or maybe she was simply trying to ease the awkwardness of the moment. After all, who went around asking maids where they lived?

Feeling embarrassed, Eddie mentally berated himself yet again. What was he doing, acting as if he had a right to know anything about her? "Hope you have a good evening."

"Thanks." She turned and walked down the front steps. But then, just as she reached the sidewalk, she turned back to him again.

"Hey . . . are you all right?"

"Yeah. Sure." When she continued to study him, he added, "I . . . I have a bad habit of living inside my head too much. It's a natural consequence of being a farmer, I suppose. I was just telling myself to stop asking you so many questions."

"You didn't ask too many. If I hadn't wanted to answer, I wouldn't have."

Eddie couldn't help but chuckle. He liked her honesty. No, he liked that she wasn't afraid to be honest with him.

"What are you doing the rest of this evening?" she asked.

"I'm not sure."

"What about November?" She looked around. "Is she about to join you out here?"

"Not at all. She's currently somewhere around the inn reading. She has a pile of four books and told me to leave her in peace."

Lilly grinned. "She sounds like a woman after my own heart."

"Not mine. I like to read as much as anyone, but she's taken rest and relaxation to a whole new level. Not only does she want to read for the next few hours, she doesn't want to go out to eat, either. She's planning to eat in her room again."

Her lips twitched. "She's an independent woman."

"She is."

"What will you do for supper?"

"I don't know, but that's okay. I mean, don't let me keep you."

Lilly stared at him for a long moment. "You know, yesterday I spent time with my friends, but tonight I'm on my own. I mean, I could've gone over to one of their houses, but I decided not to. I've been working hard, and they would probably want me to linger. I don't want to do that." She cleared her throat. "Would you like to join me for supper?"

"Are you sure you wouldn't mind?"

"I don't mind. But, um, it probably won't be anything special or expensive."

"I like cheap. I mean, I do as long as it's good."

Lilly seemed to think about that for a moment before speaking again. "I was thinking about going to get a fish sandwich. Do you like fish?"

"I do."

She looked relieved. "They have some fried fish sandwiches that are really good. They serve them on toasted sourdough. You can get some coleslaw or potato salad or a bag of chips to go with it. All for about seven dollars."

He stood up. "That sounds perfect. Thanks."

"You'll be doing me a favor. Like I said, I was going to eat alone. Now I won't have to."

"Do you have a moment for me to get my wallet?"

"I even have two moments," she teased.

He was glad she was starting to relax. "Hopefully I won't even need three. My room is nearby. I'll be right back."

"Take your time. I'm off for the rest of the evening."

"Okay. I'll see you in a few minutes."

He walked inside and headed to his room, already mentally

preparing a list of things he could talk to Lilly about. The last thing he wanted was for her to regret the invitation.

He didn't know why that was so important to him, but it was.

When he was alone in his room, he couldn't help but chuckle. Obviously the Lord had been with him again. He'd been hoping for a signal so he'd know what to do, and the Lord had given him an opportunity to be with Lilly.

"Danke, Lord. I appreciate You acting so bold and not making me guess what to do. I'll follow Your lead and hope that I'm up to the task."

8

The minute the front door closed behind Eddie, Lilly sat down in the rocking chair he'd just vacated and pressed her hands to her cheeks. What was she doing?

She'd never asked a man out to dinner in her life. And while she hadn't exactly had scores of men lining up hoping to go out to supper with her, she knew that even if she had, it would never have occurred to her to do something like that. Well, not until five minutes ago.

She couldn't even blame her sudden burst of awkward brazenness on Eddie, either. No, the blame was all on her shoulders. All day long, she'd been longing for a little space from the inn. Not only did she want to have something different for supper than some leftovers she'd saved from lunch, she realized that she needed to have at least a few minutes every day being around people who didn't see only her uniform.

But she'd never been so outgoing in her life.

What in the world was going on with her? She felt as if these new surroundings were encouraging her to be a different person. She'd never gone out and invited men to do things before. But here she was, acting bold and foolhardy. Taking risks.

Maybe being around Betsy and her life lists and goals was beginning to rub off on her? She didn't know.

"You're getting yourself all spun up for no reason," she whispered to herself. "All you did was ask if Eddie would like to join you for supper. You know why you suggested that, and it isn't because you've fallen in love. You're tired of eating by yourself."

Feeling marginally better, she rocked back and forth. Watched a family of five walk past the inn. They were all so busy talking that they didn't look her way once.

As one minute passed, then another, and then five, she began to doubt herself. Maybe Eddie had changed his mind. Maybe he'd found something else to do and hadn't felt the need to tell her. Maybe he wasn't the man she'd thought he was and was standing her up.

Or maybe she'd taken his "few minutes" too literally? She'd made the mistake of doing that before. Glancing at the large clock just inside the entryway, she decided to wait another ten minutes.

Which slowly edged into fifteen. And then twenty.

It had now been almost half an hour.

He wasn't returning. If she waited too much longer, she was just going to feel like a fool—and she might even miss getting dinner. Some places closed early in the evening since they opened early in the morning.

Standing up, she resigned herself to going back to her original plan, which was to find an inexpensive sandwich shop and read a book while she ate alone. There was nothing wrong with that. She'd done that before many times. What was important was that she was getting out of the inn.

She pulled out her sunglasses and walked down the steps.

"Lilly."

She turned. "Eddie. Hey." With effort, she tried to look completely nonchalant. She was pretty sure she was failing miserably at that too.

"Hey, I'm real sorry that it took me a little longer than expected. My grandmother was looking for me. By the time I found her and saw what she needed, another fifteen minutes had passed. I hope you weren't worried that I changed my mind."

"I guess I thought you had done that, but it's all right."

"No, it isn't. Look, I know we don't know each other too well, but you need to know that I wouldn't do something like that. I wouldn't blow you off without a word. That's not who I am."

Eddie looked so earnest and sincere, all of her doubts evaporated. Everything inside of her turned to mush. "It's not who I am, either."

His voice warmed. "I guess we have that in common then."

"I hope nothing was wrong. Is your grandmother all right?"

"She's fine. I wanted to make sure she wasn't overdoing it, so I walked her back to her room. Then she was all excited about someone she met in the gardens today. Of course she had to tell me all about that before I left. My grandmommi has never met a stranger."

That was rather an understatement. "November is friendly, that's for sure."

"Are you ready to eat?"

She summoned a smile. "I am."

"When I mentioned I was going out to eat with you, my grandmother let me know some good options. I know we'd talked about grabbing fish, but what do you think about Italian?"

"I think that sounds gut." The only thing that mattered to her was that he hadn't changed his mind.

"Gut. You don't mind walking, do you?"

"Of course not."

He gestured to the intersection and crosswalk just to their right. "We need to cross there and then walk about five blocks."

"Sounds good."

She walked by his side and crossed with him. She was a quick walker. He seemed a little taken by surprise by her pace but didn't comment on it.

When they arrived at Ricci's about fifteen minutes later, they still hadn't talked much, but Lilly did feel a little bit more comfortable by his side.

The hostess at the front took them directly to a nice table in the back of the restaurant and promised that their waiter would be with them shortly.

"They act like they know you, Eddie."

"They don't."

"Really? They seem awfully attentive."

"I might have called ahead and asked them to make things nice for us."

"Hmm." She wasn't sure what to make of his explanation, but she supposed it didn't matter. "Eddie, I just realized that I don't know too much about you. Where are you from?"

"Ohio. I'm in Geauga County."

"Eddie, I can't believe it. I live in the same county." Geauga County was just east of Cleveland. Though there was a good-sized Amish population there, it wasn't near as populated or large as Holmes County.

"Truly? What a small world. What part?"

"Middlefield."

He grinned. "I'm surprised we don't already know each other. I live on a farm about eight miles to the east of Middlefield."

She couldn't believe it. Here she was, running away from her hometown to have a fresh start . . . and the one man who caught her eye was from the same area that she was. "I guess the Lord wanted us to meet."

He smiled. "It seems He did."

"Do you think it's odd that we've never run into each other?"

"Not so much. Everyone in my church district lives on a farm too. Plus, I rarely have a reason to go into Middlefield."

Lilly supposed his explanation made a lot of sense, but she still couldn't get over the fact that they'd lived so close but only met in Florida.

The waiter walked over to their table. "Have you decided on your dinner choice?"

She looked up in surprise, realizing rather belatedly that she'd been ignoring the fancy leather menu on the table in front of her because she'd been so intent on Eddie. "I'm sorry, I haven't had a chance to look at the menu."

"Do you have any questions?" he asked in an impatient tone. "Would it be easier if I gave you some suggestions?"

The server was acting as if she was wasting his time, which was both irritating and offensive. "It would be easier if you allowed me a few more minutes. I haven't been here before."

"I see."

"We only just sat down. Please bring us some Pellegrino," Eddie said in a clipped voice.

"Yes, sir."

The moment the waiter turned away, Lilly gaped at Eddie. "I think he thought you were upset with him."

"If he thought that, I'm glad. He was really rude to you."

"Do you think so?"

"He acted as if you couldn't read, Lilly. I hate when people look at my clothes and decide that I'm barely worth their time. Don't you?"

"I . . . well, I guess I never thought about it too much."

"You should. You're great. Plus, you work hard helping other people all day. And even if you didn't, no one should talk down to you as if you aren't worth their time."

"I'm beginning to think that your grandmother is really blessed to have you."

"Because I'm not afraid to let someone know that they should treat you better?"

"Because you're not afraid to stand up for what you believe in. I think that's pretty wonderful."

"You're too easily impressed."

She didn't think so. She had seen a lot in the world. She'd seen her parents—both very good people—treat her as if she wasn't *quite* part of their family. She'd seen kids at school act as if maybe she wasn't quite as good as everyone else because she'd been adopted.

What she hadn't seen very much of was someone championing her just because she existed. As far as Eddie knew, she was only just a maid at his hotel.

And maybe that was really all she was.

Until that moment, she would've said that was enough. Now, however, she was starting to think that she was more than just her occupation. If that was so, she thought that was a very good thing indeed.

9

When he got back to the inn, Eddie almost didn't knock on his grandmother's door. It was a little later than he usually stopped by and he didn't want to wake her up.

He changed his mind when he heard the television through her door. He winced. It seemed that not only was Mommi enjoying her movie night but she'd forgotten to put in her hearing aids.

Her inability to hear well became obvious when she didn't answer the door the first two times he knocked.

"Eddie, what do you need?" she asked as soon as she allowed him inside.

And no, she hadn't bothered to turn down the volume, so she was yelling over her show. He marched over to her remote and turned down the volume himself.

She frowned. "What did you do that for?"

"Mommi, you've got the television on too loud. I could hear it out in the hall."

"Really?"

"Really." Gentling his tone, he added, "You should put in your hearing aids, ain't so?"

She nibbled her bottom lip. "I hate wearing them."

"I know you do, but you have them for a reason."

"I'll put them in tomorrow."

As much as he was tempted to point out that she would need them in if she was going to watch any more television, he knew better than to push too hard. She'd push back, and then they'd spend the next few minutes arguing instead of catching up.

"Danke," he said simply as he leaned down to kiss her cheek. "How was your night?"

"Gut. Just like every night has been. I had some supper, went for a small walk, and then settled in here."

"Would you like to rest? If so, I'll go and see you in the morning."

"I don't want to rest." She sat down on her bed. "Tell me what you did this evening. Did you go out to eat?"

"I did."

"What did you say?"

It looked like he was going to get his way after all. Fighting back a smile, he said, "Put in your hearing aids and I'll tell you."

"Edward." After a second passed, she gaped at him. "You're serious."

"Sorry, but I'm not going to yell. If you want to talk, put them in."

"Fine."

She walked to the bathroom. When she was out of sight, he noticed a few articles of her clothes strewn around and a container from supper that she hadn't thrown away. Not wanting to make a big deal about it, he hung up her dress and threw out her trash.

In a moment, she walked back out. "I can hear now," she said, pointing to her right ear.

"Thank you."

"Well?"

"Well . . . I went to the Italian place you told me about. Ricci's Grill."

She smiled as she returned to her spot on the bed. "How was it?"

"Wonderful. I had pasta."

"I had lasagna when they delivered my meal. Is that what you got?"

"No. I had fettucine, but Lilly had the lasagna."

She looked pleased. "You did it. You took Lilly out on a date."

"I did. I mean, I took her out for supper."

"Sounds like a date to me."

Already imagining his grandmother saying something to Lilly, he said, "We're just friends, Mommi."

"She's such a dear girl. Every time I see her in the halls, she takes a moment to visit with me."

"That sounds like her. She's sweet." Actually, she was a lot of things. Adorable. Kind. Caring.

"Edward, stop standing and sit down. My neck is starting to hurt from looking up at you."

"Mommi."

"What?" She placed a hand on her chest and somehow managed to look pitiful. "You know I'm old."

He knew she was something else, that's what he knew. He knew her neck was perfectly fine. His grandmother had a list of complaints she seemed to enjoy pulling out whenever they suited her needs. But just as he'd learned to pick his battles when it came to her choices, he also had learned to take her complaints with a grain of salt.

"Fine." He sat. "What did you eat for supper?"

She waved a hand. "Thai food."

"You ordered in Thai?"

"You need to try new things every once in a while, Eddie. I had chicken in curry."

"Did you like it?"

"Of course. The chicken was tender and flavorful. But the best part was that I didn't cook it . . . or wash a single dish."

He fought off a grin. Leave it to her to put things into perspective. "Well said. Now, what about tomorrow? I think we should do something together."

She looked down at the remote in her hand. "Hmm. I think we should talk about that in the morning."

"Why?"

"Because I'd rather talk about you and Lilly. That's far more interesting, don't you think?"

No, he did not. He liked Lilly. He liked her a lot. But the two of them still didn't know each other well. It was going to take time to get to the point where he was willing to discuss her with his grandmother. "There isn't anything to talk about."

"Of course there is. Did you feel sparks?"

Sparks? What did that even mean? He needed to nip this in the bud and fast. "Mommi."

Her expression was all guileless wonder. "What, child?"

"You know what. Don't make one dinner into something it isn't."

"But she's so nice. She's so down to earth and sweet."

"She is, but things are still early."

"I agree, which is why you need to spend more time with her."

"I plan to, but I'm also not sure if that's a good idea, anyway."

"Why?" Frowning, she asked, "Is it because she's a maid?"

"Of course not. I'm impressed with her job. Cleaning rooms doesn't seem easy."

"I imagine it isn't." She looked at him over the top of her glasses. "She's such a nice young lady. So different from Hanna, ain't so?"

"Jah."

"I suggest you stop looking at obstacles and begin to concentrate on solutions."

"Our obstacle is pretty big, Mommi. Over a thousand miles separate us. Lilly lives here and I don't." When she still stared at him like she wasn't following, he added, "I don't know how we could overcome that problem."

She waved a hand. "It is a problem, but locations can be changed, don't you think? After all, she did just move here. She can move again."

"I don't know if she'd want to. She moved here to be near her friends."

"Friends are wonderful-gut, but I have a feeling she would like to be with you too." Brightening, she said, "Maybe she'll want to be a farmer's wife. Have you asked her how she feels about that?"

"Of course not."

"Next time you take her out, ask. She might yearn for the peace and quiet of farm life."

He loved their way of life, but it wasn't very exciting. "I doubt she's yearning to be around a bunch of cows and chickens."

"She might be. You'll never know if you don't ask."

"I knew I shouldn't have told you about our supper."

"I would've found out anyway."

"How in the world would you do that? Do you plan to grill poor Lilly every time she stops by to clean this room?"

"No. I mean, not every time. But I wouldn't have even needed to ask her, anyway. I have a number of sources."

"Is that right?"

She lifted her chin. "I'm very friendly."

Eddie wasn't even going to touch that. Yes, his grandmother was very friendly. However, as far as he knew, she was basically holed up in her room 24/7. It seemed she had a double life. "I think your talents are wasted being Amish, Mommi. You would've been a good spy."

Her eyes lit up. "I think I would've been a good spy too. But who's to say an Amish lady couldn't be a spy?"

"Oh, for Pete's sake."

Giving up on the conversation before she said something else that took him off guard, he stood up. "On that note, I think it's time I went to bed." He kissed her paper-thin cheek. "Don't forget to get some sleep."

"I will. I always do."

"I'll knock on your door in the morning. Maybe, at the very least, we could have breakfast together."

"That sounds nice, dear. But don't knock too early."

"I'll try not to."

He left and walked down to his room, still thinking about his grandma and the way she was having a ball being on her own. As much as he was surprised by the fact that she hadn't wanted to spend more time with him, he supposed he couldn't blame her. He'd never known a time when she hadn't risen with the sun, baked bread, catered to everyone's needs, and always put her needs and wants last.

Who was he to say that she didn't deserve to spend her vacation ordering in food, watching movies on television, and putting herself first?

Maybe it was the conversation he'd just shared with her about Lilly, but by the time he'd had a shower and was lying in his own bed, he was thinking about Lilly again. He knew he could be wrong, but he had a feeling that she, also, hadn't spent a lot of time thinking about herself.

Maybe instead of focusing on romance and the future, he should try to make sure she had a good time whenever she was free. They could simply be friends.

Closing his eyes, he did his best to ignore the voice in his head saying that simply being friends with Lilly Kurtz wasn't going to be all that easy.

10

Nancy had just finished meeting with the head of Amish
Bird Shuttles. The two of them had discussed the need
to work together more often. Though some of their
customers didn't arrive in Pinecraft on either the bus or the
train, most did. Nancy spent a lot of time answering letters
and exchanging information with Amish from various parts of
the country who were concerned about getting from the train
station to the Marigold Inn.

Vanessa, the shuttle representative, had confided that she was
often asked to recommend a list of hotels and inns for people
who came down to vacation but didn't want to rent a house.
They wanted something more full service.

Still feeling good about the agreement they'd tentatively
hammered out, Nancy walked out of the conference room just
behind the reception desk to see Phillip looking agitated.

"Good. You're done," he said as he strode toward her. "I
need your help."

"Whatever you need, you've got it. What's wrong?" Mentally
she started figuring out when he might be flying out for some
sort of family emergency.

"Amber."

"Amber's your problem?" The sixteen-year-old girl was bubbly and usually helped out whenever she could. "What's going on?"

He sighed. "Her cat died, and she was a mess. I was so afraid she was going to cut herself, I sent her home."

"Really?" Nancy didn't necessarily disagree with him, but she was surprised to hear that he'd sent her on her way. Even though his intentions were good, Phillip didn't always explain himself well. Amber could be thinking that he was upset with her instead of attempting to give her a much-needed break. "Maybe I should give her a call to make sure she's all right."

"You might want to, but later, okay? I need some help." Sounding more agitated, he waved a hand. "I have dough that's rising, cookies to make, and a bunch of vegetables to chop for tomorrow's breakfast. And both Josh and Kim are about to arrive with the egg and milk deliveries. I need someone to finish all the prep so I can take care of everything else."

"I see." She hid a smile. If there was anything she knew about Phillip, it was that he always said what was on his mind. She also knew that his bark was worse than his bite. Over the years, she'd learned to go with the flow instead of questioning his concerns.

He folded his arms across his chest. "I certainly hope so."

"Give me a second." She pulled out her phone from a pocket and started thumbing through screens. "I think I have everyone's schedules on here someplace."

"No need to do that. I already have someone in mind."

"Who?"

"You."

"Me?"

While she gaped at him, his lips twitched. "How are your knife skills? Can you chop vegetables?"

"Yes."

"Perfect."

"Phillip, I can chop vegetables, but not all that well." The truth was that she'd never been very talented in the kitchen.

"That's all right."

"If my pieces aren't uniform, are you going to chew me out? Because I really don't want you to give me grief if my celery and carrot sticks aren't uniform."

"You won't be cutting up celery and carrot sticks. It's peppers."

"Same difference."

"No matter what you work on, I won't give you grief. All I'll say is thank you."

His eyes were sparkling. He was teasing her. Or maybe it was more like flirting. Flirting, Phillip style. It made her more than a little amused.

And maybe just brave enough to tease him back. "I'm going to hold you to that. I'm not going to perform better if you suddenly turn into some Gordon Ramsay clone."

"I won't turn into anyone's clone."

"Hmm."

"So, what do you say? Nancy, will you please help me out?"

What else could she say to that? "Yes."

His eyes gleamed. "Great. Come on."

She hurried to catch up to him. He was striding toward the kitchen like he was worried it was going to catch on fire. "I can't stay too long, though. I have a job, you know."

"I know, boss. You're a busy woman. Believe me, I get it. Just give me two hours, okay?"

"Fine." Seeing Penelope and Lilly in the living room, Nancy said, "Let me tell Penelope what's going on so she can answer the phones or the door if needed. I'll be there in five minutes."

"Thanks."

When he disappeared, she walked over to the girls. "Hey, you two. Just to let you know, Amber had to go home early."

"Is she okay?" Lilly asked.

"She's having a hard time because her cat passed away."

Penelope frowned. "Oh no. She loved that little cat."

"Phillip's a little shorthanded, so I'm going to give him a hand. Penelope, would you please stay near the front and answer the phone or the door if needed?"

"Of course, but what about the dining room? I was going to deep clean it today."

"I could do it," Lilly volunteered.

"Do you have time? Did you already finish your rooms?"

"I did, and I don't mind at all."

"Okay, then. You're in the dining room and Penelope is going to take over at the front desk." She grinned. "Ladies, we have a plan."

"Don't worry. I'll send Lilly to get you if there's a problem, but we'll be fine," Penelope said.

"I hope I will be. Here's hoping that Phillip won't be too critical of the way I chop vegetables. Say a prayer, okay?" she called out over her shoulder. When Nancy heard both of the women giggle, she didn't blame them. After all, just a couple days before, she was sure he was about to ask her out on a date. Now all he wanted was for her to chop peppers.

Ninety minutes later, she was beginning to think that she'd never take the tiny pieces of red and yellow peppers in Phillip's egg strata for granted ever again. Or the onions in his famous feta cheese and leek tart. This was more than just cutting up a pepper and an onion for a simple supper.

It was more like she was finely dicing and chopping for several people's suppers.

Staring at the fruit, she felt even worse.

Until this moment, she'd simply given herself a spoonful of fruit salad without ever considering who had put it all together.

She was also starting to think that she owed Amber a raise. Dicing fruits and vegetables for Phillip was neither easy nor relaxing.

Especially when he'd had the nerve to ask her to make her orange slices neater and thinner.

"How's it going?" he asked after the egg lady finally showed up. "How much fruit do you still have to slice?"

"Just the strawberries." Glancing his way again, Nancy sighed. She wasn't exactly looking for a compliment, but she did think he should at least notice that she wasn't just a one-trick pony. She might not have his skills, but she did all right.

But none of that was evident in his expression. Actually, Phillip looked rather resigned, like he'd hoped she would be finished by now.

Disappointment filled her heart. No, she reminded herself sternly. It wasn't her heart that had needed coddling, it was her ego. Shame on her.

"I'll get right on those berries. They shouldn't take too long."

"No need to try to prepare them on your own. I'll help you hull and slice them."

"Wait, you hull the berries too?"

Phillip studied her intently. "Do you honestly never look at the food you serve here?"

Was this a trick question? "Of course I do."

"Really?"

"Oh, for heaven's sake. Yes, really."

"Well, you obviously don't look at it too closely. "

"Of course I do pay attention to the food, Phillip." She realized that she probably sounded snippy, but how could she not? She ran the place. She didn't sit around analyzing fruit. "Whether a strawberry is hulled isn't exactly something I take notice of before I eat one."

He laughed. "I have a feeling you will now."

She barely refrained from rolling her eyes. "You know, we should probably just get started. The sooner we start, the sooner we'll finish. How about you hull and I slice? I'm not too fast at hulling strawberries."

"Here." He slid over about two-thirds of a cup of berries. "I hulled these while we were talking."

"I hadn't even noticed you doing that." Why hadn't she noticed? Had she really been so into sparring with him that she'd been oblivious to what he'd been doing?

"I didn't expect you to." Picking up another berry, he neatly hulled the top with a paring knife and dropped it on a plate.

She started slicing. When he neatly hulled about three berries for every one she did, Nancy started to think that he probably deserved a raise too. He really was a master in the kitchen.

"Hey, careful now. You're liable to cut yourself holding the knife like that."

That was good advice. On another day—or if, say, they were on a date and he was being flirty and fun—she would probably appreciate his concern. However, at the moment, she was just annoyed.

She wasn't incompetent, she just wasn't able to slice fruit very quickly.

She sighed. "Don't even think about giving me tips."

Up went his eyebrows. "Really?"

"Really." She wanted his thanks, not his criticism. Honestly, he should take some pointers from her when it came to treating employees.

"Wow. I didn't know you were so sensitive."

She hadn't known that, either. She lifted her chin a good half inch. "I didn't know you could be so unappreciative."

"I didn't know you could be so full of salt and vinegar." The corners of his lips curved up. "I'm starting to think that there's a lot we don't know about each other."

"I think that's a good way of putting it."

"You know, I think I've got this now. Thanks for your help, but you don't have to stay any longer."

She was being dismissed. "Great. Because I have an inn to run, you know."

"Believe me, I haven't forgotten that you're in charge."

There was challenge gleaming in his eyes, but Nancy pretended not to see it. With the way things were going, she was pretty sure she'd say something she might regret.

Given the frosty tension that was flowing from her favorite chef, she figured she'd already managed to do that.

Now all she was trying to do was prevent herself from making things worse.

11

Lilly had cleaned a lot of hotel rooms in her life and seen all sorts of messes. That said, she was still surprised when she entered November Byler's room for the first time in several days. There were towels on the bathroom floor, and both trash cans were filled. She also had several outfits lying on the chair and desk.

Taking a whiff of the room, she wrinkled her nose. Everything needed to be thoroughly cleaned and sanitized.

What in the world was going on? From her previous interactions, she'd gotten the impression that November was neat and organized.

Obviously that wasn't the case.

Deciding it wasn't up to her to try to figure out why a guest was so messy, Lilly focused on what needed to be done. First off, she was going to need a trash bag larger than the one attached to her cart. After checking that no one was around, she propped November's door open two inches and hurried down the hall to the storage closet to retrieve another garbage bag and some air freshener. While she walked, she mentally devised a plan of how to attack the mess.

Step one, dispose of the garbage.

Step two, gather up the wet towels and take them to the laundry.

Step three, deep clean the bathroom and set it to rights.

And step four, change the bedsheets, try to clear off the desk enough to dust, and then finally vacuum the carpet.

It was all going to take a full hour.

Which meant that she was not going to be able to go with Esther and Michael to visit Betsy and August at Siesta Key. "Well, that's what you get for trying to make plans. Your plans should be work," she muttered as she hurried back to the room.

Eddie was standing in the doorway. His hands were on his hips and he was wearing the type of incredulous expression that she'd no doubt worn when she'd first unlocked the door.

"Hi," she said. "I just ran down the hall to get a trash bag."

"I bet you needed it. Where is my grandmother?" he asked.

"I don't know."

"How come her room looks like this?"

"I don't know that answer, either."

"Why not?"

"I've been working on the rooms on the upstairs halls. I guess someone else has been working on this one."

"Obviously not very well."

She might have been new, but she wasn't afraid to stand up for the other employees. "It doesn't look like your grandmother has been allowing anyone to come in."

"I was in here a couple of days ago. It didn't look like this." He frowned. "I noticed a bit of trash near the desk, but I didn't think anything of it."

"To be honest, I was taken off guard too. I haven't been in here in a couple of days."

"I can't believe things have gotten so bad."

"No worries," she said. "I'll put everything to rights soon."

"I feel like I should apologize for her."

"Please, don't. It's not the dirtiest room I've ever cleaned, and it sure won't be the last." The fact of the matter was that some people kept messy rooms when they were staying in motel rooms for several days.

"Do you think I should talk to her?"

"I don't know." She and Eddie were becoming friends, but that didn't mean she had any business giving him advice about his grandmother.

After another second passed, she figured it was time to save the situation. "You know what? I really need to get started."

"It's going to take a while. A long while."

She shrugged. "It doesn't matter. I was hired to clean rooms. I don't mind."

Eddie nodded but didn't move toward the door. "Hey, do you need some help?"

Everything inside of her softened as she realized that he was being completely serious. This guy really was someone special.

But there was no way she was going to let him do a single thing. "Not at all."

"Are you sure? I don't mind."

Not only would it be awkward, but she could just imagine what Nancy would say if she discovered that Lilly had allowed a guest to help her clean a room! "I'm positive. You'd just be in the way."

"Hmm."

Hoping to shoo him out, she said, "If I see your grandmother, would you like me to tell her that you were looking for her?"

"Nee. I'm not sure if I want her to know that I saw this mess."

"All right. I won't say a word then. I'll see you later."

He turned to the door but stopped with his hand on the knob. "I feel bad, leaving you like this."

"Eddie, don't take this the wrong way, but please don't. Not only will I do a better job without your help but I would get in a lot of trouble if my boss found out that I let a guest help me do my job."

"Understood."

He backed out with a sympathetic smile. At last, the door closed behind him.

Unable to stop thinking about Eddie, she stared at the closed door for a moment. He was so nice. So nice. His grandmother was blessed to have someone like him in her life. She hoped and prayed that November didn't take him for granted—or that she wasn't attempting to keep something from him.

Realizing that the clock was ticking and that she wasn't going to be able to do anything until this room was spotless, she firmly put those worries out of her head, put on her gloves, and decided to concentrate on what she could control: cleaning this room.

Ninety minutes later, Lilly was pushing the cart out of the room just as November returned. Her face was flushed, but she didn't look unhappy or concerned to find her there.

"Oh, hello. How are you?"

"I'm very well, November. How are you?"

"Good. I decided to take a short stroll. I guess it was good timing, wasn't it?"

"Jah. Now you don't have to worry about me being here while you relax."

"Oh, I wouldn't have minded your company. I would enjoy it, actually."

There was something in the way November was watching her that gave Lilly pause. She wanted her company. Was she lonely? "Are you looking for your grandson? Would you like me to find him for you?"

"Thank you, dear, but you don't have to do that. I've been hoping that he kicks up his heels a bit while he's here. He works so hard at home."

"I don't think he'd find sitting with you to be work, though. He enjoys your company."

"I'm glad you two are getting a chance to visit." Sitting in the now-empty chair, November added, "I think I'll just sit and relax for a spell."

"That sounds like a lovely idea."

She clapped her hands together. "See? That's why you are good company. Do you have a moment to chat?"

For the last hour, all Lilly had wanted to do was get out of her uniform and see her friends. But it was too late. "I do." She sat down on the chair across from November's.

"I'm so glad. Now, it's time to tell me all about your life."

"There's not much to tell. Why don't you tell me about yours?"

"I'm a widow, you know."

"Yes. I heard that."

"I used to be very busy, but now my days are far more quiet. I spend time with my family, read, sew, cook, and do whatever everyone wants me to do." Looking torn, she sighed. "My Henry would probably not even recognize me now."

"Has he been gone a long time?"

"Oh yes." A sad, wistful expression appeared on her face. "Too long, really."

"I'm sorry."

"One can't survive on regrets, Lilly. If I've learned anything, I've learned that." Suddenly staring at her intently, she murmured, "Have you learned that yet? Have you learned not to have regrets . . . or are you still hoping that somehow everything will get better?"

"Everything in my life is just fine. I don't need it to get better."

"Ah. That's my mistake." She swallowed. "I'm glad you're happy now."

This was the strangest conversation. "I am. I have a lot of friends here."

"Friends are important, for sure and for certain." After a pause, she added, "Do you have anyone special in your life too?"

"Special, like a boyfriend?"

November's eyes twinkled. "Jah. Do you?"

"Nee."

"Maybe someone will step into your life and surprise you. Wouldn't that be something?"

"Jah." Lilly stood up. "Well, I need to put up this cleaning cart. Nancy is probably wondering where it is."

Some of the light in November's eyes dimmed. "Of course, dear. I'm sure you have many other things to do besides chat with me."

"I do need to leave, but I enjoyed our visit." Lilly hadn't lied, she did need to leave and she had enjoyed the lady's company. That said, she didn't want to talk with her any longer. November was making her reconsider too many things in her life.

Or maybe it was more like she was now debating about whether she regretted something . . . or had, indeed, started simply hoping for things that would likely never happen.

She hurried out of the room and pushed the cart down the hall.

And almost ran into Eddie.

"Sorry!"

He looked at her with concern. "Please don't tell me that you're only just leaving my grandmother's room."

What could she say? "I am, but it's not what you think. I was cleaning, but I've spent the last few minutes chatting with her too."

"So, she's back?"

"She is. I think she's going to take a rest now."

"How does she seem?"

Though warning signals were going off in her head, reminding her that he was a guest at the hotel and she was an employee and therefore need not be completely open with her opinions, she knew she wanted to answer him honestly. "She seems all right. Maybe a little tired, but who wouldn't be after taking a walk for a spell?"

"I guess you're right. Thanks for visiting with her, that was very kind of you."

"No need to thank me for that. I enjoyed her company."

Eddie gazed at her a moment longer. It seemed to Lilly that he was about to ask her something, but if he was, he must have changed his mind. "Well, I better go see her now. I hope you have a good evening."

"You too."

"Hey, do you, ah, have any plans?"

No way was she going to tell him that she'd had to change her plans because his grandmother's room was such a mess. "Nope, I'm just looking forward to being off my feet."

"I bet. Well, you take care now."

"You too."

They stared at each other another long moment before separating. But as Lilly rolled the cart back to the storage room, she felt like something new was brewing between them. She wasn't sure what it was, exactly, but it felt special.

Of course, as soon as she opened the storage room door, she pushed that fanciful idea out of her head. Obviously, she'd let November's question about having a "special" somebody get in her head.

12

Eddie wasn't sure what he'd find when he entered his grandmother's room, but it wasn't seeing her sitting on the easy chair in the corner with a book in her lap and a cup of tea by her side.

She looked peaceful and perfect. Just like always. There was also that same hint of fun in her being that he'd always loved so much. Loved since he was a little boy.

In short, she looked like she always did. It was almost as if the room had never been a mess and she didn't have a care in the world.

He wasn't sure if he was relieved about that or disappointed. He didn't want anything to be wrong with his grandmother, but he also didn't want to be thinking negative thoughts about her without reason. Was she perfectly fine and he'd been allowing his worries and imagination to get the best of him?

After he stood there like a fool for another couple of seconds, she cleared her throat. "Cat got your tongue?"

He could feel his neck heat up. "Nee. I . . ."

"Yes?"

"It's nothing."

"Hmmph. And here I thought you were a bit spun up because you might have run into a certain lovely housekeeper in the hall."

"Are you referring to Lilly?" Hearing his words, he mentally groaned. Could he sound any more stilted?

His grandmother folded her hands on top of her book. Then she peered at him over the rim of her glasses. "Yes, I meant Lilly," she said in a tone that said she knew exactly what he was doing and that his feigned nonchalance hadn't fooled her for a minute. "Or were you thinking of someone else?"

"No, I was not."

"Well then. Did you see her?"

"I did."

She smiled. "Well, what happened? Did you two talk?"

"We did, but only for a few moments."

She nodded encouragingly. "Sometimes short conversations are the best, though. So, how did it go? She's such a nice girl."

"Mommi, let's not talk about Lilly and me. I came in here to see how you're doing."

Her expression turned guarded. "I'm fine."

"Are you sure?" When she averted her eyes, he knew he'd hit a nerve. "I'm asking because I've noticed that you've seemed pretty tired of late."

"No more than usual."

"Maybe a little distant too."

She swallowed. "I don't know what you mean."

"You know . . ." His voice drifted off as he tried to think of a way to phrase her absentmindedness without actually saying it directly. "Sometimes I've noticed that you're moving rather slow."

"That's because I'm looking at eighty years old, child. My

knees and hips sometimes like to remind me that I'm not the same girl who used to play kickball with all the boys on the playground. When you're in your late seventies, I have a feeling you'll be moving slowly from time to time as well."

"Yes, I imagine I will." He paused. "It's just that when I came by the other evening, you had kind of a mess in here."

"I fear I've gotten a bit too lazy. I'm going to pick up after myself better. Let's talk about something else. How was your day?" Her voice had a bit of an edge to it.

Deciding that he'd said everything he needed to, at least for the moment, he leaned back against the wall. "Good. I ended up playing a round of golf and met a good guy named August. What about you?"

"Oh, I had an interesting day. I decided to get out of this room so the staff could clean it. I went for a little walk."

"Did you use your walker?"

"Of course I did, but I didn't even need to depend on it all that much. I'm getting around right as rain today. Hardly slow at all."

When he noticed that she was smirking, he said, "Mommi, you know I wasn't actually talking about how fast you walk."

"I know."

"I'm only concerned. There's nothing wrong with caring about you."

"I suppose. But you don't need to be too worried yet. My mind might have a few Swiss cheese holes, but overall it's working properly."

"I love you, so I'm going to keep an eye on you."

"I'd expect no less, Edward."

He pulled the chair from the desk next to her. Took a seat and then reached for her hand. She allowed him to hold it. Looking down, he felt the thin skin, the sharp bones and the tendons lying just under the surface. Noticed that her fingertips were soft. So different than his memories of her when he was small, when she was constantly cooking, cleaning, and gardening.

Seeing the beauty of the woman she was now, he couldn't resist squeezing her hand. His grandmother was the strongest person he knew. She never gave up, either. When some men or women her age would look at her aches and pains as a real problem, she always acted as if they were a minor inconvenience.

Ninety minutes later, he was standing on the beach on Siesta Key. After they'd chatted for a while, she'd dismissed him and he'd been so restless, he'd boarded the SCAT and headed out to the beach.

Because it was later in the day, wide stretches of the shoreline were empty. He took off his shoes, rolled up the cuffs of his pants, and started walking. The sand underneath his toes was slightly chilly, but every time the water lapped against his skin, he felt a hint of the warmth of the gulf.

Calmed by the tangy sea air, the breeze, and the faint sound of the seagulls squawking, he relaxed.

It was kind of a surprise.

It always made Eddie a little bit uncomfortable when he went to Siesta Key. He didn't know why—he'd been taught not to judge other people and especially not to be holier-than-thou. So, it wasn't his business if other Amish folks wanted to wear bathing suits, flirt with other single men and women, or even do a few things that were frowned upon in their own church community.

His grandmother was full of stories about people who had sowed a few oats in their teens and then became true role models in both their church and their community.

But that said, he often wasn't sure how he felt when he spied so many Amish men and women essentially acting "English" on vacation.

All that was why he usually avoided Siesta Key. He liked the beach but didn't enjoy the direction his mind sometimes headed.

But after speaking to his grandmother, he needed a break. The beach, with the soothing waters of the bay, was the best spot for him to relax and calm his mind.

After walking for almost an hour, he sat down on the sand and stretched his legs.

And then he saw Lilly.

She was sitting on a folding beach chair. She had a nylon beach bag next to her and a plastic container filled with what looked like iced tea, and she was reading a book. She had on a short-sleeved dress in a pale orange color. It was an unusual shade, almost the color of orange sherbet. A white cotton cardigan was draped around her shoulders. Her dress was pushed up around her knees and her feet were bare.

In short, she looked like she was achieving everything he'd been trying in vain to capture. Peace and tranquility.

As if she felt his gaze, she looked over at him. Blinked. And then smiled.

"Hello again."

"Hi."

"Are you all right?"

"Why do you ask?"

"No reason . . . except that you look a little tense."

He shrugged. "I guess I am. I'm attempting to relax."

She laughed. "You're the first person I've ever heard say that they have a hard time relaxing when they come to the beach."

"Right? I'm pretty sure I'm doing everything backward."

"I don't think there are rules here. Part of the reason we all come to Siesta Key is because every rule doesn't apply."

"I never thought about it that way."

She shrugged. "Maybe you should."

Enjoying their conversation—the way that they were half volleying verbal jabs and half flirting—he stood up and walked closer to her. "Mind if I join you?"

"Of course not."

"I'll tell you a secret. The first thing I thought of when I saw you was that you looked completely at ease."

"That's how I feel. I love coming to the beach and reading."

"I have a hard time reading novels."

A bit of pity entered her expression. "I see."

She didn't see at all. "I don't have a difficult time reading. It's just that I don't enjoy reading. It feels like a waste of time." And . . . now he'd just offended her. "Um, not that that's what you're doing," he added quickly. "I wish I enjoyed it more."

Luckily, she didn't seem offended by his awkward little speech. "At least you came to the beach, right? I think the worst day at the beach is always better than the best day in town."

"Hmm."

A little bit of her friendly smile faded. "What's bothering you?"

"Nothing worth talking about. Are you planning to be here for a while?"

"I think so. I thought I'd stay here until the sun started to set." Looking toward the horizon, she said, "Maybe another hour."

"I know you came to read . . . but why are you alone?"

"Why are you asking?"

Because every time he talked to her, he wanted to know more about her. "I just thought you came to Pinecraft to see your girlfriends. Going to the beach seems like something women would enjoy doing together."

She put the novel she'd been reading to one side and tucked her feet under her. "We did have plans, but I had to break them."

"That's too bad. Oh well, I bet you can reschedule."

"I hope so. I did come to Florida to be with them." She was frowning.

"I feel like you're trying not to add something else."

"I guess that's true."

"If you'd like to share, I'd like to hear it. I really do want to get to know you better."

"Okay, but it feels silly to even mention it."

"Tell me anyway."

"Fine. When I was planning this move, I forgot that my girl-friends' lives are different than mine. They don't have too much free time anymore. They're all married now."

He felt sorry for her. "Maybe they'd still want to do some things with you without their men. Or you could join them?"

She smiled. "I could do either, but it's more than just them having husbands. They're busy and, well, sometimes I feel like they're in such different places in their lives than I am. They're discussing houses and sharing closets and couple get-togethers and I don't know. A bunch of things to do with married life I can't relate to. Sometimes I find myself struggling to appear interested when I'd rather sit by myself." With a groan, she pressed a hand to her face. "I know this sounds horrible, but I don't always find them especially relaxing to be around."

"I know what you mean."

"Do you?"

"My brother and one of my sisters are married. When we all get together, I suddenly feel like I'm the awkward teenager when we're all about the same age."

"You do understand! That's it exactly. Sometimes all I want to do is talk about my job or a book I read. My girlfriends don't mean to be rude, but I've seen them exchange looks, like they think it's cute that I'm not concentrating on grown-up things."

"And since you're outnumbered, you just keep your mouth shut."

"Yep."

"It's too bad that things are working out that way. I'm sorry."

She waved a hand. "There's nothing to be sorry about. It's life, you know? Everything changes, whether one is ready for it or not."

"My grandfather used to say that change is the only constant."

Lilly's smile was beautiful. "Indeed."

13

His conversation with Lilly had stayed with Eddie for the last two days. They'd ended up talking about a wide variety of topics until the sun bled into the sea. Then they'd gotten mugs of hot chocolate and warm pretzels from a vendor and boarded the SCAT for Pinecraft.

The bus had been about half full of Amish. More than one older couple had smiled at them knowingly. No doubt they'd thought they were either married or a courting couple.

Which had made him think about courting . . . and their single statuses.

When he'd taken a walk this afternoon, he'd come across a street vendor selling flowers. Impulsively, he'd picked some up—two dozen daisies with a smattering of baby's breath.

His brother had always sworn by daisies. More than once James had told the story of how Sally's heart had melted when she'd spied a bouquet of daisies in his hand.

Until that moment, Eddie had always thought his brother was full of it. After all, Hanna had never cared that much about flowers.

Then he remembered that she'd left him for someone else.

Holding the bouquet of jaunty white flowers, Eddie frowned at them. Yes, the bouquet was rather charming. The florist had collected two dozen stems, wrapped them together in an attractive black-and-white polka dotted bow, and even added a few sprigs of greenery.

So the bouquet was lovely. But it didn't feel right. He was plagued by second guesses. Maybe Lilly would know that his bouquet hadn't been very pricey and she would wonder why he hadn't spent more.

Or perhaps she didn't even like daisies. After all, didn't a lot of women like roses or tulips?

Or at the worst, he feared that Lilly would think that he was trying too hard and she'd be turned off by that. He was pretty sure women didn't like men who were too effusive.

Maybe he should play it cool. He mentally scoffed. Like he had any idea how to do that.

Of course he had to be standing on the sidewalk outside of the inn when Lilly's friend's husband walked by. August Troyer was Betsy's husband and managed the public golf course, where he'd just happened to have met his wife.

Feeling even more foolish, Eddie gave August a chin lift. Hopefully the man would simply walk by without any questions.

That wasn't the case.

The moment August spied Eddie—and the bouquet of daisies in his hand—he stopped.

"Going courting?"

August wasn't exactly smirking, but there was a light in his eyes that signaled he knew exactly what Eddie was about and found a bit of humor in it.

Eddie was tempted to say the flowers were for his grandmother, but he wasn't going to back down now. Especially since walking around with flowers for a grandma was sweet . . . but not the type of man he was. Or at least not at the moment.

"I suppose I am."

August grinned. "Are you finally making your move on Lilly then?"

Finally? "I am. Just to let you know, she and I haven't known each other very long. One must be seeing each other for a bit before flowers are involved."

"I reckon that's true."

Why was August looking so amused? "Does Lilly hate flowers?" A terrible thought entered his head. "Oh no. Is she allergic to them?"

August's cheeky smile grew wider. "Lilly's allergies haven't come up in conversation, but I don't think so. I think she likes them fine too."

"Sorry, but I feel like there's a joke that I'm not catching."

August shook his head. "No, it's not that at all. It's just, ah . . . you standing here brings back memories for me. Courting ain't for weaklings. Ain't so?"

"I don't know who it's for. All I do know is that it's harder than it looks."

The man's unusual gray eyes filled with compassion. "Eddie, I'd like to tell you something. And if Jayson and Michael were here, I'm fairly sure that they'd all say the same thing."

"What is that?"

"That you're in good company. Each of us made our moves fast too. These women are really special. I fell for Betsy practically the moment she almost got hit by a golf ball. By the time I spent ten minutes with her, I knew she was the woman I'd been waiting for my whole life."

"You fell for her that fast, huh?"

"Jayson said he knew Mary Margaret was for him when she didn't back down from him when he was kind of rude to her."

"And Michael? When did he fall for Esther?"

"When he first caught sight of her on the beach. He walked right over to her and started a conversation even though he was with his friends and he's a couple of years younger than she is. He thought she was perfect."

"I never knew men could be such romantics."

August laughed. "I promise, I'm not making fun of ya. I just wanted you to know that you're in good company."

"Thanks, but Lilly and I aren't serious yet. I mean, I like her, but I don't know where our relationship is going."

"Oh. My mistake."

"Yeah. I'm only giving her these flowers because they happened to be available."

Something in August's expression faded. "Hey, no worries. I shouldn't have presumed that you were in the same boat as the rest of us."

"Thanks for saying hi, though."

"No problem." He lifted a hand, obviously about to turn away . . . then paused. "Hey, Eddie, since I've already trod where I had no business stepping, let me say one more thing."

"Okay . . ."

"Lilly Kurtz is a sweet girl. We're all really fond of her."

"I know she's a good friend of your wife's."

August shook his head. "No, you misunderstand. Jayson, Michael, and me . . . well, we all think of her as a little sister. A very sweet little sister with a soft heart. She hasn't had an easy life up until now. I'd sure hate to find out that you didn't treat her well."

Thinking of his younger sister Meg, Eddie knew he'd probably feel the same way. At the moment, though, he was feeling put on the spot, especially since he didn't know August all that well. "Thanks for the advice, but I'm not really used to seeking four men's approval when I take a woman out."

"I guess not. See you around."

Watching August walk away, Eddie closed his eyes and looked up at the sky. He'd just messed this up. Chances were good that August was going to tell his wife about their conversation and she'd tell the other women—or he would tell one of the men and word would get around that way. No matter what, he realized that not a one of them was going to be happy with his attitude.

And if it got back to Lilly? Well, she could very well take it all wrong and immediately think the worst.

That would be on him too. Hanna had twisted his head and heart in so many knots, he'd sometimes felt as if he was going to need open heart surgery in order to get himself back to rights.

He trotted up the stairs and opened the front door to the Marigold Inn.

And found Lilly sitting on one of the chairs near the window. She'd just watched his conversation with August. Though there was some comfort in the fact that she hadn't overheard his words, she'd likely observed their body language.

Their eyes met, and she looked concerned instead of giddy about receiving flowers.

"Hi," he said.

She stood up. "Hello."

"I brought you some flowers."

"That's very kind of you. Thank you."

"It was no big deal." Handing them to her, he added, "I think they need to go in water."

She'd been just about to smell them. Straightening, she replied, "Oh. Yes, I should probably go do that. I'll be right back."

She turned without another word, leaving him alone in the inn's living room.

No doubt Lilly had just arrived at the same conclusion that he had. As far as romantic gestures went, this one was off to a bad start.

He really should've practiced what he was going to say.

14

Phillip and Penelope both stopped what they were doing when Lilly entered the kitchen.

"Whatcha got there?" Phillip teased.

Fighting off her embarrassment—and Penelope's knowing looks—Lilly threw out a little attitude. "I would've thought it was obvious," she teased. "Any idea if there's a vase in here?"

"There's a whole cabinet full of them," Pen said as she walked over to a cupboard above the large stainless refrigerator. "Phillip, pull the green glass one down, wouldya?"

He put down his carving knife, walked to the cabinet, and reached up high to pull down the vase. "Here you go."

"Thank you. Come on, Lilly, let's put these daisies in some water."

Lilly joined Penelope at the sink but wasn't much help. All she did was stand next to her while Pen cut the bottoms off the stems, filled the vase with water, then competently arranged the flowers. "There you go, dear."

"Thanks." Almost wishing they were asking questions instead of looking at her in such an amused way, Lilly picked up the vase and headed back to the door. "I better get back out there."

"Eddie's waiting on ya, then?" Pen asked.

"Yes. How did you know the flowers were from him?"

"It's pretty obvious that he's smitten with you, honey," Phillip said.

"I don't know . . ." Yes, he'd brought her flowers, but he was acting so strange.

"Would you like me to bring you out some drinks and snacks?" Penelope asked.

Lilly thought about it for a minute, then shook her head. "I don't think so. I'm afraid if you come out with a tray, he's going to feel even more on the spot than he already does."

"As long as he knows we're all looking out for you," Phillip said. "He better be nice to you."

"Oh, brother." She walked back to the living room. When she didn't see him sitting on the couch, a lump formed in her throat. She'd taken too long.

"I'm over here."

She turned to find him sitting in a nook over in the corner.

"I thought this might give us a little bit more privacy," he explained. "I hope you don't mind."

"I don't." She carried the vase of daisies to their new spot and set them down in the exact center of the table. "I'm sorry it took longer than I expected. I had to find a vase."

"I didn't mind. I think they look great in there."

"Me too." She smiled at him as she sat down in the chair to his right.

"Actually, I'm kind of glad that took you a minute, because I've been thinking about what to say to you."

"Oh?"

"I've been wanting to tell you about my ex-girlfriend Hanna. I think hearing about what we went through might help you understand why I'm pretty rusty at romance."

She liked the way he'd phrased that. "I'm pretty rusty at romance too."

"Really? You're so pretty, Lilly. I noticed a couple of men on the SCAT staring at you when we were coming back from Siesta Key the other night."

"I didn't notice anyone doing that." She shrugged and smiled. "I don't have much courting experience. What happened with you and Hanna?"

"We were in school together. That's how we met. She had dark hair and matching eyes and dimples." His voice grew soft. "She was smart and a little sassy. We became friends almost instantly. By the time we graduated our eighth-grade year, we were something more."

"Ah." It was a rather feeble response, but that was the best she could come up with, most likely because she was fighting an unwelcome jolt of jealousy. This Hanna sounded perfect.

No, Hanna sounded perfect for Eddie. He obviously still had strong feelings for her.

Pulling herself together, she said, "So, you began courting her when you were fourteen?"

"Nee. Not quite that young. I waited until I was seventeen and then proposed when I was eighteen. She said yes. Our families were thrilled. We decided to marry the following year."

He exhaled. "Lilly, I honestly thought everything was perfect. I was so full of myself, I even had the nerve to tell some of my friends that I thought relationships were easy and that they were going about things all wrong."

She had to smile at that. "I'm guessing that didn't go over very well."

"Not at all." Embarrassment and humor filled his gaze. "I'm embarrassed to say that I thought everything in my life was perfect. I worked on the farm, talked to my grandmother about moving into the dawdi haus, and basically counted the days until the big day." He swallowed. "But then, ah, six months later, Hanna broke up with me."

"Why? What happened?"

"She'd met another man." He wrinkled his nose. "Someone she met at some family reunion. They started writing, and one thing led to another."

Lilly looked at him, trying to imagine what that would do to her in the same circumstance. "Eddie, I'm so sorry. No one deserves to be treated like that."

Eddie gave her a small smile. "Thanks. It was really bad. Not only was my heart broken but my family was upset as well. Everyone knew how I felt about her, so there were a lot of knowing looks and comments. I was publicly embarrassed."

"Everyone shouldn't have acted that way. You were innocent."

"I wanted to think I was, but now that so much time has passed, I wonder if I could've been better. Maybe I could've been more romantic or spent more time with her." He waved a hand. "Or, I don't know, been the man she wanted."

She hated that he was accepting part of the blame. "I've never been engaged, but it seems to me that Hanna must have thought you were the man she wanted. If not, she wouldn't have let you court her, and she never would've said yes when you proposed."

"I think the worst part about it all is that when she broke up with me, she said she'd been feeling like she'd made a mistake for a while but hadn't wanted to let me know. Then, when she'd met this other man, she tried to fight her feelings but couldn't help herself."

"I guess not." Though if Hanna had been writing to her mystery man, it was pretty obvious that she hadn't been trying very hard.

"I wish she would've told me the truth. I hate secrets." His voice hardened. "She not only broke my heart, she made a fool of me. And, yeah, I know I shouldn't care about pride, but it wasn't easy being the jilted fiancé."

"I bet it wasn't."

"I just don't know how I could have missed all that."

His words were painful to hear. What about her secrets? Would he think the same about her? All she'd ever heard when she was in Middlefield was that she was lucky and blessed to be adopted. Then there was the knowledge about the type of man her birth father was. He'd been incarcerated her whole life. Though his choices had nothing to do with her life, she'd always felt like everyone inadvertently held that against her. She'd ached for someone to see her as simply "Lilly." To realize that she was more than her parents' past.

Now that it was finally happening, she wondered if keeping her secret was going to one day come back to bite her. She didn't think that Eddie needed to know everything about her past, but what if she was wrong?

Oh, why was she so confused?

"Did what I shared make any sense at all?" Eddie asked, returning her to the present.

She smiled. "It did."

He sighed. "It's made me pretty cautious now—even when I meet someone as wonderful as you."

She shook her head and tried to give him some reassurance. "Eddie, you're a wonderful man. Even though we're just getting to know each other, I can already tell that any woman would be blessed to have you court her. I think Hanna made a bad decision, but maybe it was meant to be."

"I think so. After all, if I was married to her now, I wouldn't have taken my grandmother to Florida—and we would've never met."

Until just a few minutes ago, Lilly would've said the same thing. At the moment, however, she was wishing that they'd never met. If they hadn't, then she would never have started hoping for something better.

No, that wasn't the complete truth.

She would've never started to imagine a future with him . . . or to imagine how he would look at her if he knew that she was the daughter of a prison inmate.

"God is always so good," she murmured. "I guess He had a different future in mind for you all along."

"Exactly. I'm so glad you feel the same way."

The way he gazed at her was so sweet, like she was wonderful.

No, like she was special.

It took everything Lilly had to return his smile and not run to her room.

15

He'd made a big mistake with Lilly. Eddie wasn't sure what he'd said or done that had spooked her, but he definitely believed that she was spooked.

It was his fault too. Even though she could be spunky, he'd known that she was also wary. He should have thought about that wariness and not have come on so strong. He didn't know if it was the flowers, the way he'd shared his feelings for Hanna, or the fact that he'd pretty much put his heart on the line with her.

He groaned. It was probably all three! It had been too much, and now she was avoiding him. It was driving him crazy.

And, because he was on vacation, he had nothing but too much time to dwell on it. He'd started thinking of all sorts of things that he should be saying to her. At the top of the list was to apologize for whatever he'd done wrong that had upset her.

Unfortunately, he didn't get that chance.

In the three days that had passed, he'd "just" missed her at breakfast service, she was too busy in the back to spare him five minutes, and then she had a day off and was with her girl-friends.

When Esther had looked at him in sympathy that morning, Eddie knew his suspicions had been correct.

Which made him feel even worse, and each day feel even lon-ger. He was alternating between being frustrated with himself and bored. Although his grandmother had started walking with him a bit every day, she was still most content in her room or reading on the property.

On Saturday morning, he decided to go back to the Snow Bird Golf Course. Not only did he need something to do that would take up a good portion of the day, he was hoping he might have the chance to speak to August Troyer again.

August knew Lilly and was married to one of her best friends. Hopefully he would be able to shed some light on what was going on with her.

He found the course easily enough and was delighted to see August behind the counter when he walked in the clubhouse a little after nine in the morning.

After giving the four men in front of him their tee time, August greeted him warmly. "Hey, Eddie. How are you?"

"I'm all right. How's the course? Is it full? Any chance I could get on?"

August looked down at the schedule in front of him. "Do you want to be a fourth teeing off in twenty minutes?"

"I was hoping I could play alone. I'll need to rent some clubs too. Do you have any available?"

"I'm pretty sure. Let me double check." He went to a back room then returned a few minutes later. "We've got a right-handed set. That's good for you, yeah?"

"It is."

Looking back at the schedule, he tapped a time with the end of his pencil. "Now, as for tee times, I think you could get on in forty minutes, if you don't mind playing just nine holes."

"That's fine. I'll take anything as long as it gets me out of my head."

August put down the pencil. "Any chance you want some company? I've got a couple of guys here helping out. They'd have no problem covering the front desk for a couple of hours."

Eddie breathed a sigh of relief. "If you could join me, that would be great. I, uh, was actually hoping that we could talk sometime today."

"Let me guess. You've got some flower problems? Especially one named Lilly?"

He grinned. "Do I ever."

"Since I was going through the same thing just last year, I'd love to commiserate. These women can run us guys through the wringer."

"Danke. I'm starting to second-guess every single thing I've said to her."

"That much, huh?"

"She's avoiding me," Eddie added.

The shop's front door opened, and a group of four couples walked in.

August grabbed a set of clubs and handed them to Eddie. "Go hit balls or putt if you want. I'll meet you right outside here in forty minutes."

"Thanks. See you then." Carrying the golf bag on his shoulder, he headed over to the driving range. He hadn't played golf in two years. Warming up sounded like a great idea.

They were playing the back nine. By the fourteenth hole Eddie had decided to stop worrying about his shots and simply use the time to appreciate how well August played. Every time the guy swung his club, it was fluid and smooth. The way his golf balls sailed through the air, continually hitting the green, was impressive too. But what Eddie liked the most was August's easygoing manner. He shrugged off Eddie's compliments, easily chatted with other players on the course, and essentially looked as if nothing in the world had ever bothered him.

The guy was relaxing to be around, for sure and for certain.

He was also, unfortunately, making it really hard for Eddie to admit just how mixed up he was feeling.

After he skimmed the top of his ball and the thing went right into a sand trap, Eddie groaned. "I'm so sorry. I guess I'm a lot rustier than I'd realized."

"Nothing to apologize for."

"Do you have any tips for me?"

"Sure. Keep your head down when you tee off and start talking about what's going on with Lilly."

"Are you sure you want to hear about it?"

After Eddie used his wedge and popped his ball onto the green, August laughed. "Eddie, when Betsy and I were courting, I was debating whether or not to follow my parents to Africa for missionary work. Then she ended up in the hospital. That's when I had to come to terms with my feelings for her and how far I was willing to go to be the man she needed me to be."

"Wow. That's a lot."

"Oh yeah." He pulled off his hat, ran his hand through his dark hair, then adjusted the hat on his head again. "During that time, I also had to stand up to both her parents and mine.

116

I'm not going to lie—there were a few moments when I didn't think I was strong enough to handle it all."

"But you did."

"Jah. I did." He pulled out his putter and easily shot his ball into the hole. "With the Lord's help."

After he retrieved it, August turned to him. "Just to let you know, Jayson and Mary Margaret had a few dark moments as well."

"So what you're saying is that I shouldn't expect things with Lilly to be easy."

"I guess I am. But more importantly, now that all that is behind me, I'm even glad we went through it," August said after Eddie made his shot. "But I bet that doesn't come as a surprise, does it? I mean, nothing worthwhile ever comes easy. Not even playing a sport well."

After two more strokes, Eddie pulled his ball out of the hole, and as he followed August to the next tee, he explained about his last meeting with Lilly. The flowers. His past. His hopes for the future. And her silence since then. "So what do you think I should do? I mean, you know Lilly pretty well. Or at least Betsy does."

"What do you want to happen, Eddie? Are you hoping she'll fall in love with you and want to get married? Or do you just want to end your vacation on a good note?"

"I don't know! I'm not ready to make that choice. It's way too early."

"You sure about that?"

"I'd known my fiancée for most of my life, and everything still ended."

To his surprise, August only shrugged. "Sounds like the Lord knew better than you."

"I'm sure the Lord did, but that doesn't mean that He thinks Lilly is the better choice. You don't know anything about what happened between Hanna and me."

August looked hard at him. "I know that you haven't once said that you wish you had Hanna back. I know that you're thinking about Lilly. I know that you care enough about her to play a really sorry game of golf in order to have the chance to make things better."

While Eddie thought on his words, August walked to the men's tee box, steadied his golf ball on a tee, and swung. It sailed in a perfect straight line and landed on the putting green.

When he turned back to Eddie, August looked very amused. "I know enough."

Eddie might be completely confused, but he hadn't turned into a fool. "I'd say you're right about that."

Slapping him on the back, August chuckled. "Don't be so hard on yourself, Eddie. Relax around Lilly, don't rush things, and pray. Whatever is meant to happen will happen. The Lord is always right."

"The Lord is always right," he repeated under his breath. "I'm going to remember that." When he swung, he peeked at August.

Which, of course, made his ball go short and land in the brush.

"Might be helpful if you remembered to keep your head down too, man. The Lord's going to be busy enough sorting out your love life. He might not have too much time to help you with your golf game."

16

"Nancy, I think we have a problem," Phillip said as he strode into her office.

She'd been concentrating so hard on a set of bills, she jumped. Which made the pencil she'd been holding fall out of her hand and eventually roll off the edge of her desk. Growing more flustered by the second, Nancy jumped to her feet to try to save it.

But the only thing that happened was that Phillip had a close view of her acting like an idiot. The thing fell to the floor with a clatter and then rolled under a file cabinet.

Just like the dozen or so other pencils that were already there.

"Argh!"

"You okay?"

"Yes. I mean, I am, other than I'm really wishing that the floor of this office was level."

"It's not?"

"Nope. It used to be, but when we had that tropical storm a couple of years ago, the foundation on the right-hand side started to sink. Now it's like living in a fun house."

His lips turned up slightly as he pointed to the pair of heavy, solid oak file cabinets. "Let me guess—the file cabinets are now home to all of your unwanted writing utensils?"

"Not unwanted. I actually like them a lot. But yes. Somehow they all manage to roll under the cabinets, which are so heavy and big that the pencils are doomed to rest there for years to come."

"That's a pity."

"I think so too." She frowned for a long moment before collecting herself. Here she was, discussing her office furniture like it was a big deal. It wasn't.

There was obviously something wrong, though, since Phillip was still standing in front of her desk and visibly biting his tongue until she finished.

"Phillip, please forgive me. You came out here for a reason, and all I've been doing is mourning a pencil. What's wrong?"

"What's wrong is that it's Saturday night, the inn is full, and you're in here."

She had no idea what he was acting so agitated about. "You've lost me. None of what you said is a surprise. Plus, having a full house is a good thing. I get to stay in business that way."

"I know. I get to keep my job that way too." He shifted on his feet, bringing her attention to him. Today he was wearing a pair of soft-looking khakis that had to have been washed several dozen times at the very least. On his feet were a pair of leather Birkenstock clogs, his shoe wear of choice whenever he was spending the majority of his day in the kitchen. He also had on a faded light blue T-shirt that fit him like a glove and molded to his chest and biceps. As usual, his skin was lightly tan and his hair in need of a trim.

So, he was pretty much looking the way he always did to her: perfect.

She walked around her desk so they could face each other without anything between them. "Phillip, I've been working on bills, schedules, and reservations for the last three hours. I'm afraid you're going to have to be a whole lot clearer about this Saturday night problem. My mind is a jumbled mess right now."

"What's going on is that Esther and her husband are here, and they just volunteered to watch over the place for a few hours since they're hanging out with Lilly."

"Sorry, but why are they here?"

"Obviously, to do us a favor. You've been working, I've been working, but neither of us has been enjoying the fruits of our labor. It's clear that we need to go out to eat tonight."

All this was about dinner. He wanted to take her out. "Are you asking me on a date?"

Finally his expression warmed. "Yeah, Nancy. I'm asking you out on a date tonight. Will you go out with me?"

"Yes."

"Really? You mean I'm not going to have to stand here and list about twenty reasons why this is a good idea?"

"I'm not going to make you do that. I'd love to get out of here. And even though I kind of feel like a new mom learning to trust her baby with the sitter, I'm excited."

"I'm glad. I'm excited too."

"Do you mind coming to get me at my place?" She gestured to her tailored outfit that looked very much like what a hotel manager would wear and nothing like what a woman about to go out on a date would wear.

"I don't mind at all . . . if you take one piece of advice."

"Okay . . ."

"Go out the gate. If you go into the main building, something or someone is going to take your attention."

He had a good point. And while she probably should check in with Esther and Michael, Nancy decided to take Phillip's advice. It was time to think about herself for once.

Even if just for three hours.

17

I t was nice to meet you," a middle-aged lady from Indiana
said as she and Lilly slowly followed the other parishioners
out of the Amish community church.

"I enjoyed meeting you as well," Lilly replied with a smile.
Bending down to the lady's two adorable little girls, she added,
"I hope you find a starfish soon." Before the service, they'd
told her all about their visits to the ocean and how much they
wanted to see a real starfish on a rock.

"Danke," the older one said before shyly hiding her face in
her mother's skirts.

As the line slowly moved forward, Lilly decided that she
enjoyed going to the community church very much.

The first week, going to a building in the center of town had
been so strange. Worshiping next to women she'd never met had
felt awkward too. It was so different than being in a neighbor's
barn and standing next to someone she'd known for years.

But she'd taken a cue from Mary and learned to embrace all
the differences. That change of heart had worked wonders too.
The next week, women around her, seeing her smile, had been
just as eager to make a friend. Now it was becoming almost

easy for her to casually ask the women around her where they were from.

Those conversations always seemed to lift her spirits, especially on days like today when she couldn't seem to stop thinking about Eddie and their conversation about Hanna. Whenever her mind settled, she could hear his words, telling her about all the things he'd loved about her.

Which, in her darkest moments, reminded Lilly that Hanna was a lot of things she wasn't.

To top it off, she kept remembering how much he didn't like secrets. His voice had been so harsh. Firm.

What was she going to do if he ever learned about her past? Would he think worse of her because of her birth father? She didn't like to think that he would hold something like that against her.

Just how well did she know Eddie Byler, anyway?

"Blessings to you," the lady murmured, interrupting her thoughts.

"Hmm? Ah, yes. Blessings to you all as well."

The woman smiled as she took hold of her daughters' hands and walked through the crowd to find her husband.

"There you are!" Mary Margaret called out. "I lost you for a moment."

"There's a big crowd here today."

"Now that it's getting closer to the holidays, more and more snowbirds are arriving," Mary's husband Jayson said. "By the time New Year's Day arrives, you'll be thinking of this crowd as small." He shifted Tricia in his arms. Their babe was fast asleep.

Lilly playfully groaned as they headed to the sidewalk. They'd made plans to meet at church and then spend the afternoon together. "That means the inn will be crowded all the time too. I'll have to go to your house for some peace and quiet."

"Not *mei haus*," Mary said with a laugh. "When Tricia is awake, there's only chaos."

Lilly knew that wasn't true. Mary was a wonderful mother and never seemed to get too rattled. She didn't argue the point, however. Instead, she simply enjoyed listening to Mary and her husband tease each other about little chores that never seemed to get finished, thanks to the antics of a busy toddler.

Just as they walked in the door, Tricia woke up. Lilly played with her while Mary and Jayson prepared lunch. To her surprise, Betsy and August joined them. Their lunch was a simple meal of grilled hot dogs, chips, and fruit. Lilly's contribution was a container of oatmeal cookies that Phillip had made the day before.

Eventually, Tricia went down for a nap. The men went inside while the three women sipped lemonade and ate cookies in the warm October sun.

"I received a letter from my mother yesterday," Mary said. "She said they've already had snow. What do you think about that, Lilly? Are you excited not to have to worry about shoveling snow this winter?"

"I am, though I can't say I hated shoveling snow that much."

"I did," Betsy said.

"You got snow in Kentucky?"

"Of course we did. Not all the time, but we had at least one or two good snowfalls a year." She playfully shivered. "I don't miss the cold weather in the slightest."

When Lilly just smiled, Mary seemed to study her more intently. "What's going on, Lilly? You look like you have something on your mind."

"I'm afraid I do. The other day, I went to the beach for a spell and ended up seeing Eddie."

Betsy smiled brightly. "August met him on the golf course! He said he was nice."

"He is nice . . . but I'm afraid he's also nursing a broken heart." Knowing that she needed to hear their opinions, she shared her and Eddie's conversation.

By the time she finished, both of her girlfriends were looking at her in concern.

"Lilly, you are not responsible for anyone's actions other than your own," Betsy said.

"I know, but I'm afraid he's going to be upset with me for not telling him everything about my past."

"What past?" Mary asked. "You grew up in a small town, have an older brother and sister, and sometimes felt like a wall-flower. You've done nothing to be ashamed of."

"I don't know if he'll feel that way. He kept saying that he was disappointed that Hanna wasn't the person he'd thought she was."

"Of course he was disappointed," Mary retorted. "His fi-ancée had wandering eyes."

Betsy nodded. "Mary's right. No one is perfect, but it does rather sound like this Hanna was especially imperfect." She paused to take a sip of her drink. "But Lilly, her story has nothing to do with yours. It's like comparing today's humidity with the chance of snow up north. Both aren't necessarily welcome news, but they are two very different things."

"They are also two things that not everyone in the world thinks are bad things," Mary added. Reaching for her hand, she whispered, "Lilly, I think that you're letting your fears get the best of you. Being adopted is a blessing."

"Yes, but what if he doesn't think that?"

"If he's the right person for you, he'll understand," Betsy said. "That's all there is to it."

Lilly hoped her friends were right. Feeling like she'd painted a poor picture of Eddie, she said, "He's a good person. You should see how he is with November, his grandmother. They've got a fantastic relationship. It's almost like they're best friends."

"I'm glad to hear that, but all I really care about is how he treats you," Mary said. "You're important too, Lilly. Don't forget that."

"I won't." Ready to talk about something else, she turned to Betsy. "What have you been doing lately?" A little over a year ago, Betsy had begun to work on her "life list"—a list of activities that she wanted to try. Some, like swimming, were things that she enjoyed very much. Others, like kayaking, hadn't gone so well.

"Quilting," Betsy replied with a frown.

Mary chuckled. "I didn't know you liked to quilt."

"That's because I don't. After seeing last year's quilt benefit auction, I decided that I should make one for charity, but I'm afraid I'm not cut out for it."

"What don't you like? The design, piecing it together, or the actual quilting?"

"None of it." After peeking at the glass door, presumably to make sure her husband couldn't overhear, Betsy added, "Even August has asked me when I'll put the project away."

Lilly and Mary exchanged amused glances. "It's that bad?"

"Oh yes."

"We should have a quilting bee," Mary said. "I'll ask Esther and Jayson's sister Joy to join us too."

"And Betsy's friend Brianna," Lilly added, remembering that

Brianna was August's best friend's wife. "If we all got together, we could fix it up and get it done in no time."

Betsy frowned. "I don't know if that's going to be possible. It's a really big quilt and none of it looks too good."

"I'm up to the challenge if you are," Mary said.

"Oh, I am," Betsy said. "I want it out of my life."

"I guess making quilts for charity isn't going to be in your future," Lilly teased.

Betsy shook her head. "As much as I want to make something warm for others, I'm never attempting to make a quilt again. I mean, not if I can help it."

Mary looked like she was trying not to laugh. "Do I dare ask what the next item on your life list is?"

Betsy's pretty dark eyes brightened. "Knitting."

Mary's eyes lit up with mirth. "Knitting?"

Lilly felt the same way Mary obviously did. Betsy with a pile of yarn and sharp needles sounded like trouble. "Are you sure you want to tackle another craft project?"

"Jah. I mean, how hard can knitting be?"

"I guess we'll find out," Mary said as she started to laugh.

Unable to help herself, Lilly joined in. Betsy did too. As their laughter filled the air, she realized that her burdens felt lighter and her mood had lifted. These two women had done that.

No matter what happened with her and Eddie, she realized she was going to be all right. The Lord had given her wonderful friends who were going to be by her side no matter what happened. She was grateful for that.

18

It was only Tuesday, but so far Lilly believed it was shaping up to be a really good week. After she returned to the inn on Sunday afternoon, she'd discovered that Phillip had left her a meal in the refrigerator. Monday had been nice because she and Esther had been able to eat lunch together. Because of the staff's schedules and the general busyness of the inn, coordinating meals with one of her best friends was a rare occurrence.

However, the best part of her week had been when she'd discovered the note Eddie had left for her at the front desk on Monday afternoon. It had been simple and to the point.

Lilly, are you free on Tuesday afternoon? If so, want to go out for ice cream? Say, at four o'clock?

Since Nancy had been right there, Lilly had asked if she could get off a little bit early. When Nancy had said it would be no problem, she'd written Eddie back that she would meet him in the lobby.

She'd been fighting a batch of butterflies in her stomach all day. They were good ones, though. Betsy's and Mary's pep talk on Sunday after church had done her confidence a world of good.

So did Penelope's encouraging smile when Lilly had walked through the kitchen just moments before. Lilly knew she felt pretty and fresh in her pale green dress and white flip-flops.

Eddie's expression when he spied her made her pulse race too. He was looking at her like there wasn't another person in the entire inn.

"Hi," she said softly when she got to his side. Eddie was wearing a pair of loose navy pants and a bright white short-sleeved shirt. His face and arms were tan. He looked so handsome.

He also looked a little nervous.

"Hi, Lilly. I'm so glad you agreed to come! I thought you might be avoiding me."

Lilly's smile stopped before it started. Of course she had been avoiding him, but she hadn't thought it was obvious. "Why would you think that?"

"Every time I went looking for you, you were out or too busy. I worried I'd done something wrong." His blue eyes, always so striking, looked directly into hers, and she sensed he was hoping she'd deny it.

She realized she had two choices. Admit that she'd been skittish and wary . . . or move on by telling a little fib. "I haven't been avoiding you at all. It's just really busy right now." When he still looked skeptical, she smiled. "I'm glad you left a note about today. I . . . I like being with you, Eddie."

Sure, she was still rattled by some of the things he'd said to her about secrets, but she was going to trust the Lord with the outcome.

"I can't tell you how glad I am to hear you say that. So, are you ready?"

"I am."

He held the door open for her and stayed by her side as they walked down the short flight of stairs from the front porch. "Tell me what you've been doing. Hopefully not just working."

"Let's see. I went to church and then spent Sunday afternoon with my friends Mary and Betsy. Yesterday, Esther and I were able to have lunch together. What about you?"

"I played nine holes at the golf course with August, which was humbling. He's a great golfer."

"I bet."

"I also convinced my grandmother to go out to lunch yesterday."

"Where did you go?"

"We went to a sandwich shop near the water and spent two hours just watching all the boats and such travel in and out of the harbor."

"Isn't that the best? It's snowing up north, but here you get to sit outside in the sun."

"We said the same thing. Mommi smiled the whole time. The seagulls even made her laugh."

Before she knew it, they were at Olaf's Creamery. Eddie paid for their ice-cream cones and they sat down at one of the small tables to enjoy the treats.

Lilly knew that something special was happening between them. Eddie was kind and fun. He smiled at her often and seemed to appreciate everything she had to say. She was so glad that he'd asked her out for ice cream . . . and that she'd gotten over her worries and said yes.

As the late afternoon sun started to descend, she even began to wonder when they'd see each other again. Maybe she could take him to meet her friends. He'd already met August, so chances were good that he'd probably get along with Jayson and Michael too.

Eddie finished his cone quickly and turned to Lilly. "You know, after we talked, I realized I didn't give you much chance to tell me about your life."

And just like that, all of her optimism faded. Lilly could practically feel her guard go up. "There's not much to say. I've told you that I have an older brother and sister and that they're both married."

"What about your parents?"

"What about them?"

He raised his eyebrows. "Well, what are their names? What does your father do?" He waved his fingers. "I just want to know more about your family, Lilly. What are they like? You know . . . like, do you have your mother's eyes? That kind of stuff."

She knew his questions were simple—so why did answering them feel like an obstacle course? "My parents' names are Fran and Gabe. My father is the manager of an Amish-made furniture store."

"Is he a carpenter too?"

"Nee. He is just the manager. But he's a mighty gut one. It's a very big store. There's almost fifty people working there. He makes sure everything runs smoothly. Now, my mamm spends most of her days taking care of the house. But she also bakes things like muffins and cookies and pound cakes to sell at the furniture store on Fridays. Some people only come to the store on Fridays so they can purchase her treats."

"You sound close to them."

She shrugged. "I think so. I guess I'm as close as most girls are with their parents."

"Did you inherit your mother's love for baking?"

"Nee."

His eyes became shadowed as he seemed to process her answer. "Oh."

Lilly knew that Eddie didn't care whether she could bake or not. It was the fact that she was barely answering his questions. Feeling more uncomfortable, she added, "Like I said, there isn't much to share."

"I've been thinking a lot about how brave you've been. I don't know too many people who would leave their family and all their friends to move to a new state."

"I wouldn't say I was brave."

"But wasn't it hard?" He leaned back. "I mean—I'm just trying to understand why you wanted to move away."

"It wasn't too difficult. I have friends here." Since she really hadn't had any good friends to speak of back in Ohio, leaving them hadn't been hard at all.

"And you weren't dating anyone?"

"I didn't have a boyfriend, Eddie." Glad that the conversation was moving on, her pulse took a quick leap. "And I already know you are single too," she teased.

Instead of grinning, he barely acknowledged what she said. "Have you ever had one?"

"Eddie, I'm starting to feel like this is an interrogation. Why are you asking me so many questions?"

He drew back, stung. "All I'm doing is trying to get to know you better."

She attempted to laugh, but it came out sounding fake and flat. "I've been answering your questions for ten minutes now. I think you know me as well as anyone does."

"I doubt that."

"I'm a pretty simple person. There isn't too much to know."

He shook his head slowly. "I think the complete opposite. I think you're one of the most interesting women I've ever met."

"You do?"

"I do. But I think I've made you uncomfortable, and I never want to do that."

"If you're talking about right now, I have to admit that you're probably right. I'm not used to people asking me so many personal questions."

Eddie leaned forward, placing his hands on the table. Close, but not too close to her own. "Well, I'm asking. I'd love to know what you think. I'd love to know more about you."

"You know I grew up in Middlefield," she said impatiently. "You know what my parents do. You know that I have an older sister and brother."

He sighed. "And?"

And they weren't adopted. They were "real." But even to her ears those descriptors didn't come close to describing her older brother and sister. It didn't say a thing about the type of people Katie and John were, which was a shame. Katie and John were fine. Decent people Lilly might not be close to, but that didn't mean it was their fault. There was an age gap. John was ten years older and Katie was nine. John had been apprenticing at a carpentry shop and courting Samantha when Lilly entered kindergarten.

"Their names are John and Katie. They're both quite a bit older than me."

His focus on her never wavered, but he smiled, encouraging her to keep going.

She swallowed. "And they're both married. John lives a couple of miles away. Katie and her family live a little farther out. Katie has five *kinner*. She's busy."

"What else?"

She laughed. "Eddie, that's everything!"

"Come on. All the information you just gave me could have been on a library card or something."

"I doubt that."

He waved a hand, as if the example wasn't relevant. "What I meant was, what do you like to do with them?"

His question felt like an intrusion. Not because he was wrong. In a lot of ways, he was right. She really hadn't given him any information that was personal. But the problem was that she didn't have a wealth of memories or a catalog of interests in common with her siblings. "I don't really see John and Katie all that much."

"I see."

Feeling helpless, she said, "I'm not like you, Eddie. I don't have the gift of gab."

"I wasn't looking for entertaining stories, Lilly. I was hoping to get to know you. The real Lilly, not just things one could read on a resume or something."

She knew Eddie wanted her to open up more toward him, but she just wasn't ready. Even though Eddie seemed genuinely kind, she'd been burned before by supposed friends gossiping about her. "I'm sorry if you're disappointed with our conversation, because everything I've told you is all I've got to share."

His lips pursed. "Are you close to John and Katie?"

"I don't know. I guess." But even she didn't believe her words. Of course, how could she? For most of her life, she'd barely felt as if she even belonged in their house.

He blinked. Then, for a split second, almost looked pained. "I'm one of four kids. My older brother's name is James. He's married, has a baby, and lives on a farm nearby. I have a sister named Alice who is married and lives in Missouri. Finally, I have a younger sister named Meg. She's shy and has been courted by the shyest man I've ever known. They're a perfect match, but I don't know if Mason will ever get the gumption to actually propose because he sometimes can hardly speak four words to Meg in a row."

"I think that's sweet."

Eddie grunted under his breath. "Of course you do. I promise, you wouldn't if you were her older brother, though."

"What do you think of Mason?"

"I think that he's a nice guy but that if he really likes her, then he should do something about it. They've been seeing each other for years. I feel like he's been stringing her along."

"That's hardly fair. I mean, if he's courting her then he isn't stringing her along. Maybe he wants to be sure."

He shook his head. "Nee. That's not good enough for me."

"Eddie!"

"I know I sound like a caveman or something, but Meg is so sweet and she's been waiting and waiting for him to propose. What if he changes his mind?"

"Then that will be for the best, jah?" She lifted an eyebrow.

"I don't know," he grumbled. "I just don't want to see my little sister get hurt, you know?" He lowered his voice. "Sometimes I think Mason is waiting until he feels like everything in his life is perfect and that we'll accept him without reservation."

She bit her lip. "You can't rush Mason or your sister."

"I agree, but I also don't want Meg to settle for a man who is always gauging everyone else's reactions before doing what he wants. He needs a backbone, Lilly."

"I don't think it's that easy."

"Of course it is."

136

"Nee."

"Lilly, no offense, but if Mason believes that he's good enough for my sister then he should be man enough to ask for her hand in marriage."

She gazed at him. "And you genuinely believe that?"

"Of course I do." Lowering his voice, he added, "I believe in love. I believe that there's something perfect about love that means more than insecurities or self-doubts or wishes or dreams."

Eddie sounded so sure. "Have you been in love before?"

For the first time, he didn't meet her eyes. "I thought I was, but I wonder if I just wanted to be in love." He frowned. "Now—I'm hoping for the future." Turning to face her, he softened his voice. "What about you?"

She gulped, then nodded. He was saying things she hadn't believed could ever come true for her. No—Eddie was saying things that she'd imagined would only be realized in her dreams. She wanted to tell him everything about her past, right then. But the words refused to come.

As seconds passed, Eddie started to look doubtful. "I guess I came on too strong. Again."

"What could have given you that idea?" And yes, she was being sarcastic.

"Oh, I don't know . . . maybe because yet again I've been sharing all my mixed-up, jumbled thoughts while you are barely speaking."

"That isn't true."

"Lilly—I really like you. I want to spend this trip getting to know you. But some of the time I feel like I'm only getting to know a carefully filtered version of you. You never grumble, you don't seem to struggle, and you always take care of everyone else."

"I do struggle, and I do complain. Of course I do those things."

"I haven't seen you do much of either."

"You act like that's a bad thing. It's not."

"Never seeing you get upset or irritated might be bad . . . if a man is looking to know about you—even the parts that aren't lovely and perfect. I want to know you, Lilly. I want to know all of you."

She flinched and scooted back in her chair a bit. "Eddie, do you hear what you are saying? You're asking too much, too soon."

"I don't think so. I don't understand why you think so, either."

His words sounded harsh. Almost impatient.

She felt his disappointment but wished he could sense how she was feeling too. What if she said something that made him walk away? Why did she need to share things that made *her* feel unloved? It was too much to risk. Much too much. "I'm sorry then."

"I'm sorry too." He stood up. "Let me take you home."

Lilly got to her feet, but she felt off-kilter, like she'd gone four days without sleep. Like something had happened that had put her into such a fog that she couldn't see things clearly. But the rest of the world was continuing on at the very same pace.

It felt confusing and upsetting.

Or maybe it just felt familiar. After all, hadn't she felt some of the same things when she'd been a wallflower back home? Like she'd been standing in the dark, just waiting for someone to see her clearly.

"You don't need to walk me back. I know where the inn is from here."

"Of course I'm going to walk you back there. Don't argue."

"I'm not arguing, you're just not listening to me. What I'm saying is that I don't wish you to walk me back, Eddie. I'd rather walk alone than by your side."

He stared at her for a few seconds, then threw up his hands. "You know what? Fine. Walking by yourself is probably what you're used to anyway. It seems you'd rather be alone."

"Congratulations. You've successfully questioned me, analyzed me, and found me wanting. I hope you're pleased with yourself."

She turned and walked away. Tried to take comfort in the fact that she didn't hear footsteps behind her. But all she felt was her hopes getting crushed. She'd let herself believe that she was close to having a boyfriend and maybe even a fiancée and husband one day. Like Mary and Betsy. Like Esther. Like John and Katie.

She'd been so wrong. Maybe the Lord did intend for her to have those things one day, but it wasn't today. It wasn't anytime soon.

For now, she really was going to have to walk by herself.

Huh. She supposed Eddie had been right about everything after all. She was used to this. It was familiar.

Not comforting, not what she wanted. It felt like she was wearing a wool coat in July.

But that coat was hers.

19

Two days had passed since her awful date with Eddie. Two days of doing her best to think only about work. Everyone had seemed to notice that she'd been working extra hours and dusting and polishing everything in sight.

Nancy had even pulled her aside that morning with firm instructions to clock out at one o'clock.

Which was why she was feeling pretty bored at three in the afternoon. Lilly knew she should be exhausted from all the work or simply just be pleased that she was in sunny Florida.

Ever since she'd left Pinecraft for the first time, she'd dreamed of returning. When each of her girlfriends decided to make Florida their home, her dreams of living there intensified.

She'd honestly thought that working at the Marigold Inn was going to make her so happy that she wouldn't even mind spending her days cleaning.

She had been wrong.

Even if she wasn't still reeling from her argument with Eddie, Lilly knew she'd been wrong.

She liked her job just fine, but it didn't fill her heart.

No, it was more like she had begun to realize that her dreams had been too small. She didn't want to simply live in Pine-craft and work hard. She wanted what her girlfriends had. She wanted to fall in love with a man who loved her back, get married, and begin a life together. She had secretly hoped to one day be like Mary and start a family. That's what she'd been hoping for when she'd been back in Middlefield, Lilly realized. It wasn't simply living in Pinecraft or being near her girlfriends. She wanted everything.

Lilly was beginning to feel like she'd asked for a hot fudge sundae and had been served a scoop of vanilla ice cream instead. The treat was good and she appreciated it, but it wasn't what she'd hoped for.

That realization had made her feel restless and maybe even a little blue. Hoping to shake off her doldrums, she'd gotten through her work day and then went out on the front porch. Usually she enjoyed the opportunity to simply sit, especially since she had a book in her hands, but that wasn't the case this afternoon.

It felt like there were too many hours in the day now, especially since she'd already read the book and it hadn't been all that good in the first place.

When the front door opened, Lilly straightened, expecting to see one of the inn's guests. Although she was out of her uniform, there was a good chance a guest might recognize her and either ask her to clean something . . . or have a problem with her taking a spot they believed was reserved for guests.

Instead, it was Phillip.

She relaxed again. "Hi, Phillip," she murmured, expecting him to walk right by. He didn't. Instead, he stopped in front of her. "Hey."

As usual, he looked serious and a little intense as he scanned

her face. At first, the way he looked at the world had kind
of freaked her out. She'd assumed he was in a perpetual bad
mood. Now, she knew that his expression was his usual look.
The Marigold Inn's cook wasn't a smiler.

He didn't usually seek her out, either.

Concerned, Lilly closed the book on her lap. "Is something
wrong?"

"Not at all. I was looking for you, though. One of the guests
told me you were out here on the front porch."

It looked like her fear about being on the porch had been
justified. "Sorry," she said as she stood up. "I was a little ap-
prehensive about reading here, but Nancy never told me I
shouldn't. I'll go—"

"Sit down, kid."

Taken aback by his tone, she sat back down.

His expression softened. "Sorry. I didn't mean to bark at you.
But listen, you live here, right? This is your home. Of course
you can sit wherever you want."

"Oh." His words were sweet, but everything about their conversation was confusing.

His lips curved up for a second, like he was trying hard not
to smile. "Lilly, I was looking for you because I'm done for the
day too . . . and I think you need a break from this place. Let's
go to the bookstore."

"I'm sorry. What did you say?"

"You heard me. Go grab your purse or whatever you need
and meet me in the parking lot in five minutes." His voice softened. "I drive the green Jeep that's usually in the back row. Do
you know it?"

His Jeep was the type that had a soft top that could be re-
moved. It was a dark forest green and always shiny. She might

be Amish but even she had felt a pang of longing to have such a vehicle. It was the perfect way to drive along the boardwalk at the beach. "I know it."

"Good." He turned to walk back inside. "See you in five."

"Hey, wait! I can't go shopping."

He turned on his heel. "Why not?"

She wasn't really sure why. "Are you sure about this? I mean, someone might need me to do something."

He stuffed his hands in the pockets of his worn khakis. "I have it on good authority that you are done for the day. I am too. Get your stuff together and let's go."

"But . . . why?"

"Because you read as much as me. That's why. Come on, girl. Don't make this weird. I promise, I'm trustworthy. I would never hurt you or anything."

"I wasn't worried about that."

"Stop overthinking things then. I want some new books and I don't feel like going to the library. Plus, there's nothing wrong with getting out of here from time to time, right?" He arched an eyebrow.

She felt like he was issuing a challenge.

At least she was up for this one. "Right. I'll see you in five."

"Good." He grinned. A full smile with teeth and everything. It transformed his features and made him appear suddenly approachable. It was so rare to see that she stared.

Oblivious to her thoughts, Phillip walked inside without another word. The action didn't surprise her but did make her smile. He was abrupt and more than a little rough around the edges but nice.

She was starting to think that the Marigold Inn was feeling like home. Or maybe it was just more familiar. In any case, she wasn't going to pass up a trip to the bookstore—or getting to know the enigmatic man whom Nancy seemed to have a close partnership with.

Glad she'd already taken off her gray uniform dress and had on her favorite yellow one, Lilly hurried past the kitchen and down the short hallway to her room. Once inside, she put down her book, pulled out her envelope of cash from tips, and put a twenty-dollar bill in her wallet. Then, she hurriedly backtracked her steps and walked to the parking lot.

She was pretty sure that Phillip didn't mean five minutes in a general, ten-minutes-is-just-fine way. His five minutes actually meant five minutes.

Sure enough, when she got out to the parking lot, Phillip was already standing next to his vehicle and texting on his phone. He stuffed it in his pocket when he spied her.

"Look at you. You got here in five minutes, on the dot."

"I didn't want to get left behind," she teased.

His expression warmed. "I wouldn't have left you. But I do appreciate you not making me wait." He opened the driver's side door. "Hop in, buckle up, and we'll go."

She did as he asked and carefully buckled in as she surveyed the interior of the Jeep. It had tan leather and a chrome dash. It was also surprisingly comfortable. She hadn't expected that. "I like your Jeep."

"Yeah? Me too." He put the gearshift into reverse and backed out.

"Have you had it a long time?"

"Two years," he said as he maneuvered out of the parking lot and then turned right. "My old one was twelve years old and had a ton of miles on it. I was worried about my grandkids' safety."

"You have grandchildren?" Though she knew he'd just turned fifty, that still surprised her. He had such an independent way about him that Lilly had a hard time imagining him surrounded by little kids.

"I do," he said as he stopped at a stop sign. "Five of them."

"Five? Wow!"

"I've said that same thing from time to time. It's hard to believe." He grinned. "My son and his wife didn't lie when they said they wanted a large family."

"I didn't know you were married."

"I'm not." A muscle in his jaw tightened. "I mean, I'm not anymore. My wife died fifteen years ago."

"I'm sorry."

"I am too." He shrugged. "We were happy for a lot of years and had a great kid. Even though Annie didn't get to see it, she would've been thrilled to know that Evan married a great woman and they've produced a bunch of kids." He waved one of his hands in the air. "Those are all things to be grateful for, right?"

"Right." Remembering his comment about needing a safe vehicle, she asked, "Does Evan live nearby?"

"Close enough. Evan and Jamie live in Fort Myers. Their oldest is twelve." He grinned. "Before long, that kid is going to be asking to drive this. I know it."

"What are you going to say?"

He laughed. "I'm going to go into full grandpa mode and say that he can drive it as long as he's with me . . . and if it's okay with his mom." Phillip grinned. "My daughter-in-law watches her kids like a hawk. There's no way Jamie's going to let him drive my Jeep around Sarasota or to the beach."

She giggled too. "So you'll get your way but don't have to be the bad guy."

"Pretty much. It's a grandparent's prerogative."

"I think I'd want to do the same thing."

"Trust me, you would. Parenting is hard. Grandparenting is the reward for all the sleepless nights you have when you raise your kids. I've given thanks to God more than once for only giving Annie and me Evan. He was relatively easy and turned out great." As he slowed down to merge in traffic, he added, "I'm sure your parents will say the same thing."

Like always, the mention of her parents made her think of her birth parents first. Not eager to dwell on that, she quickly shook off those thoughts and said, "I think they already do. My older brother and sister are already married with kids."

"See? There you go."

Five minutes later he was pulling into the parking lot of a shopping center. In the middle of it all was a Barnes & Noble. Phillip slipped his Jeep into a spot a little away from most of the other vehicles. "Here we are. You don't mind walking, do you? I don't want anyone to ding my doors."

"Of course not."

"That's what I thought. I mean, you're on your feet all day every day at the inn."

Lilly was starting to think that he knew more about her than she'd realized. Not because he'd known that she was on her feet a lot at work—that was obvious. It was everything else. The way he'd said she'd needed a break from the inn. His offer to take her to a bookstore because he knew she liked to read.

As she unbuckled, she said, "Phillip, I'm really glad you asked me to come with you, but I don't understand why you thought about me in the first place."

He'd been just about to get out of the vehicle but turned to face her instead. "Pardon?"

"What I mean is that we don't really know each other. I'm just the new girl at the inn. I'm not trying to make going to a bookstore a big deal, but it kind of is to me." Feeling more foolish by the second, she blurted, "I don't even know how you knew I liked to read."

He chuckled. "You're kidding, right?"

She shook her head.

"Lilly, all of us have seen you either walking to the library or pulling books off the shelves in the living room. And before you try to defend yourself, I hope you realize that I think reading is a good thing."

"A lot of people have said that I should be talking to real people instead of keeping my nose in a book."

Phillip shrugged off her comment. "Who cares about what other people think? The only thing that matters is that you're happy. I'm just glad there's now someone at the inn who likes to read as much as I do."

"I'm glad about that as well."

"Then try not to worry so much, yeah? Let's go get a couple of books and take a break from the inn."

Smiling at him, she nodded. "I think that's a great idea."

He winked at her. "Stick with me, kid. I've got lots of great ideas."

Getting out of the Jeep, Lilly relaxed at last. Phillip was right. Everything didn't need to have a reason or be a big deal. She really did need to stop overthinking every little thing. All that mattered was that she was making a friend, and she'd learned that one can never have too many of those. It was better to count her blessings instead of worrying so much.

An hour later, she had a latte in one hand (courtesy of Phillip) and two books from the clearance bin in the other. Phillip was holding the same. She also thought they probably looked like father and daughter because of the way they both looked so happy.

"Lilly Kurtz, you are now my favorite person to go to the bookstore with."

"Any special reason why?"

"You didn't ask me when I was going to be ready to leave, and most importantly saw the value in getting a too-expensive but really fattening latte to sip on the way home."

"You're responsible for that one," she joked. "I wouldn't have bought the coffee if you hadn't offered to buy me one."

Phillip pretended to look offended. "It's good, though, right?"

It was some kind of coffee with sprinkles and whipped cream. "Of course. It's wonderful."

"Everyone needs a treat now and then."

After they got in the Jeep and buckled up, Lilly said, "Phillip, how did you end up becoming a chef?"

"It's a long story but a good one. Do you really want to hear it?"

"I really do."

He started talking, telling her about trade school and his wife and how he loved to fish and then was trying to find a way to cook it. The stories were interesting and lighthearted. He seemed to enjoy making a little bit of fun of himself too.

But what she was struck by the most was that the conversation was easy. For once she wasn't worried about saying the wrong things or making a good impression. She was simply relaxing. Phillip Shaw was a gifted conversationalist. Or maybe he was simply a nice man who happened to notice that she could use a small act of kindness.

Whatever the reason, Lilly felt that their little field trip had done her a world of good.

When he pulled back into the Marigold Inn's property, Lilly turned to him. "Thanks again for the field trip. You were right. Getting out of here did me a lot of good."

Phillip looked pleased by her words but a little embarrassed too. "It was nothing."

She'd heard his words, but she also knew that there was more to what had happened than "nothing." "Phillip, really. Danke."

"You are very welcome, Lilly. I enjoyed getting to know you better. Don't forget—you have a friend here."

"I won't forget."

As she walked back to the inn, holding her bag of books and the remains of her drink, one of the guests sitting on the front porch called out to her.

"Hi, Lilly."

"Hello, Mrs. Martin."

"How was the bookstore?"

"It was great!"

"I've been meaning to stop by there. Maybe tomorrow."

Lilly smiled at the woman as she walked inside. For the first time all day, she felt at ease. No, she still wasn't falling in love, but what she was experiencing was really good. She was making friends and gathering great memories. Both were things to be grateful for.

20

The end of his week had not been going well. Since he'd messed up with Lilly, Eddie had decided to check on his grandmother more often. No way did he want her leaving towels and trash on the floor again. He also wanted her to get outside and get more fresh air.

He was getting mixed results.

On a positive note, Eddie had been able to convince his grandmother to leave her room and go out for a walk with him.

The bad part was that she hadn't been shy about her feelings about leaving the inn. She hadn't seemed impressed with either the very nice lunch, the beautiful weather, or the fact that he was practically doing backflips in order to make sure she was happy.

Instead, she kept glancing at the clocks and hinting that it was time to go back home.

"Mommi, come on. Give today a try."

"I am. I enjoy being around you and I'm grateful for your time, Edward. It's just that I don't like that you're wasting all your time with me when you could be doing something else."

"Such as?"

"Oh, I don't know. Getting to know a certain young lady a

little better." Her expression warmed. "Dear, I might be old, but I remember when your grandfather courted me. Every conversation we shared felt priceless to me. Now, even though he's been gone for a long time, I treasure those memories. There's something almost magical about getting to know a special person in your life, one tidbit at a time."

Eddie couldn't deny that everything his grandmother said was true. He had friends who were already engaged or married. Each of them had said that they'd enjoyed the experience of getting to know the love of their lives very much.

But with Lilly it was different.

First, he wasn't positive she actually was the love of his life. He was attracted to her, yes, and liked a lot of things about her. But there were a lot of things about her that he just wasn't sure about. That wasn't a criticism, either. It was simply how he felt. And right now, he was pretty sure how she felt about him.

November frowned. "Eddie? What's wrong?"

"Nothing."

"Come now. The truth, if you please."

It was on the tip of his tongue to admit that getting to know Lilly really wasn't easy. She was a closed book and she acted as if she didn't trust him, and that hurt. He wanted to know her better. Just as important, he wanted her to want to know him. Not just in a superficial "let's just be friends" way but in a more meaningful one.

It was both discouraging and stressful to realize that she didn't want the same things from him.

"I've been trying to get to know her."

"Jah. I know." She smiled sweetly, but there was a new intensity shining in her face. She wanted to encourage him, but she didn't want any fibs or lies, either. She wanted the truth. "But . . ." She arched one brow.

But what? But . . . he wasn't sure? But . . . he wasn't sure if she felt anything close to the way he did? He wasn't sure she was speaking to him now? Those statements might be true, but that didn't mean he wanted to share them with his grandmother.

So, he settled for something else. Something far less meaningful but safe. A statement that would protect his feelings, at least for now. "But . . . we're taking things slowly, Mommi. I mean, Lilly is busy, right? I want to give her space. After all, we don't have to see each other every single minute of the day." Liking his response—and the fact that it was both firm yet evasive—he nodded.

Like he was approving his own statement.

His grandmother stared at him for a long moment then looked away. "Yes. I suppose you're right."

Her words were what he wanted to hear. So how come he felt like he'd just let them both down? "How about some coffee and a stop by the library before we head back to the inn?"

"That sounds nice, dear."

They stopped at a small coffee shop near the edge of Pinecraft. The Blue Star Café wasn't too big and had a good menu. It was slowly becoming one of his favorite places to get a quick bite to eat. "Would you like to sit outside or inside?"

She moved her walker toward one of the empty tables on the patio. "Outside. There's just enough of a chill in the air to make sipping a cup of hot chocolate delightful."

"I agree." After helping her to her chair, he added, "I'm going to see if I need to order inside. If so, would you like a cookie or a scone?"

"Sure, dear."

"Anything specific?"

She shrugged again. "Anything sounds fine."

Still feeling deflated, he walked inside and realized that customers did, indeed, need to place their orders at the counter, and did just that.

"I'll bring your order in a few minutes," a green-eyed Mennonite woman said with a sweet smile.

"Danke."

"Of course." Her gaze was warmer.

He smiled back, both taken aback and a little flattered that the server had obviously found him attractive.

Walking back outside, his thoughts turned quickly to Lilly. It was nice to be noticed—but he wasn't interested. She wasn't Lilly. There was only one woman he wanted to pursue, and she was a little prickly, a lot secretive, and could maybe even break his heart.

He really didn't want to go through that again.

However, it was starting to feel like the Lord was in control and he wasn't. No, that wasn't true. The Lord was always in control. It was that finally—at long last—he was listening to what He had to say.

21

Lilly woke up at dawn. When she entered the kitchen to get a cup of coffee, she found Phillip standing at the griddle in the back of the kitchen. He was muttering under his breath.

"What's going on, Phillip?"

He didn't turn around. "Amber's got some kind of stomach bug so we're shorthanded."

Noticing that there were two trays next to him, she said, "Do you need me to start my shift early?"

"I can't answer that," he said as he placed two pieces of French toast on the plate next to him.

"But do you need help?"

Before he could reply, the door swung open and Nancy strode in with an empty tray.

"Hey, Phillip, how close are you to having another tray ready?"

"Eight minutes."

"Eight?"

"It's going to be longer if you keep bothering me."

"I hear you. It's just . . . oh, hey, Lilly."

"Do you need another set of hands?"

Nancy frowned. "Honey, why are you asking? You're off this morning."

"I know, but I heard that Amber's out. I can clock in, if it's needed."

"That's very generous of you dear, but—"

"It's needed!" Phillip called out.

Looking sheepish, Nancy nodded. "We could sure use your help if you don't mind clocking in early. Some of our guests are starting to get grumpy."

Lilly chuckled. "I'll be back in ten minutes."

"Thank you. I owe you."

"You don't owe me. I'm glad to help."

"Bless you, Lil," Phillip said as she hurried back down the small hallway to her room.

Glad she'd already gotten dressed for the day, she switched out the blue dress she was wearing for her gray uniform and put on tennis shoes.

When she arrived back in the kitchen, Phillip was making eggs and the tray of French toast was gone. "Where's Nancy?"

"Back out in the dining room."

"Okay, I'll go check in with her."

"Thanks for helping out. The inn's completely full this morning."

"It's more than full," Nancy said as she walked back in. "A big group of ladies decided to sleep more people in their rooms than is allowed . . . which means we have more people to feed than we should."

"Oh no."

"Things like this happen from time to time. It wouldn't be too bad, except they all decided to eat right now."

"Where would you like me?"

"Back in the dining room. Could you bus some of the tables? Penelope and I set up a couple of extra tables in the living room."

Lilly walked out to the living room, noting where Nancy and Penelope had set up the portable card tables and covered them with cream-colored linen tablecloths. "Oh wow."

Some of the guests didn't look pleased to be sitting at those places, but Lilly figured they would enjoy the location. They'd put the tables in the living room, and the fireplace was on. Lilly thought it was very charming.

She wished she could've had a moment to appreciate it, but there simply wasn't time. She began doing everything she possibly could to help.

During the next two hours, she was not only clearing places but wiping tables, refilling coffee cups, and bringing out serving platters. When she wasn't doing that, Nancy had her in the kitchen helping to rinse dishes and silverware.

Phillip looked like he was counting the minutes until the breakfast rush was over.

Eddie was sitting with his grandmother at one of the living room tables. They seemed to be enjoying every moment and in no hurry to get up, but Lilly kept hoping they'd leave before she got to their table.

No such luck. Each time she walked their way, November stopped her for something—an extra plate, more coffee, more water. She could see Eddie trying to catch her eye, but she just nodded at them and hurried away to fill the request.

Finally, when the worst of the rush ended, Eddie stood up and placed himself in her path. "Lilly—please stop for a moment." He lowered his voice. "I want to apologize. I was way too overbearing when we went out for ice cream. I'd like to start over. When do you get off today?"

"Around three, I think. There's a lot to do. Why?" Since she'd started early, Lilly kind of hoped that she would get to leave early but she wasn't sure.

"I want to take you out to supper. What do you think?"

She wasn't sure if going out with him was the best choice for her heart but she knew she would regret it if she refused. "All right."

Relief—and desire—showed in his face. "Thanks."

Turning to his grandmother, she said, "November, will you be coming too?"

"Of course not. This is for you two young people."

"I wouldn't mind if you would like to join us."

"Danke, but I'd prefer to be back here."

"I guess it's just you and me then," Lilly said to Eddie.

"I suppose we'll have to manage as best as we can."

"Lilly Kurtz, is that really you?"

Lilly turned toward the voice—hoping against hope that the voice wasn't who she thought it was.

But *of course* it was Gretta Walker. Her high-pitched, slightly nasally voice was distinctive—she would've recognized it anywhere.

"Gretta?"

Gretta dropped her bag and suitcase on the ground and rushed to her side. "What a nice surprise. I can't believe you're here."

"I didn't know you were coming down to Pinecraft."

"It was a spur of the moment decision. I'm meeting two of my cousins here. They're arriving tomorrow, and we all got a house together. Unfortunately, it wasn't ready today so I decided to stay here. And here you are."

Yes. Here she was. "Let me tell the owner that you've arrived, and she'll get you checked in. I'm not sure if your room is ready, though."

"That's okay. I'll just hang out with you. We can catch up."

"I'm sorry, but I can't. I'm working."

All of a sudden Gretta seemed to realize that Lilly's dress was a gray uniform and that she had a coffeepot in her hands. Her manner changed.

"For some reason, I thought you were staying here as a guest. Are you cleaning rooms here too?"

Gretta's tone wasn't mean, but it did feel cutting, like she'd pointed out Lilly's job on purpose. It didn't make her feel good, but what could she say? The truth was the truth.

"Jah."

"That's too bad."

"Lilly?" Nancy called out. "We need you when you're able."

"I'm sorry, but I've got to go help with this breakfast service."

"Oh. Yeah, sure." Her smile was tight and it didn't reach her eyes. "Would you pour me some coffee before you go?"

"Where are you sitting?"

"I'm not sure . . ."

"Why don't you sit with us, dear?" November asked. "A friend of Lilly's would be a friend of mine. Right, Eddie?"

"Right."

Her school friend smiled directly at Eddie. "Thank you. That's so nice of you to say. I'm Gretta Walker, by the way."

"Good to meet you. I'm Eddie Byler and this is my grandmother, November."

"It's so nice to meet you," Gretta said as she sat down. "Where are you from?"

"We live on a farm outside Middlefield, Ohio."

Gretta paused. "Wait, is your father's name Hank?"

"It is."

"Eddie, it's like we were supposed to meet! My father is Jeremiah Walker. He's Doc Hershal's vet tech."

November smiled. "Hank talks about Jeremiah all the time."

"What a small world." As if she suddenly remembered that Lilly was standing right there, Gretta lifted her cup. "May I have some coffee?"

Feeling wooden, Lilly filled it then hurried away. She sure didn't need to hear any more.

When she got to the kitchen, Nancy was handing Penelope a plate of fruit. Both looked her way.

"You were frowning at that girl," Nancy said. "Was she being difficult?"

"Nee. She was just being herself. Gretta's from my hometown. I was pretty shocked to see her."

Nancy nodded and said, "Listen, since Esther just arrived, I wanted to let you know that you can get off at one."

"Are you sure?"

"Very sure. You started at seven instead of nine. Help out with the last of the breakfast service and then get started on the rooms." Playfully wagging her finger, she added, "And then get out of here at one o'clock."

"I will."

After Nancy left, Lilly said hello to Esther and then they both went back to the dining room. A few more tables were filled. Esther volunteered to pour water, so Lilly picked up the carafe and started filling coffee cups.

November and Eddie were still sitting with Gretta when she walked by. November was looking at a brochure she must have picked up in the lobby, and Eddie looked like he would rather be anywhere else.

Stopping in front of them, Lilly held up the carafe. "More coffee?"

"None for me, dear," said November.

"None for me, either," Eddie replied. He smiled warmly at her. "I'm going to take off soon, but I'll see you late this afternoon. Is it okay if we meet at five?"

Everything inside of her seemed to settle back into place. Gretta hadn't turned Eddie's head. Not a bit. "Jah. That is fine."

"When do you get off today?" Gretta asked. "Maybe we could go somewhere and catch up."

"That would be so nice, but I'm afraid I can't," she replied, keeping her tone even. "It's a really busy day."

Gretta looked from her to Eddie. "I guess so."

When November coughed, Lilly hid a smile as she returned to the kitchen to get a fresh coffeepot.

"Are you friends with that girl?" Esther asked the moment they got back to the kitchen.

How would she describe her relationship with Gretta? "Kind of."

"Kind of, like you put up with her? Or kind of, like you wish she wouldn't have followed you to Pinecraft?" Esther asked.

"She didn't follow me. She looked as surprised to see me as I was to see her."

"That's amazing that she's sitting with Eddie."

"Yeah, but I guess they have a lot to talk about. Their fathers know each other."

Esther put her hands on her hips. "She shouldn't have sat with Eddie and November, though. It was pushy."

"She's sitting with your beau, Lil?" Phillip called out.

160

"He's not my beau, but yes."

He grunted. "That was gutsy."

"It kind of was," she admitted at last. "At least Eddie looks miserable."

"He definitely looked stuck," Esther agreed. She sniffed. "She sure had you pour her a cup of coffee fast enough."

"There's nothing wrong with that. It's my job." Even more embarrassed, she reached for a fresh carafe of coffee. "I'm going to do another round of refills then clear more tables. Does that sound good, Nancy?"

"That would be wonderful, dear. Thank you."

Practically feeling all three of their gazes settling on her, Lilly walked back out to the dining room.

All she had to do was concentrate on her job and her date with Eddie that evening. She needed to remember that.

Well, and hope that Eddie wouldn't suddenly become charmed by Gretta's smiles.

Eddie was not a fan of Gretta Walker. He didn't like how she hadn't said more than two or three words to his grandmother. He didn't like how she kept trying to flirt with him even though he'd made it obvious that he had no interest in her. But most of all, he didn't like that she seemed to take a lot of pleasure in having Lilly wait on her. It was so blatant and rude, he was tempted to say something to Gretta.

Or tell Lilly that she didn't need to wait on them anymore.

Of course, he didn't do either of those things. He didn't want to be rude to Lilly's friend or make his grandmother uncomfortable. But their easy, low-key breakfast had sure taken a turn for the worse.

161

Gretta's voice turned silky. "You know, now that we know we live so close to each other, we should make plans for when we return to Ohio."

"What kind of plans?"

"You know, silly. To see each other."

He knew one thing—he didn't want to do that. But how to convey that without sounding terrible was another thing. "I guess we'll see what happens."

A line formed in between her brows. "What do you mean by that?" She chuckled. "Surely you don't spend all your time on that farm. I mean, you do get out quite a bit, don't you?"

"Some."

"Some?"

Growing more uncomfortable by the second, Eddie debated about how to answer. "I am on the farm a lot. It's impossible for me to make future plans now anyway."

"Really?" She smiled softly as she leaned closer.

"Really."

"Well, maybe I could come see you. I could meet your parents. I'm sure your mother and I would get along well."

"Why do you think that?" November asked.

"I get along well with everyone."

"Hmm. Even Lilly?" Mommi added.

Gretta smiled. "Yes, of course."

"I could be wrong, but it didn't seem like you were close."

Gretta looked uncomfortable. "I wouldn't say we were close, but we have known each other for a long time. Practically from the time her parents adopted her."

Eddie couldn't believe this woman was so brazen as to share something so personal about Lilly. "Are you almost finished, Mommi?"

"Almost." She put her napkin beside her plate. "Just for the record, I'd like to share that I think Lilly's a lovely young woman. It's a shame you haven't gotten to know her better."

"I've had my reasons. There were rumors about her, you see." She cast a look around the room, then her expression turned to stone when she spied Lilly approaching. Abruptly getting to her feet, she smiled at Eddie. "I'll look for you later."

Eddie barely resisted rolling his eyes. The woman was acting like she was a catch. He personally couldn't imagine anyone he wanted to be with less. "Enjoy your time with your cousins."

"It was good to see you again, Lilly. Maybe I'll see you two on the beach soon."

"Yeah. Maybe."

When Gretta was out of sight, November said, "Don't you dare spend another moment with her, Edward."

"Mommi, of course I won't." Getting to his feet, he said, "Lilly, I don't want to be mean, but I didn't care too much for Gretta."

"I didn't care for her too much at all," Mommi said.

"She's never been one of my favorite people," Lilly murmured.

"I'm sorry she's staying here."

"It's fine. I'm kind of surprised I don't run into more people from Middlefield. A lot of families come here in the winter."

Eddie smiled at her. "Well, we're going to take off, but I'll see you later."

The look Lilly sent him was so sweet, Eddie knew he'd made amends with her. When she walked away, he couldn't resist watching her graceful maneuver around the tables.

"The more I get to know that girl, the more I like her," Mommi said.

"I was just thinking the same thing."

"I think your parents would like her too, Edward. I think everyone in the family would."

He thought so too but didn't want to encourage his grandmother. Next thing he knew, she'd be calling home and telling his mamm all about his new girlfriend.

"I'm still getting to know Lilly. Don't push."

"I hear ya, but mark my words, girls like that are special. She's sweet and hardworking and kind. She would be a perfect helpmate through life."

"Let me walk you back to your room, Mommi."

"Danke, Edward." She lowered her voice. "But let's go the long way, okay? I don't want to run across that Gretta again."

"I think that's a terrific idea." He didn't want to do that, either.

Her chuckle sounded so pleased that more than one person looked over at his grandmother and grinned. She really was a special lady.

22

Ever since she'd said goodbye to Eddie, Lilly had felt as if she were floating on air. He'd apologized and asked her out again and hadn't even been shy about asking in front of his grandmother. Then he hadn't even looked twice at Gretta.

Maybe things were going to work out. Maybe her secret hope had a chance.

Looking at the clock, she smiled. It was a quarter to one. All she had to do was finish this room and then she could be done for the day.

"Hey, Lilly?" Esther called out from the doorway of the room Lilly was cleaning.

Looking up from her crouched position by the reading table in the corner, Lilly called out, "Jah?"

"May I speak with you for a moment?"

"Sure, but could you come in? I'm in the middle of polishing the legs on this table."

"I think it would be best if you came over here."

There was something odd about Esther's voice. Lilly quickly got to her feet and walked to the door. There she found Esther with Mr. and Mrs. Martin. They were about the age of her parents and had been staying in the nicest room in the inn, the suite on the second floor.

"Hi there," she said.

Mrs. Martin smiled, but it looked a little sick. "Hello. Your name is Lilly. Is that right?"

"Yes." The slight concern that had been playing in her head grew. She put down the can of furniture polish and rag she'd been holding. "Is everything all right?"

"I'm not sure," Esther said.

"How can I help?"

"Did you clean the Martins' room this morning?"

She glanced at Mr. and Mrs. Martin curiously. "I did. I was there about eleven. It was the first room I cleaned as soon as I finished with breakfast service."

"Did anyone enter while you were there?"

"No. I mean, I don't believe so. Did something happen?"

"When we returned to our room, it was unlocked," Mr. Martin said. "Furthermore, my wife's sweater was missing."

Lilly exchanged a look with Esther. It was taking a moment, but she was finally understanding what they were insinuating. That someone had left their room unlocked and an interloper had come in and stolen Mrs. Martin's sweater. Not only did that seem unlikely but the problem did seem rather odd. All of the housekeepers took care to lock rooms after they were finished cleaning, but no one was going around stealing articles of clothing.

"I'm not sure what could have happened. All I know is that I locked the door when I finished."

"Did you notice my sweater on the chair by the desk?"

"I'm sorry, but I don't know if I remember seeing it or not.

I cleaned another room after that. And now here I am in this one."

"That's only three rooms."

"You're right. But I'm afraid that I don't notice too many things. I'm usually focused on my job."

"Which is?"

"Cleaning the bathroom, dusting, changing sheets, vacuuming." It all sounded very obvious to her. She smiled weakly. What else was she supposed to say?

"Is there any chance that you could have forgotten to lock the door?"

"There's a chance, but it's doubtful. I'm not the fastest housekeeper on staff but I'm very thorough."

"We'd like to check your cart then," said Mr. Martin.

"Why?"

"We're looking for the sweater."

They thought she'd stolen it? After glancing at Esther, who was looking away, Lilly turned back to the Martins. "I didn't take it."

Mrs. Martin seemed to be looking everywhere but at her. Mr. Martin, on the other hand, looked extremely aggravated. "We don't have all day to search for items." He tapped his foot. "I'd like to take care of this now, if you don't mind. Once it's settled, we won't have to get the police involved."

Police? "I do mind because I haven't stolen anything. I would never do that."

Ignoring her protests, he reached for the trash bag that was attached to the side of the cleaning cart. "Maybe it's in here."

"I promise, it isn't."

"If you're sure about that, then you shouldn't mind if we look." He waved a hand. "Jill, start digging through."

Jill Martin was wringing her hands together. "I don't know. Maybe we should be rethinking this, Don."

He sighed. "Start looking." Before she could stop him, he pulled down the trash bag and handed it to his wife. "Oh, hold on. I need to take this call." He walked back into the hallway.

Lilly felt like she was in the middle of a very odd movie or play.

After watching Jill Martin tentatively look inside the bag, Lilly had had enough. She pulled her friend a few steps over. Taking pains to keep her voice low, she said, "Esther, does Nancy know about this?"

Looking pained, she nodded. "She does. She told me to take them over here to talk to you."

Hearing this news was worse than having this couple think she was a thief. "She really thought I might have stolen something?"

Esther bit her bottom lip. "I don't know what she thinks. I know you didn't do a thing wrong, but I guess we have to go through the motions."

"Did you find it?" Don asked his wife.

"No."

"I was afraid of that." He folded his arms across his chest. "It looks like we're going to get more people involved. We're also going to need to take a better look around this inn. Maybe even look at the dumpsters."

"Maybe you hung it up in the closet?" Esther asked Lilly.

"I didn't touch any one of our guests' sweaters."

When Mr. Martin rudely rolled his eyes, Lilly lost her temper. "I don't know what happened, but all I did was clean your room!" she retorted. "I didn't touch any of your personal things."

A muscle jumped in his jaw. "I can see we're going to have to speak to the manager." Pointing to Esther, he said, "Go find her, please."

"Esther, I'm right here," Nancy said from the doorway.

Lilly breathed a sigh of relief. At last, someone was listening to her! She reached for her cart and for the trash bag that Jill Martin had looked through. "I'll take care of this now."

Just as Mrs. Martin started to hand the trash bag to her, Nancy took it out of her hands. "No, I'll take care of this. Lilly, please go to your room."

"Excuse me?"

Stepping closer, Nancy lowered her voice. "I heard the way you talked to our guests from out in the hall. It was unacceptable."

"But—"

"That is enough." Her voice hardened. "Don't make me repeat myself."

Stunned, Lilly stepped away from the cart. Though she could feel Esther watching her in a concerned way, Lilly didn't dare meet her gaze. Instead, she walked out the guest room door and down the hall to the set of small staff rooms just beyond the kitchen and large pantry. With each step, the enormity of what had just happened settled in harder. She'd been accused of stealing from the guests at the inn. She'd been sent to her room like a wayward child.

No doubt she was just hours away from being fired and then kicked out of her room.

"Lilly, is that you?" Phillip called out just as she reached the door that separated her room from the kitchen area.

"Jah."

"I made some key lime bars. Want to tell me what you think?"

"Nee. I . . . I'm sorry, but I can't."

"Why not?" The moment he saw her face, his voice softened. "What happened?"

"Everything."

He walked to a cupboard and pulled out a thick stoneware mug. "How about this? I'll pour you a cup of tea and you can sit down and talk to me." He winked. "I promise, I won't even offer advice. I'll just listen."

Phillip really was a blessing. The more time they spent together, the more she appreciated him. But as much as she wanted to tell him the whole, confusing story, she needed to do what Nancy said. "I wish I could, but I can't. I'm supposed to go straight to my room."

His eyebrows rose. "What? Who said?"

"Nancy." It had been tempting to not tell him, but there was no reason to lie. Phillip would find out anyway.

"What happened?"

As briefly as possible, she told him about the Martins and the missing sweater. "I can't believe this is happening."

"Me neither." He looked as shocked as she felt. "What—"

She interrupted him. "I can't talk about it, Phillip. I just can't." She turned and kept walking.

Only when she got to her room and closed the door behind her did the enormity of the situation hit her full force. She'd cleaned motel rooms for years. Almost five full years by now. She'd worked for Amish people and Englishers and had come in contact with all sorts of people while she'd done her work. She'd met some really kind people who told her they appreciated how well she cleaned their hotel rooms. Others had acted as if she didn't exist and then surprised her by leaving a tip on the dresser.

She'd met tired families and young adults who left a big mess and no tip. Some of her managers were very kind. Others not so much.

Even though she wasn't all that old, she'd really believed that she'd experienced almost everything that the world had to offer, at least in terms of human interaction.

It was obvious that she'd been very wrong. Until now she'd never been accused of stealing.

Sitting down on her small single bed, she pressed her hands to her face. What in the world had happened, anyway? How could everything go so wrong, so fast?

She had no idea.

Dropping her hands, she stared at her plain walls. "God, why would You give me this trouble? Why did You decide I needed it? I've been as good as I possibly could and tried my best. I learned to accept that my adopted mom and dad love me but will never completely think of me as their own. I've been teased and felt like I wasn't good enough but still kept going." Swiping a teardrop from her cheek, she added, "I thought I finally had my own chance to be happy."

She thought of her friends and Eddie. She really liked him and had been starting to think they might have a future.

But she knew he wouldn't think that if everyone in the bed and breakfast thought she was a thief.

She'd lost him too.

"Why are You taking it all away? Why?"

She lay down on the bed and tried to feel guilty for the things she'd said. Deep in her heart she knew that the Lord didn't work like that. He didn't divvy out good things to good people and bad things to those who needed to be taught a lesson.

She knew that.

But even though she did know that, it was hard to ignore the truth. And that was that she was once again alone and at a loss as to what to do.

So she did what she'd always done. She curled up in a ball and hugged herself close. And pretended that everything was going to be okay soon.

It was just too bad that she knew that wasn't going to be the case. All she could do was wait for Nancy to knock on her door and tell her that she was fired.

Lilly didn't know if she'd ever dreaded something so much.

23

After she'd sent Lilly to her room, it had taken Nancy another fifteen minutes to calm Don and Jill Martin down. Though Nancy had usually adhered to the belief that the customer was always right, she'd known that something wasn't true about the whole story.

First of all, there was too much emotion for a missing sweater. Though Nancy could sympathize with Jill for being upset for losing a special piece of clothing, she and her husband were acting as if the item had been a priceless heirloom or an envelope filled with thousands of dollars of cash.

Then there was the whole idea of the door being left open and someone going in and taking the item. The rooms were old-fashioned in the sense that guests still had to carry keys and lock the doors after themselves. Lots of her guests never did that. It had bothered her, and she'd often thought about switching all the guest room locks to electronic keypads. But the cost would be fairly high, not to mention many of her guests liked how old-fashioned and charming the B and B was. She knew that she'd hear many complaints about the change.

But it seemed she'd made a big mistake. If she'd trusted her judgment, it was very likely that the sweater would never have gone missing and Lilly wouldn't have been blamed.

After promising to reimburse them for the missing sweater— once Jill was able to find a comparable item online—Nancy had given the couple a gift card for the Boardwalk, an upscale restaurant in Sarasota. At last, only slightly mollified, the couple had calmed down. It seemed the thought of a free meal was going to take away the sting of a thief in their room.

She and Esther had stood outside the hall while they'd gotten themselves together. When they left, Don had made quite the showing of locking his door securely.

Nancy remained where she was until she'd heard them walk through the lobby and at last pass through the front door.

Only then did she smile at Esther. "Well, that was horrible."

Esther didn't smile back. If anything, she looked even more angry than the Martins had.

"Lilly did not steal anything."

"Esther, you know I didn't have a choice. I had to take the guests' side. At least for the moment."

"You sent Lilly to her room. Now they know she lives here."

"I needed to get her out of here before they made her cry."

"They are horrible people. You had to know that woman was lying."

"I don't know anything. All I do know is that they were missing an important item and that someone left the door unlocked."

Esther raised her eyebrows. "I doubt that."

Nancy inhaled sharply. "Excuse me, Esther?"

"Nancy, you like us to tell you the truth, and the truth is that I'm sure something wasn't right with their story. One of them was lying."

"We don't know that."

"I know that they were rude to you and mean to Lilly." Her voice thickened with emotion. "And now you went and gave them a free meal where my husband is the assistant manager. They'll probably run everyone ragged all night. How could you do that?"

"The Boardwalk is one of the nicest restaurants in town. I had to give them some kind of compensation for their troubles."

"You mean for lying." Looking even more perturbed, Esther added, "I wouldn't be surprised if they found fault with their meal and complained to Michael."

"Esther, it's not my fault that your husband works there." Before Esther could say anything else, Nancy said, "Please take care of the cart and put it back and then finish Lilly's work for the day."

"All right. I think she was almost done with the guest room she was in. I'll double check, then dust and straighten the living room."

"Thank you."

Esther didn't move. "Hey, Nancy, what are you going to do about Lilly?"

If Nancy was being completely honest with herself, she wasn't sure. But no matter what, she wasn't going to talk to Esther about it. "I'd rather not discuss this with you, Esther."

"I think I have a right to know, though. I mean, I encouraged her to work here."

"Well, I took your word that she was completely trustworthy. That might not be the case."

To her shock, Esther didn't back down. "I know you called her references too. Everyone thinks well of Lilly."

Nancy had called her references and also believed that

everyone on staff liked Lilly. But something was missing from the Martins' room, and Lilly was the most logical person to suspect. "Esther, I know you and Lilly are good friends, but you're out of line."

Esther blinked. But instead of backing down, her normally easygoing employee lifted her chin. "Are you going to fire Lilly?"

She didn't know what she was going to do, which didn't sit well with her. She didn't want to let Lilly go, but she also didn't want to have someone on staff whom she didn't completely trust. What was right didn't seem clear at the moment. "How I decide to handle this situation is none of your concern." Inwardly, Nancy hated how harsh she sounded. When she'd taken over the Marigold Inn, she'd planned to be the type of manager whom her employees saw mostly as a coworker. Unfortunately, it was times like this that reminded her that wasn't always possible. Someone had to do the hard stuff. It looked like this whole episode was falling into that category.

"You are, aren't you?" Esther's eyes flashed as she waved a hand. "Over a sweater that probably didn't even exist."

"Esther, go do what I asked you to do."

"I will, but I'm telling you now. If Mr. and Mrs. Martin are horrible to Michael or if you fire Lilly, I'm quitting."

"You're threatening me?"

"No. I'm only giving you notice. I refuse to work for someone who can be so unfair."

Stunned, she watched Esther stride over to the cart and push it down the hall. How could a missing sweater turn into this?

Nancy walked toward the lobby. She was exhausted. She needed a break and some space for a few moments. Maybe then she'd know what to do about Lilly.

Then, after pausing for a few moments to chat with a group

of guests who were returning from a day trip to Naples, she walked to the kitchen to get a cup of hot tea.

As she'd hoped, Phillip was at the stove stirring a large pot when she walked inside his realm. Like always, she was surrounded by appetizing scents and a vision of an incredibly organized chef. Small bowls were neatly lined up on the counters, some of which were still full. She knew enough about him by now to know the bowls held all the ingredients he'd already prepped.

"Boy, that smells good," she exclaimed. "Are you making fish chowder?"

"I am. I had a bunch of fish in my freezer from the last time I went fishing. I decided to make some chowder for the staff before it went bad."

"I love that chowder."

"Everyone does. So, any reason you came in here?"

His voice was noticeably cooler. "Not really. I only came in for some hot tea."

"You know where everything is."

"I suppose I do." She smiled at him.

Instead of smiling back, he looked irritated.

"I was going to hang out in here for a few moments, but I'll get my drink and then get out of your way."

Phillip didn't even look back at her.

Walking around him, she collected a mug and tried not to take his attitude personally. It was sure strange, though. Phillip usually stopped whatever he was doing to get her tea for her. And often added a cookie or some other treat he'd recently made to accompany it.

She walked to the electric tea kettle, saw it was empty, and filled it with fresh water. After she pressed the button to start it heating, she leaned against the counter. "Where's Penelope?"

"She left for the day."

Nancy glanced at the clock. It was almost two. "Wow, I didn't realize it was so late. This has been such a crazy day. Time has flown by."

"I bet."

She was finally realizing he was irritated with her. Really irritated. Since she hadn't spoken to him since breakfast service hours ago, she was confused.

"What is that supposed to mean?"

"I'm not sure I should say anything."

"Because?"

He put down the wooden spoon he'd been using. "Because I've heard that you've been acting pretty difficult."

"Pardon me?"

"Sweatergate."

Sweatergate? He'd already given her crisis a name? "How did you hear about what's been going on?" Before he had a chance to answer, she put two and two together. Lilly had to walk through the kitchen to get to her room. She must have told Phillip everything. Annoyed, she felt her temper rear. "I guess Lilly couldn't resist telling you about everything that just happened?"

He turned down the burner and walked to stand in front of her. "It was more like Lilly looked devasted when she walked through here on her way to her room. I encouraged her to talk to me about it."

"So she did?"

"Only a little bit. Only enough for me to know that you sent her to her room."

Nancy felt her cheeks heat. She really shouldn't have done that. But that said, she didn't need Phillip wading in. Not yet. "You don't know the whole story, Phillip. I'll figure it out."

"You better."

She sure didn't appreciate his tone. "I know that you two have become friends, but she doesn't work for you here in the kitchen. This problem had to do with one of the rooms she cleaned."

"I guess you've forgotten how breakfast service went this morning. You seemed pretty happy to have her in here then."

"All I'm saying is that I wish she wouldn't have talked to you about it. Not while I'm trying to find a way to salvage the situation."

"Nancy, do you hear yourself? Lilly was near tears. Of course she needed to tell someone something."

"Do you think I'm enjoying myself? Because I'm not."

"I don't think you're enjoying this one bit. But that doesn't really matter. Talk to Lilly again. Talk to that couple again. Look around the inn. Maybe the guest inadvertently left that sweater on a chair or it dropped in the hall or something. Nancy, treat that girl in there like she matters, because she does."

"I know she matters." Nancy realized that she was starting to feel like she was close to tears as well. Why wasn't Phillip even trying to see her point of view?

"The kettle's whistling."

She quickly pushed the button to silence the noise as Phillip walked back to the stove. He wasn't going to talk to her about this any longer.

Feeling bereft, she found a tea bag, tossed it in her mug, and added the hot water. Then she walked back out feeling like part of her heart was left behind in the kitchen with Phillip. Maybe her father had been right all those years ago when he'd proclaimed that it was never good to mix business with pleasure.

Not wanting to return to her office, she took over at the

reception desk. Between the normal work and an engaged couple who asked for a tour, time flew by. Just after five o'clock, Eddie and November stopped her.

"Have you seen Lilly, Nancy?" Eddie asked. "She was supposed to meet me here about fifteen minutes ago."

"I believe she's still in her room."

"How can we get ahold of her?"

"Her room is past the kitchen. Phillip should be able to show you where it is."

"Okay, thanks," Eddie said.

As he strode off, November walked closer. "Are you all right, Nancy? You seem upset."

It was tempting to tell her that everything was fine, but she didn't think she could do it. "I'm dealing with a small issue here at the inn."

"Do you want to talk about it? I'm a good listener."

"Thanks, but I'm afraid this is something I need to figure out on my own."

"You mean you and God."

"Pardon me?"

November blinked. "I said you and God, dear. After all, it's not like we need to handle everything on our own, is it? That's what He's there for."

Walking out to her little she shed, Nancy pondered November's words. At first it felt like her advice was a little too simple. Yes, she believed in God, and yes, she believed He answered prayers. But she'd never believed that He stayed by her side all day and tried to help her out with day-to-day staffing issues.

Her steps slowed. But maybe that was the problem after all. This wasn't a staffing issue; it was bigger than that.

She also had to admit that she wasn't doing so well on her own.

After she unlocked her office, she walked inside and left the door propped open a bit to let in the day's last rays of sun and some fresh air.

Then, instead of sitting behind her desk, she sat on the couch and took a sip of tea.

"All right, God. I sure could use some help right now. Would you mind helping me work through some problems?" After a pause, she felt the muscles in her back ease.

That was all the encouragement she needed. Taking a deep breath, she began telling Him the whole story of Sweatergate.

24

Phillip, who Eddie now knew was the chef's name, looked up when he stood in the doorway of the kitchen.

"Need something, buddy?"

"Yes. I'm sorry to bother you, but Nancy said I could ask you how to find Lilly."

"She told you that?"

"Was she wrong?" Feeling kind of put out—after all, couldn't Nancy have knocked on Lilly's door for him? Or, better yet, at least get the girl a cell phone for work so she wasn't relying on staff to summon her with a knock on the door? "Lilly and I had plans this evening, and I guess she's running late. I'm worried that maybe something's wrong."

Some of the irritation in the man's expression eased. "Yeah, I guess you could say that."

"Is something wrong? Is she sick?"

"She's not sick." After fussing with the knobs on the range, he said, "Come on. I'll walk you down to Lilly's room."

"Appreciated."

After taking a few more steps, the man turned around. "Hey, I'm sorry for acting like a jerk. There's some stuff going on, and I took it out on you." He shook his head, like he was still frustrated with himself, then reached out a hand. "I'm Phillip Shaw."

"Eddie Byler." Eddie shook his hand. "It's good to meet you. You're the chef here, right?" When Phillip nodded, Eddie grinned. "Lilly's told me a lot about you. She's a fan."

Phillip's expression eased a little more. "I'm a fan of her too. She's a nice girl and a real good addition."

Eddie had been so intent on Phillip, he was only now looking at his surroundings. Unlike the area where he and his grandmother were staying, this hall was dark and the hallway was narrow. There were only two doors. One had an impressive lock on the outside. The other was painted white and was six paneled.

"Here it is," Phillip said.

"Thanks."

"Yeah, I know. It seems a little depressing around here but a lot of us have lived here at one time or another while we were getting on our feet."

"You too?"

"Yeah. Even me. That was a few years ago, though. Anyway, here's Lilly's room."

"Thanks for walking me down here."

"No prob." He paused. "Hey, ah, listen . . . just to let you know, Lilly's had kind of a bad afternoon. You might want to keep that in mind."

A dozen questions filled his head, but Eddie pushed them aside. If Lilly was having a problem, he wanted her to be the one to tell him about it. "I will."

"Good." Phillip turned around and walked back to the

kitchen. His steps were about double the pace of what they'd been when he'd been escorting Eddie.

Starting to wonder what he was walking into, he knocked softly on Lilly's door. When he heard someone moving around but the knob didn't turn, he said, "Lilly, it's me."

"Eddie?"

"Jah. We had plans for this evening, remember?"

"I remember but I'm, ah, afraid I'm not much good company right now."

"Open the door and let's talk."

"I'm not sure that's a good idea."

"Talking or opening the door?"

"Maybe both."

He looked both ways down the hall. "Come on, please open the door. I don't want to talk to you while I'm standing out here. Anyone could overhear."

"That's doubtful, but all right."

When he saw her face, splotchy with tears, he wanted to hurt someone. Not waiting another second for her to invite him in, he pulled her into his arms. Her starched white kapp brushed against his chin. It made him wonder how it would feel if she had it off and he felt nothing but her soft hair against his bare skin.

When she trembled, Eddie drew her in closer. He was half expecting her to pull away, but she did the opposite, like it had been far too long since anyone had given her a decent hug.

"Hey," he murmured. "I don't know what's wrong, but everything's going to be okay."

"I don't think that's possible."

They were still standing in the hallway. Though he appreciated the fact that he was able to hold her to him, he wanted to be able to have a real conversation. For that they needed privacy. "Come on," he murmured. "Let's go sit down."

Lilly turned without argument. However, she did seem to shrink into herself a bit. "This room ain't much."

"I don't care what it's like. I only care about you."

She sat at the foot of the twin bed and pointed to a chair. "You may sit there."

He did as she suggested, looking around the room as he did so. In a way, it was nicer than he'd thought it would be. Though it was small, there was a sunny yellow and violet quilt covering her bed. There were also three fluffy pillows covered in white cotton. There was an additional quilt, this one a crazy quilt that looked soft and well-loved.

The room's floor was wood, but there was an oval-shaped braided rug in the center of it. The designer had used shades of green and blue. The walls were painted white, and the window was small. Glass blocks replaced the standard windowpane, but it didn't look bad. Off to the side was a doorway leading to a small bathroom.

"Phillip told me that lots of people who work here have stayed in this room."

She brushed a piece of hair away from her face. "Yes, that's true. When I moved in, everything was almost like this."

"Almost? What did you change?"

"There's a closet that has extra items for rooms." She waved a hand. "Lamps, quilts, pictures, clocks . . . Nancy let me take whatever I wanted to make this room feel more like mine."

"Did you not bring items from home too?"

"I did but it was mainly personal items. Books and stationery and clothes." She bit her bottom lip. "I grew up in a fairly plain house. I didn't have a lot of items to bring."

"If I moved, I wouldn't have a lot to bring, either."

"Ah."

"Lilly, what's going on? Why are you so upset?"

Her bottom lip trembled. "I'm not sure if I'm supposed to share."

"Phillip already told me that you were upset."

"He did?"

"Of course he did. He cares about you. So that means the cat is already out of the bag. Plus, I'm not here for information, Lilly. I'm here because I care about you, too."

"Some guests have accused me of stealing from their room."

He couldn't have been more shocked. "You've got to be kidding."

"I wish I was."

"What happened?"

She folded her hands in a tight knot on her lap. "It was so awful. A couple accused me of taking a sweater."

"A sweater?"

She nodded. "The husband accused me of leaving their guest room unlocked."

"And they thought someone wandered in and stole a sweater?" Was he the only person who thought that was a stupid idea?

"Yes. Or that I stole it and left the door unlocked because I'm irresponsible."

"I'm sorry, Lilly but none of that seems very likely. I don't understand why you're in trouble."

"The couple was really upset and got Nancy involved. She sent me to my room. I'm pretty sure I'm going to get fired."

"I hope not."

She shrugged. "Eddie, you have to believe me. I would never steal from anyone."

Unable to watch her struggle all alone, he sat down on the bed next to her. "Of course you wouldn't," he whispered. "Of course not."

A tear ran down her face, breaking his heart. "I think that's what makes me so upset. Nancy didn't believe me. She thought I was a liar."

Reaching for her hand, he said, "There is not a doubt in my mind that you're innocent. Plus, if Nancy wants to fire you over something so silly, then I think you're better off without this job. You'll find another one."

"I've been sitting here feeling so foolish. I moved down here with all these grand plans. I was going to have this job, see my friends, and eventually make enough money to get my own little place. I was finally going to be independent and do what I want. Now it's all blown up in my face."

"Don't say that. We'll figure something out."

"We will?"

"You don't think I'm just going to leave and not try to help you, do you?"

"Eddie, we hardly know each other."

"You know what? You're right, and it's time we did something about that." Standing up, he said, "We're going to go on our date."

"Wait—"

"Nope. There's nothing to wait for. Nothing between us has changed, Lilly. I still want to get to know you better, and you still need to eat supper." He laughed. "What am I saying? We both do."

A line formed between her eyebrows. "But . . ."

Eddie knew for sure and for certain that if he hadn't shown

up, she would've stayed in her room all night without even getting a glass of water, let alone supper.

That made him so mad. What was Nancy thinking? Ordering Lilly to her room and expecting her to remain there? It was not just mean, it wasn't right.

Realizing that if he gave her any sort of choice, she would retreat back into herself, he cut her off. "I'm serious. Get up and get ready. I'll wait outside in the hall for you."

To his relief, she stood up. "Has anyone ever told you that you're kind of bossy?"

"Truth?"

"Of course."

"No. I'm usually not the bossy type."

"You could've fooled me."

"Maybe I only boss around people I care about." He smiled at her. "Get ready and don't take too long. I think you already look beautiful. Plus, I'm starving."

"I'll be right there."

"Gut."

Just as he opened the door, she called out to him again. "Hey, Eddie?"

He turned back to face her. "Yes?"

"Thank you for coming to find me."

"I'm glad I did." He closed the door behind him and then leaned against the wall in the hallway to wait for her. As the minutes passed, Eddie realized he didn't care how long he was going to have to wait. He was learning to be patient with her and put her needs first.

Another day he was going to have to figure out why she meant so much to him and why he wanted to fight all her battles and make everything better for her when they hardly knew each other.

But he wasn't going to allow himself to think about that now. All he wanted to do was focus on what had just happened, which was that he'd helped make her feel better and now he was going to make sure she ate something and didn't sit alone and cry.

She'd needed him tonight and he'd made things better.

Hanna had never needed him like that.

Only now was he realizing that the Lord had known what was right for both of them even when he hadn't. Hanna hadn't been the right woman for him, just like he hadn't been the right man for her.

About fifteen minutes after he'd stepped out, Lilly opened the door. She was now dressed in a pale rose-colored dress and matching flip-flops. She'd obviously redone her hair and put on a different kapp. Everything about her looked fresh.

After turning to lock her door, she faced him. "I'm sorry it took me so long. I decided to change clothes."

"No need to apologize. I didn't mind waiting."

Relief filled her expression. "Danke."

"Are you ready now?"

"Oh yes." She blushed. "I mean, sure."

He grinned. She was obviously embarrassed about showing him how pleased she was to be by his side, but what she didn't realize was that her response made him happy. He needed to know that she felt the same way he did.

"Let's go, then."

"Do you mind if we go out through the kitchen?"

"Of course not, Lilly. Lead the way and I'll follow."

As they did just that, Eddie realized that he'd meant those words. He didn't know where the future would take them, but he didn't want to leave her side anytime soon.

Maybe not ever.

25

Jacob's On the Water was on Longboat Key and looked very upscale from the outside. Inside was a different story. The tables were mismatched, and the floor was cement. All the servers wore either black pants or shorts and untucked button downs in Easter egg colors.

When they sat down at a table in the screened patio near the harbor, Lilly smiled at the strands of bistro lights over their heads and the soft instrumental music floating around them. It mixed in with the sound of seagulls outside and the laughter of a group of kids near one of the boats on the pier.

"I hope this table is to your liking?" the host said.

"Lilly?" Eddie asked. "Are you good?"

"Yes. I mean, yes, thank you. This is fine."

Only then did he hand them each a simple menu. "Your server will be with you shortly."

"How did you find this place?"

"I asked around. I don't know about you, but whenever I go on vacation, I like to explore a bit. More than one person told me that taking a car out to Longboat Key was a good idea."

"I love it, but you didn't have to go to so much trouble. I would've been happy with a sandwich shop."

"I know. You're easy to please."

"I don't know if I am or not. I hope so, though." She liked that simply being with Eddie made her happy.

After they looked at the menus and a server took their orders, Eddie said, "How are you doing, really?"

She shrugged. "I don't know. I'm upset and hurt but mainly confused, you know? I feel like the Martins' accusation came out of nowhere."

"It sounds like it." Thinking about his life on the farm and the seasons when things had been financially difficult because of corn prices or bad weather, he said, "I guess if they were missing an envelope of money, I might understand the panic, but not all of this for a missing sweater."

She looked out at the boats in the marina. "I don't blame them for wanting that sweater back. But I don't know how a missing sweater turned out to be so much more important than me. I feel like Nancy let me down."

"You should feel that way. What are you going to do?"

She sighed. "I don't know. Wait and see, I suppose." Meeting his gaze, she said, "I don't want to live back at home."

"You want to stay here no matter what?"

She thought about it. "Ever since I first met Mary Margaret and Betsy on that bus, I've wanted to be near them. I've never had best friends like them before. When each of them settled here, and then Esther did too, coming felt like the right choice."

"I see."

"Eddie, I'm not saying that Pinecraft is the only place that

191

I'd be happy. It's simply what I've been thinking about for two years."

"I guess you could find another job."

"Maybe so." Her stomach sank. As upset as she was about Nancy and the day's events, Lilly realized that it already had started to feel like home. "If I have to leave the Marigold Inn, I don't know what I'll do. Part of my pay was the room here. I don't have enough saved to afford my own apartment."

"Maybe another inn?"

"Nee." Just the thought of being put in the same position again made her feel sick to her stomach. "I don't think I can clean rooms again. I would always worry about something like this happening again."

"Yeah. I can see how you'd feel that way. I'm sorry."

"I am too." Tired of dwelling on her sad situation, she cleared her throat. "So, um, when do you head back to Ohio?"

"My grandma and I go back in three days."

"So soon."

"Mommi wanted a nice, long vacation, and everyone in the family wanted to give her that." He paused, obviously searching for the right words to express himself. "It was a blessing to be able to spend this time with her."

"You'll always have this memory."

He smiled. "I will. We both will. But I have to get back to the farm. Even in late fall, there's a lot to do. The livestock . . . upkeep. There's a lot, and *mei bruder* is getting tired of doing everything."

"You are settled there, aren't you?"

"I am. As much as I sometimes wished I had other options when I was growing up, I've always known that the farm is where I belong."

He sounded almost apologetic, which she hated to hear. "There's nothing wrong with that. Knowing where you belong is a good thing."

He leaned forward. "Tell me about growing up, Lilly. Tell me about your life in Middlefield."

Her mind spun. She'd neatly sidestepped a lot of details when Eddie had asked before, but now she knew she had no choice.

The server approached their table just then. "Here's your meals. Redfish with grits and vegetables for you and grouper with a baked potato and soup for you, sir."

"Danke."

They closed their eyes in silent prayer when he left. Lilly gave thanks for the food they were about to receive then said another prayer, asking for strength to finally tell Eddie the truth—and the strength to be okay if it turned out that her past was too much for him to handle.

"My birth parents are English, Eddie," she said when they both picked up their forks. "My father was in prison when I was adopted."

"Is he still there?"

"I have no idea. I didn't know anything about my birth parents until my rumspringa. I went to the children's home without my parents' permission and learned about them."

"What about your mother?"

"She was young, just a teenager. But she was sick. She had kidney disease. I guess it was a miracle she was even able to bear a child. She was in too poor of health to care for me, and I guess her parents were more concerned with her welfare than with caring for a baby."

Eddie stared at her intently. She wondered if he was shocked by her revelation. If he was, she supposed she couldn't blame him. "I'm sorry. I know it's a lot." Still feeling awkward, she looked down at her plate. "There's no good way to share that, so I usually don't."

"Nee, it's okay. I'm glad you told me."

His words were sweet, but they seemed stilted. He didn't look like he was glad. Actually, Eddie looked like he could have gone the rest of his life without knowing about her birth father. The realization made her sad. She should've known that learning about her past would make him uncomfortable.

She took a bite of her fish, though it didn't taste especially good to her anymore. Some of the beauty of the moment had vanished.

She was tempted to apologize, but she didn't. She'd long ago come to terms with the fact that nothing about her parents' lives was her fault. Who knows? Maybe some of what happened to them wasn't their fault, either. She believed that it was wrong to judge others without walking in their shoes. She was living proof of that—so many people had judged her for being adopted when they had no idea about the questions she'd grappled with about her heritage.

Glancing at Eddie again, she noticed that he, also, wasn't eating. Instead, he looked as if he was struggling to tell her something. She put down her fork and waited. If he was going to tell her that he didn't want to ever see her again, she didn't want to have food in her mouth when he said the words.

"Hey, Lilly?"

"Jah?"

"I have an idea about something."

"Okay . . ."

He took a sip of water. "It's a bit of a risk for you, but it might work."

"What do you mean by a risk?"

"Maybe not a risk, exactly."

"Eddie, you're talking in circles."

"I know. But listen. Will you do something for me? Will you promise to hear me out before saying anything?"

"I don't want to promise you anything just yet. What is this about?"

"Please? Just promise me."

"All right. But—"

"Don't say anything else. Just listen."

She crossed her arms over her chest. "Fine. What is it that you have to tell me?"

"Well, my grandmother and I are traveling on Monday. When we get home, my grandmother will continue to live in the dawdi haus and I'll go back to helping my parents with the farm."

"I understand." She wasn't sure why he was feeling compelled to give her all the details, though.

"Nee, I don't think you do. See, the dawdi haus is actually kind of big. There are two bedrooms there and a full kitchen, living room area, and a cozy hearth room off to the side too. The whole thing is painted a pale, pale blue. It's nice." He took a deep breath. "Lilly, here's my thought . . . come back with us."

He might as well have taken the rest of the air out of the restaurant. She gaped at him and had to remind herself to catch her breath. "You want to see me again?"

He laughed under his breath. "Lilly, I don't want to just see you again, I want to see you all the time."

"Eddie?"

He rushed on. "I know leaving with me would mean that you wouldn't get to be with your friends, but I think you would be happy on our farm. My parents are wonderful. They're wonderful-gut people. And you already know what my grandmother is like."

"November is a nice lady."

"You'll like my brother too. He's already married so he lives in his own place. I know you're used to working, but maybe you could help out on the farm some until you decide what you want to do. My grandmother needs some help and looking after and it's hard for my mother to do everything that needs to be done because of all the responsibilities on the farm."

"I don't understand why you want me there."

"I hate the idea of you being alone. I hate the idea of you being stuck at the Marigold Inn when you don't trust Nancy or living in that little room off the kitchen when you could have your own space at our farm."

"But what about your family? Your parents? Won't they think it's odd that you invited me to move there without talking to them first?"

"I'll call them tomorrow. Honestly, I think you'll be an answer to my mother's prayers, Lilly. She's been worried about my mommi. We all have. That's one of the reasons that I took her to Florida on vacation. I was starting to wonder if she really was doing as well as we thought. Now I realize that she's fine most of the time, but she needs some help. I called home and spoke to my parents. We agreed that we want her to be happy but that she needs more help than any of us can give her in our spare time. She needs to be taken care of too."

"So you'd want me there as a caretaker?"

"Not only that." He bit his lip. "Lilly, if I haven't made it obvious yet, I really do like you. I don't know what's going to happen with us. Maybe we'll ultimately decide that we don't suit or you'll decide that you don't want to live on the farm. But maybe everything will work out."

She felt silly but she also felt like she needed to confirm everything he was saying, just to make sure she was understanding what he meant. "You mean work out for you and me."

His expression warmed. "Jah. If you and I decide that we were meant to be together. If that happened—if the Lord gave us that gift—it would make me really happy."

She never expected him to receive the news about her past so easily. How could she? For most of her life, she'd felt as if she wasn't quite good enough because she wasn't a Kurtz by blood. Added to that feeling was the fact that she'd had a parent incarcerated. Though her brain had always told her the things that Eddie had just said, she'd always felt somehow at fault. "But what about my parents? My birth parents?"

He shrugged. "What about them?"

"You don't think worse of me because of them?"

"Lilly, you were a baby. There's nothing to think worse about. Honestly, I think they must have been smart because you were raised by parents who cared about you, and now we've met."

"I never thought about it that way."

"Maybe you should, jah? I've never had a child, but I reckon that if I had to give it up, it would be a real hard thing to do. Painful, even. If someone loved you so much to want a better life than he or she could give you, then I think that's a pretty special gift, indeed."

Her mouth had gone dry. Somehow Eddie had just flipped everything she'd held to be true on its side and made her rethink it all.

And now he was giving her another gift—a chance to have

everything she'd always hoped for—to be a wife and eventually have a family. To be part of his family. It wasn't what she'd been hoping for when she'd boarded the train to Pinecraft, but she wasn't going to turn his offer away.

"So, what do you think?"

"Will you speak to your parents and November about this idea and then let me know if you still want me to visit?"

"They're going to be fine with it. My grandmother knows you and likes you, Lilly. If either of my parents has questions, she'll answer them too. I'm sure of it."

"Please, just ask and do some thinking and praying before you talk to me again."

"Do you really not think I'm telling the truth?"

"I know you're telling the truth. It's just that I've learned that sometimes people change their minds."

"All right." He pushed his plate away. "What are you going to do about your job and Nancy?"

Surprised that she hadn't even been thinking about the inn for the last several minutes, she shrugged. "I'm going to go back to my room and get some sleep. I have tomorrow morning off and then I am only supposed to work about five hours. I guess I'll see what happens. If Nancy intends to fire me, I'm pretty sure she'll do that first thing in the morning."

"I hope she doesn't do that."

Gazing into his eyes, Lilly realized that while she was still very upset about the situation with the Martins, she was no longer thinking that she was about to lose everything. Eddie had given her that gift. He'd not only offered her a visit and the possibility of a future with him, he'd also gifted her with a new way of thinking about her past. And that new view had lifted her heart in a way he would never fully realize.

"I hope she doesn't, either," she said at last. "But if that's Nancy's decision, I think I'm going to be okay."

"I'm proud of you. You're so strong. It's a beautiful thing."

She'd never believed she was strong and wasn't positive she was strong now. But she sure did feel stronger.

She smiled at him. "Danke."

26

As usual, the morning had dawned bright. Nancy usually loved waking up at five, taking a hot shower, and then heading to the inn with a cup of coffee in her hands.

Most of the time, she sipped her coffee, gave thanks for the many gifts in her life, and admired either the weather or the flowers she passed on her ten-minute walk.

Unfortunately, today was different. The short walk to work felt like both the longest and the shortest journey of her life. Maybe she shouldn't have been surprised. All night she'd tossed and turned, reliving every conversation she'd had about the Martins' accusations and her responses. Not only did she now have a slight headache but her entire body felt sore. She supposed that's what happened when one was wrestling with a big decision all evening.

Though Chris, the nighttime manager, had texted her that everything was quiet, Nancy knew that wasn't going to be the case for long.

As she walked the final block to the inn, Nancy began to pray for the Lord's guidance. As miserable as she felt about the whole situation, she wanted to at least feel like she was doing the right thing. She hadn't felt so unsure about what to do in years.

The front walkway and porch still looked sleepy in the early morning sun. Though it wasn't quite six yet, there were days when one of her guests had gotten up early and was sitting on the porch when she arrived.

This morning it looked as if Chris hadn't even unlocked the front door yet. Just as she walked up the stone steps, the front door opened, and Jill Martin stepped out. When she spied Nancy, she gripped the railing and waited.

Nancy fought back a look of irritation. What in the world was going on now? Couldn't the woman have waited a little while longer to seek her out? Like, at least another hour or two?

Oh well. If she'd learned anything in all her years of running this inn, it was that a small percentage of her guests were simply difficult. There was nothing she could do about it except try to make them as happy as she could without losing her mind or her temper.

"Good morning, Jill," she said as she climbed the steps.

"Hi, Nancy. I hope you don't mind, but I've been waiting for you to arrive. The night manager told me you usually get here about now."

"How may I help you?"

Jill gestured to the chairs on the porch. "May I speak to you out here? It won't take long."

"Of course." Nancy sat down on the chair closest to her. Glad she had an insulated cup for her coffee, she took a fortifying sip and steeled herself for whatever complaint or problem Jill was about to raise.

When Jill didn't speak right away, Nancy tried to hide her annoyance. What was going on with this woman? After another couple of seconds passed, Nancy set her cup down. Just as she was about to remind Jill that she had other things to do, she remembered her morning prayer. Worried about Lilly and the way she'd handled the entire problem with the Martins, she'd asked the Lord for guidance.

Jill's appearance on the porch was no coincidence. She was pretty sure the Lord was currently reminding her to be patient.

Just like He was with her.

As another few seconds passed, she took another sip of coffee.

"Nancy, there's no easy way to tell you this." Jill ran a hand through her short bob. "The fact is . . . I lied yesterday. I . . . I threw out that sweater."

"Pardon me?"

"I've always hated it, but Don gave it to me as a birthday gift. It's some fancy designer and was expensive." She wrinkled her nose. "Actually, I have a feeling he got it on sale. The price he told me it was worth was ridiculous. He would never pay so much for an article of clothing."

Nancy couldn't care less about designers or prices. What did matter was the lies Jill had told and the repercussions they had on her, Lilly, and the inn. "So . . . just to be sure I understand, you made up a story about an unlocked door and even accused one of my maids of stealing . . . all so you didn't have to tell your husband the truth?"

"I'm afraid so."

"Everything you said—the stuff about your door being left unlocked—that was made up as well, wasn't it?"

"Yes." She sighed. "Last night, I kept thinking about how upset your maid looked. Plus, knowing how mad Don was, I started thinking that my story could cost her a job. I would hate that."

"You would."

"She's such a cute little Amish girl. I heard that they don't have a very good education. So, it's not like she has a lot of options, right?"

Everything about this conversation was making her mad. The lies, Jill's attitude . . . and the knowledge that she'd bought that story so easily . . . and had half planned to let Lilly go that morning.

Feeling her heart race, Nancy took a deep breath. She had to calm down before she lost her temper. "So, just to be sure we're both on the same page. Am I correct in believing that you've now told Don the truth?"

Looking shocked, Jill shook her head. "Oh no. He would be so upset. I just wanted you to know the whole story. You know, so you wouldn't blame that cute maid."

"And now? What do you expect me to do?"

Jill's eyes widened. "Nothing. I just wanted to let you know." She crossed her legs and fiddled with the diamond on her finger. "I'm sure you understand my dilemma."

"You're not intending to tell Don the truth, are you? You're going to let him think that someone who works at my inn stole it."

For the first time, Jill looked really uncomfortable. "I'm sorry for the trouble, but—"

"But you'd rather spread lies about my employees instead of talk to your husband." As the woman's blasé attitude sunk in, Nancy felt her temper rise. Unable to sit calmly, she got to her feet. "Jill, I don't think you realize the trouble you caused."

"Of course I do. That's why I decided to speak with you this morning." She smiled. "Listen, we leave tomorrow. I bet this whole episode will be forgotten in no time."

"And you won't have to worry about wearing a sweater that you didn't like," she said sarcastically. Realizing what she was going to have to do, she picked up her coffee. "Mrs. Martin, I'm sorry, but if you don't choose to tell your husband the truth, I will."

"You can't. This is none of your business."

The door opened, startling them both.

"Jill, what are you doing out here?" Obviously noticing Nancy's irritated expression, his voice deepened. "Is she badgering you?"

"Well . . ."

Nancy couldn't take it anymore. "Mr. Martin, your wife was just explaining to me how she made up yesterday's story."

He looked as confused as she had been. "I think you must have misunderstood. My wife would never—"

"Nancy is right, Don. I made it all up."

He shook his head. "No. You wouldn't—"

"I did." Looking weary, she pointed to the chair on the other side of her. "Sit down and let me try to explain."

Realizing that the conversation was about to get uglier, Nancy walked inside. She paused as she reviewed everything that had occurred in the last twenty-four hours. It had been ugly and confusing on several different levels. Not only had Jill upset Lilly, the episode had disrupted so many other relationships.

Nancy frowned. She and Phillip had said things they shouldn't have. And Esther had gotten upset with her. And then there was the way she'd sent Lilly to her room like she was a disrespectful teenager. She'd really messed up.

Not only had she overreacted but she'd never even tried to reassure Lilly. Lilly had gone to bed thinking that she wasn't trusted. Nancy grimaced. What had been wrong with her yesterday?

Why couldn't she have taken a deep breath and considered how her words and actions were affecting Lilly?

How could she have only thought about the Martins ruining the inn's reputation instead of the big picture, which was that one of her employees' reputations had been run through the mud and she should be doing everything she possibly could to make things better?

Boy, she had a lot of apologizing to do.

She walked into the kitchen for a fortifying cup of coffee before going to her office to figure out how to make things right with Lilly. Nancy knew that she normally would've walked down the hall to share the news update with Lilly, but she knew it was Lilly's "late" day so she would probably be asleep.

That was likely a silver lining because Nancy knew she was going to need to think about what to say to that girl. A simple apology wouldn't be enough.

The kitchen was quiet. Phillip was dressed in his usual uniform of slightly wrinkled khakis, a well-fitted T-shirt, and clogs on his feet. He had a large plastic container in front of him and was carefully arranging fruit on a tray. Penelope was standing opposite from him at the counter. She was placing pastries and slices of coffee cake on a platter.

Neither gave her more than the most cursory of glances when she walked into the room.

"Hi, you two. Please tell me there's fresh coffee already made."

"There's fresh coffee," Phillip said.

A little hurt that he didn't offer to get her a cup like he usually did, Nancy walked over to the industrial-sized coffee maker that sat off to the side. "I was hoping you'd say there was. It's already been a morning and it isn't even seven yet."

"That doesn't bode well for the rest of your day."

"I was thinking the same thing." She filled her to-go cup, added a liberal amount of creamer, and then walked to Phillip's side. "You would not believe what just happened."

"You got coffee?"

His voice was sharp. Not exactly mean, but it really wasn't welcoming.

Stung, she noticed that he wasn't looking at her. It was actually more than that. Phillip didn't look like he wanted to see her at all. She supposed after their words yesterday that she couldn't blame him.

"I did get coffee. How may I help you in here?"

"Pen and I are doing fine with breakfast prep. You don't need to stay."

So, things between them were even worse than she imagined. "Uh, may we talk in the hall for a sec?"

"I'm busy now, Nancy."

"Please? This won't take long."

Releasing a sigh that sounded like he was carrying the weight of the world on his shoulders, he nodded. "Fine. I'll be right back, Pen."

"Okay."

She led the way out to the hall. Phillip shut the kitchen door after he followed her. "What do you need?"

"You know. What can I do to make things right between us?"

Phillip folded his arms over his chest. "Nancy, have you forgotten everything that happened with Lilly last night?"

"Of course not."

"Well, I haven't, either. Actually, I've been having a pretty difficult time coming to terms with the way you treated Lilly."

"I feel bad about it too. I'm going to apologize to her. But guess what? Mrs. Martin admitted to lying about the whole thing. Isn't that something?"

"So Lilly spent the evening upset because one of the guests is a liar."

"As soon as Lilly comes on shift, I'm going to speak to her. I'm sure she's going to be so relieved."

"Why would she be relieved? She knew she hadn't taken anything."

"Phillip, I don't know what else I can say. I made some poor choices yesterday and I feel bad about them. I've just told you that I intend to apologize to Lilly."

"Look, we're going to have to talk later. We're in the middle of breakfast service. I've got to go." He turned and walked back into the kitchen.

Leaving her to wonder just how badly she'd messed up everything with him . . . and how in the world she was going to make everything all right again.

At the moment, that seemed like an impossible feat.

27

The first thing Lilly noticed when she woke up in the morning was a folded note that had been slipped under her door.

Lilly,

I spoke to my grandmother last night when we got home. She was so pleased about the idea of you living with her she insisted on using the inn's phone to call home.

We intended to leave a message, but Mamm answered so we filled her in. Then Daed got on the phone. And my brother! Basically, everyone is excited for you to come. And (I hope this doesn't make you uncomfortable) they are excited for you and me too. Though I know both time and the Lord will guide our future, I am selfishly pleased that you are considering moving there at all.

I'm going to be around the inn all day. Come find me and my grandmother when you can and let me know what you think.

Eddie

After reading the letter twice, Lilly pulled out a sheet of paper and wrote her reply. She kept it short.

I'm glad you spoke to your family. I still want to come to your house. Even if we decide it's not a good fit, I want to try. I'll find you later so we can talk about things.

Thank you, Eddie. You don't know what your offer means to me.

Lilly

Then she hurried down the halls, slipped the note under Eddie's door, and then dashed back to her room to take a shower and get ready for her day.

Esther knocked on Lilly's door forty minutes before she was supposed to go on shift.

"Oh good. I was hoping you were still in here."

"I'm being lazy today. I haven't even put on shoes yet."

"Good for you. I feel like I've already walked two miles today," Esther replied as she walked into the room. "The breakfast service has been so hectic, and Phillip's been in the worst mood."

"Sorry I missed it," she teased.

"He's been like a bear with a sore paw. No one can do anything right."

"That's too bad."

Sitting down on Lilly's extra chair, she said, "When did you get breakfast? I just realized that I didn't see you come into the kitchen to grab a plate."

"Penelope brought a basket of goodies around eight. It had a carafe of coffee inside."

"That's so nice. Phillip must really like you, Lilly. He never did things like that for me when I lived here."

"I think he felt bad about everything that's been going on with the Martins."

"And Nancy?" Esther whispered.

"Yeah. And Nancy." Lilly didn't really want to talk about it, but she supposed she didn't have a choice. Sitting down on the side of her bed, she pulled out a pair of white socks and slipped them on her feet and then put on her new pair of Converse tennis shoes. They were too worldly for back home in Ohio, but here no one seemed to care that she was wearing white canvas Converse shoes. Lilly was thrilled about that because she really liked them and they were very comfortable. Plus, they made her feel a little less "Plain Jane" and a little more spunky. "I'll be on shift in less than an hour."

"I know. But, um, I thought you might want to know something before you went out."

"What's that?"

"There's a rumor going around that Mrs. Martin lied about the sweater getting stolen. She tossed it in the trash because she hated it but didn't want to tell her husband."

"Seriously?"

Esther nodded. "I've never heard of going to so much trouble about an ugly sweater."

"Was it ugly?"

"I don't know. All I do know is that she told Nancy before she told her husband."

"I guess Nancy's relieved."

"I think she is. She seems better than when I talked to her last night. What matters, though, is how you're feeling. How are you?"

"I'm okay." What was funny was that she didn't even need to think about it. Last night's dinner and conversation with Eddie had been really special.

"You know what? You kind of do look like you're okay. What's going on?"

"I saw Eddie last night. He took me out to dinner."

"And?" Esther's voice rose an octave. "Lilly, did he kiss you?"

She laughed. "Nee. But we did talk a lot . . . and he said a lot of nice things." Lilly paused. She still wasn't sure if she wanted to share her news but decided that she needed to get someone else's perspective. "Esther, he invited me to his house."

"To visit?"

"To live."

"You're going to have to backtrack. What do you mean? Are you going to marry him?"

"We didn't talk about marriage. I mean, not yet. It was more like he wanted me to have an option. He said his grandmother could use someone in the dawdi haus with her and said I could live with her."

Esther whistled low. "That's so nice of him. Odd, but nice."

"I didn't think it was odd, Esther." Meeting her gaze, she said, "I think I'm going to do it."

"No. You can't." Reaching for Lilly's hand, she squeezed it hard. "Come on, I know you're upset, but you aren't thinking clearly."

"I am."

"But you've had plans. We've all had plans to be here together, and now you are."

"Plans can change."

"I know, but this is different." She blew out a breath of air. "Listen, I know this whole mess with that couple and their

211

stupid sweater has made you upset, but it's about to blow over. Don't make more of it than it is."

"Esther, a couple accused me of stealing and Nancy didn't take my side. That isn't going to blow over."

"All right. Fine. But there are other places to work besides here. All of us will help you figure it out."

"I've already made up my mind." Spying the mutinous look on her friend's face, Lilly softened her tone. "I know you think this is a knee-jerk reaction to everything that's happened, but it's not. Not completely, anyway. I like Eddie. I like his grandmother a lot. I also like the idea of helping her. I know I can help her."

"I'm sure you could, Lilly, but you should do something for yourself."

"Esther, this will be for myself. I can see myself being happy to help November for a while. I think I could be happy living there even if Eddie and I eventually decide that we shouldn't be together after all."

Esther frowned. "There are other men besides Eddie. It's different here in Pinecraft. New men come into town all the time."

Lilly laughed. "Esther, do you hear yourself? I'm not going to start hanging out by the parking lot just to see who hops off the latest Pioneer Trails bus."

Esther flushed. "I know. I'm sorry. I'm being ridiculous, aren't I?"

"A little."

"I guess I feel responsible for you. I encouraged you to work here."

"Thank the Lord that you did. If you hadn't, I would've never had a way to come to Pinecraft any time soon. Or met November."

"Or Eddie."

"Or Eddie." They were still holding hands. Looking down at their clasped hands, Lilly felt a lump form in her throat. For so long she'd felt alone, but here was a woman who'd done so much for her. Who'd turned into a really good friend. It was such a blessing. "Esther, I may go to the Bylers' farm, be there a week, and decide it was a bad choice."

"And if you do?"

"Then I'll think of something else to do. Don't you see, though? All my life I've been hoping to fit in and be given choices. Now, I suddenly have lots of choices. And sure, everything isn't wonderful and easy, but I don't need it to be."

"I understand."

"Really?"

Esther got up from the chair and hugged her close. "Really." Stepping back, she said, "I better get back to the breakfast service. Phillip is going to wonder where I ran off to."

"See you later."

"Definitely."

An hour after Esther left the room, Lilly knocked on Nancy's office door and walked inside.

Nancy looked exhausted. "Please have a seat, dear. We have a lot to talk about."

Lilly sat and for the next ten minutes listened as Nancy filled her in about Mrs. Martin's lies, the Martins' subsequent apologies, and the fact that they had already checked out. In addition, Mr. Martin had even left Lilly a sizable tip in an envelope, supposedly for her pain and suffering.

"I haven't even opened it, Lilly, but I hope it's a decent amount."

"All I cared about was being believed. I don't steal."

She sighed. "I know that, and I'm sorry for the way I behaved." Looking more uncomfortable, Nancy continued. "I realize I should have done things differently, and I wish I would have. I wish I would've stood up for you from the very start. I don't know what to say except that I truly felt that I had to take things one step at a time. My first reaction was to get you out of the room so you wouldn't have to stand there while they accused you of leaving a guest room unlocked. I shouldn't have sent you to your room, though. I'm sorry."

"I am too."

"I hope one day you'll forgive me for not reacting better."

"I already do." She was still hurt, but she felt Nancy was sincere.

"Thank you, dear. If it's any consolation, I've learned a lot from this whole experience. It's made me want to be a better manager. I promise, next time you or anyone else is faced with an angry guest, they won't feel so alone."

Nancy was telling her all the things that she'd needed to hear. They did make her feel better too. But she also realized that she was ready to do something else.

Taking a deep breath, Lilly said, "I'm giving you my notice. I'm going to quit."

"Oh, Lilly." Nancy's eyes filled with tears. "Please don't quit because of all this. I'm not just telling you words. I meant what I said. I will get better."

"I was upset, but I'm not anymore. You can't control what other people do." She smiled softly. "Or the lies they tell. But I have another opportunity back in Ohio. I'm going to see how that goes."

"Your mind is made up?"

She nodded.

"All right then. I wish you the best."

"Danke, Nancy. Thank you for hiring me too. I appreciate it."

A pair of tears fell down Nancy's cheek, but she didn't argue. Only nodded.

Lilly walked out of her office thinking that she was already so different than she was just a few weeks ago when she was a nervous wreck about even knocking on Nancy's door. She was growing and changing and getting stronger and more sure of herself.

So many things she'd been hoping for. She was so thankful for that. She couldn't wait for what this next opportunity had in store for her.

28

To Eddie's surprise, his grandmother wanted to go out to supper with him that evening instead of being holed up in her room. They decided to go to Yoder's. Not only was it fairly close but the food was good and the prices were reasonable. The large assortment of pies that were available was a bonus.

Before they walked over, she asked if they could spend a few minutes in the inn's backyard. Eddie didn't have to ask why. It was a beautiful evening. Back home, the weather was about to turn. Before long, their evenings would be spent inside.

After meandering along the path that snaked through the yard, November sat down on a wooden bench and kicked her feet out. He sat down next to her.

Since she seemed content to sit quietly, Eddie did the same. He was actually very pleased to have a minute to simply rest and enjoy the moment. He wished he did that more often. Psalm 46 came to mind: Be still and know that I am God. There had been many times in his life when he'd known that he needed to relax and lean on the Lord. He hadn't felt as strongly about it as he did at this moment, though. He'd acted so impulsively over the last twenty-four hours. He didn't regret asking Lilly to come home with him, but he hoped it was the right decision. He didn't want her to regret it.

"I'm proud of you, Edward."

"Why?"

"Hmph. That's so like you, child. Always looking for reasons."

"Mommi, of course I'm going to look for a reason. I need to know what you're proud about so I can do it again."

She smiled. "I don't know how you'll be able to do this again." She raised an eyebrow. "Or do you intend to ask another woman to live with me?"

"Mommi, the things you say. I don't intend to ask anyone else to come to our farm."

"I hope Lilly will be very happy with us."

"I hope so too. I think she'll be a good companion for you."

"And maybe for you as well?"

"Yes." Spying a glint in her eyes, he said quickly, "But we're going to take things slowly, so don't start meddling."

"I won't meddle."

"Hey, Mommi, did Mamm or Daed ask you a lot of questions about Lilly?"

"Some. I told them the truth. She is a lovely girl and a hard worker."

"And?"

She looked away. "Only . . . that if you and she got together, that wouldn't be a terrible thing."

"Mommi, you shouldn't have said that."

"Why not? You know it's the truth." Shifting to face him, she added, "And you might think I'm a silly old woman, but we both know that you would never have suggested she move if you didn't think the same thing."

"Fine." There was no use arguing. But that didn't mean he'd wanted to be that open with his parents. "When Mamm and Daed ask a dozen questions, help me shield Lilly from them. I didn't ask her to the farm just to be interrogated." He felt himself blush. Lilly had accused him of interrogating her—and she'd been right.

"Calm down, child. Don't make it into something it ain't. All of us love you and are going to be interested, ain't so?"

He nodded. "Are you ready for supper?"

She smiled brightly. "Of course."

Standing up, he took her arm. Bypassing the inn, they walked out through the garden gate and headed down the sidewalk. Yoder's was three blocks away.

"I just realized that you're walking a lot better than you were when we arrived. Is it the warm weather?"

"I reckon so. I've been trying to walk a little bit more. After I left that mess in the room for Lilly, I decided to leave my room a lot more often."

"I didn't know that."

Her smile was a little smug. "I know you didn't."

"Who's been walking with you?"

"Amber."

"Amber?"

"She's another one of the maids that I've befriended. She kept me company on my walks from time to time."

"She volunteered to do that?"

"Jah. Well, she volunteered, plus we stopped for lattes. Amber really likes caramel macchiatos."

"I have no idea what that is," he said as they crossed another street. The Yoder's sign was up ahead.

"Of course you don't, Edward."

He didn't say another word, but he couldn't help but grin. His grandmother was something else. She was also one of his favorite people in the world. All his life she'd been his bedrock. He loved his parents—of course he did—but he was also one of four kids. His mother had had four of them to raise plus a garden and a whole house to take care of. His father had the farm. Eddie had always felt an affinity with his grandmother. They shared the same sense of humor and liked to do a lot of the same things. None of his siblings would have taken her to Disney World or had as much fun as he'd had with her.

"Ah, the line ain't bad at all today," she murmured. "That's a blessing."

"Hey, Mommi?"

"Jah?"

"I'm really glad we went on this trip together. I'm glad we went to Disney World and came here to Pinecraft. I'm even glad we met Lilly at the same time. I love you a lot."

His grandmother didn't say anything for a moment. When she did, her voice was gruff. "I love you too, Edward. Never doubt that."

29

Two full days had passed since Sweatergate, but Nancy was still suffering the consequences. Of course, everyone had heard about Lilly's decision to leave. Though Lilly had told everyone that she was looking forward to being back in Ohio and living with November, it was pretty obvious that no one believed her.

Nope, the blame for Lilly leaving was firmly on Nancy's shoulders.

Since she felt so guilty about her handling of everything, Nancy didn't try to shift the blame too much. Someone had to carry the burden, and so it might as well be her.

Besides, what bothered her more than taking the blame for Lilly's departure was the continued cold shoulder from Phillip. That hurt a lot.

When she walked into the kitchen to get her first cup of coffee, only Phillip was there. He was sitting down on a stool and frowning at his phone.

"Good morning," she said.

"Hey." He didn't look up.

"Everything all right?"

"Yeah."

That was obviously a lie. He still looked worried. Walking to the coffeepot, she filled her to-go mug and then added a healthy amount of cream. And then debated about whether to leave him alone or not. If things between them weren't so strained, she would prod him a bit, simply because it looked like whatever he was focused on was heavy on his mind.

But things weren't good. She also had no desire to make matters worse by encouraging him to share when he didn't want to.

So she concentrated on the breakfast service. At least she could give him a hand.

"What can I do to help you this morning?"

At last their eyes met. "With what?"

"Breakfast service. I can arrange platters or cook bacon or something."

"What time is it?" He glanced at the clock and groaned. "Seven? Sorry." He stood up and strode to the refrigerator. "I'll get everything out within thirty minutes."

"Phillip, I didn't ask if I could help because I'm your boss. I asked if I could help because we're friends and I care about you."

"I know." He winced. "Not that I feel like much of a friend right now. I've been pretty hard on you." He looked down. "Hard and judgmental."

He was right. He really had been. "You had an opinion and you wanted to share it. There's nothing wrong with that."

"Maybe . . . maybe not. I waded into things that weren't my business." He pulled out a tray that already had fruit neatly arranged on it. "I'll be right back."

"What can I do?"

"Get out the container of muffins from the storage room and start placing them on a platter, okay?"

"Okay." She took a sip of coffee and then started following his directions.

When he returned, they worked side by side. She filled the trays while he cooked bacon in the oven and cracked eggs into a bowl and started beating them.

After she delivered the muffins and greeted a few of their early morning risers, she started prepping the chafing dishes for the eggs and bacon.

"Is Penelope off this morning?"

"Yeah. I told her not to worry about anything." He frowned over the pan of eggs on the stove. "And then, of course, I promptly forgot about all I had to do."

"Ah."

"You're not going to ask me what happened, are you?"

"I want to ask, because I care about you, but I don't want to push you to share if you don't want to."

He stared at her. He said nothing, but he didn't need to. His expression told her that he was mentally weighing the pros and cons of divulging his secret. Nancy realized as well that he wasn't as concerned about her being able to keep a secret as he was with how it would feel to verbalize whatever was troubling him.

She could relate to that. There had been more than one time in her life when she didn't want to talk about something because talking about it made it "real." Sometimes the knowledge that the Lord already was sharing her burdens was enough.

Finally he came to a decision. "It's my daughter-in-law Jamie," he said around an exhale. "Evan called me late last night. Jamie went in for a routine mammogram and got some troubling news. They found a spot on the film that they're concerned about."

And just like that, all her problems faded away. "Oh no. I'm so sorry, Phillip."

"It's shaken me up." He ran a hand through his hair. "It's so hard when your kid calls you for support and you don't know how to respond. I want to make everything better, but I can't."

"I would feel the same way." After debating a moment, she said, "Listen, I know it's difficult, but please don't lose hope yet. Sometimes all the techs have to do is do an ultrasound or another scan and then they discover everything is fine."

He grunted. "When I was talking to Evan, Jamie got on the phone and told me essentially the same thing. She told me not to worry yet." Fussing with one of the serving platters, he lowered his voice. "Actually, she pretty much repeated to me everything that the nurse told her—but it's still bothering me."

"Of course it is."

"This is going to sound foolish, but sometimes I hate reaping the consequences of raising an independent kid. When I offered to come be with them, Evan said that they were fine."

She winced. "Ouch."

"Right?"

Stirring the eggs in the pan, Phillip sighed. "Don't get me wrong, I trust Evan and I know Jamie is strong and has a good support system with her family. It's just . . ."

"It's just hard to wait for a phone call."

"Exactly." He scraped the pan with the silicone spatula. "Evan said he'd give me a call if they need anything."

Nancy covered her mouth to try to temper her giggle. Phillip noticed and scowled. "Sorry, but it sounds like the kind of thing I would have said to my parents. I wanted to prove to them that I could handle everything on my own."

"I know they can, but part of me wants to drop everything and run to their sides."

"You could do that, Phillip."

"Yeah, I could. But then I'd be in the way."

"I'm sorry."

"Yeah. Me too." Some of the humor she was used to seeing in his eyes returned. "I should be thinking of the positives. I know it. But aside from praying, I'm feeling at loose ends."

"I'm glad you're confiding in me."

"Yeah, right." Fussing with the pan again, he said, "I know I hurt your feelings this week."

"I'm glad you told me how you felt. I needed a push to get my head on straight."

Phillip seemed to think about her words while he took the bacon out of the oven. "Do you still have time to help?"

"Of course."

"Put the bacon on paper towels for a moment, then place it all in the chafing dish."

"On it."

He grinned as he returned to his position behind the skillet.

Esther entered. "Good morning. When can I tell everyone to expect eggs and bacon?"

"Five minutes," Phillip replied. "Take the chafing dish of bacon out as soon as Nancy puts the bacon in. I'll bring the eggs in a minute."

"All right." Turning to Nancy, Esther asked, "Would you like me to finish that for you?"

"Thanks, but I've got it." She picked up the silver tongs and placed the last six strips of bacon in the chafing dish. "This is ready."

"Danke," Esther murmured as she turned and walked back into the dining room.

Nancy said, "She and Lilly are such good friends. I think Esther's really going to miss her. I am too."

"I feel the same way," Phillip said as he began spooning the eggs into a chafing dish. "I have a feeling that Lilly would be pretty surprised by the impression she's made around here in such a short amount of time."

"She has made a good impression, hasn't she?"

"She's made one around me. I would have never guessed it, but that timid girl has a spine of steel. She handled the Martins with a lot of grace and dignity. Instead of getting bitter or lashing out, she held her tongue."

"I should've been more like her."

Turning to make sure the range was off, he shrugged. "We all make mistakes. All you can do is pray for guidance and move on."

Unable to help herself, Nancy reached out and squeezed his arm. "I think that's good advice for you to follow now."

Looking puzzled, he said, "For what?"

"For Jamie."

He slowly smiled. "I think you're right. Now, I better take these eggs out to the dining room before everyone decides to complain to the inn's manager that they're paying for a hot breakfast."

"Thanks."

Standing alone in the kitchen for a few minutes, Nancy had to admit that their conversation had brought Phillip and her close and had served as a reminder that there were hiccups and problems and worries in every stage of life. She needed to remember that no problem lasted forever. Problems always came up and they always got solved one way or another. Somehow or some way, each conflict got dealt with and then would eventually fade into a distant memory.

However, she didn't have to do everything on her own. She could ask for help and advice from the many people in her life who cared about her.

And, of course, from the One who never left her side, even when she was making mistakes. It was time she remembered that.

30

Esther and Michael had volunteered to host her going-away party. Though she was very touched by their gesture, Lilly had tried to persuade them not to do it. After all, only a few weeks ago her friends had thrown her a welcome to Pinecraft party. Now, here she was, leaving them already.

It didn't feel like a cause for celebration.

But no matter how much she tried to protest the gesture, none of her friends even considered not giving her a proper send-off. Esther had been especially vocal about her desire to host since she and Lilly had gotten close while working together.

To her surprise, Eddie had admitted that he felt the same way as her friends did. Any reason for friends to get together was a good one, he said.

Unable to argue with that and realizing that arguing wouldn't do any good anyway, Lilly had finally given in gracefully.

As they walked the short distance to the couple's apartment on the top floor of an older building in downtown Sarasota, Eddie said, "Are you feeling better about this?"

"About the party? Nee. I feel guilty, especially since none

of them would accept my offer to help pay for the food at the very least."

"Did you really think they would?"

"No."

"Then maybe you should save the regrets for something else."

She couldn't help but smile at that statement. "That's probably a good idea."

"I'm full of them." When they reached the door, Eddie wrapped an arm around her shoulders. "Lilly, I know you're torn, but let's have a good time."

"Okay." Although she knew that Eddie was encouraging her, she also realized that he was probably asking her because of his own reasons. He'd taken a leap of faith in asking her to his home. She didn't want to do anything to make him regret his invitation—or his feelings for her.

"That was easy."

"I want the same things you do, Eddie."

Their knock was immediately answered by Michael. "Come on in," he said with a smile.

"Thank you for hosting."

"Our apartment is small but mighty," he teased. "We can hold a surprising number of people in here."

"I think I need to hear how you discovered that," Eddie said.

"I'll be happy to share, just be warned that it has to do with a company Christmas party," he said.

While Eddie joked with Michael, Lilly looked around the apartment. She was impressed. It was wide open—essentially an open space with just a partial wall separating the bedroom from the living and kitchen area. The only truly separate room was the bathroom, and it was off to the far back.

The entire room was decorated in shades of sand, blue, and

silver. It was an unusual combination that made her think of the beach. There were few items on the walls. Just a couple of hooks adorned the wall near the door, along with a calendar and a large, modern-looking clock made out of metal.

Their furniture was all light oak. A pair of candles filled the air with a mixture of lemon and mint. Several kerosene lights illuminated the room, casting a pleasing glow.

"Wilcom!" Esther exclaimed as she hugged her tight.

"Danke for hosting. Esther, your place is gorgeous."

Esther smiled at Michael. "Thank you. Before we chose the space, we discussed the things we wanted in our home. At the top of the list was lots of room."

"Every time I come over here, I rethink all the trinkets I have laying around our house," Betsy said. "It makes me want to go home and put half of them away."

"Your house is adorable. Plus, it's on Siesta Key."

'I know. I guess I just wanted to point out that each of our places has some pros and cons."

"I completely agree," Lilly said. Of course, she couldn't help but think about her own living situation. She wasn't living in a cute, modern loft in the middle of a city or in a darling cozy bungalow near one of the nation's best beaches.

Inadequacy filled her. She was leaving her small room at the inn for a place that she'd never been to.

What was she doing?

Half feeling like she was about to experience a panic attack, Lilly started to speak. But luckily Mary Margaret approached.

"You're looking far too serious for a girl about to begin a new adventure," she teased. "Are you all right?"

"I'm fine. I was just thinking yet again about how much I'm going to miss all of you."

Compassion filled her gaze. "Are you getting nervous?"

"I've been nervous. Now my nerves bounce up and down between almost calm and almost panic attack." Standing up, she waved a hand in the air. "Why in the world did I think this was a good idea, anyway? I mean, I barely know Eddie and November. I've only known them a couple of weeks."

"That is true," Mary murmured.

Esther spoke up. "I know you don't know Eddie's family, but don't you remember that Gretta's family does?"

She nodded. "When Gretta mentioned that, I was upset, but now I think that maybe God brought her to the inn just to tell me that news. Her father works at the Bylers' vet. Their two daeds have become friends."

Esther nodded. "I think that's a very good sign. You and Gretta might not be the best of friends, but I think she would've said something if she'd thought that Eddie's parents weren't decent people."

"As much as I feel like this is the right decision, I'm still having second thoughts. I mean, I've been wanting to come here for two years. It's all I've been talking about."

"Which is a long time," Betsy said.

She began to fret some more. "Then there's my whole family. What are my parents going to say when I tell them that I've decided to live in a dawdi haus with an older lady?"

"They'll probably be surprised," Mary said.

Mary sounded far too calm. Giving her a chiding look, Lilly said, "They're going to be really surprised. Shocked, even."

"I reckon so, but then your parents will get over it. Mine did."

Still thinking about how upset they were going to be, Lilly turned on her heel. "I don't know how I'll be able to explain myself. Won't they think I've lost my mind?"

"I can see how they might think that . . . at least for a few minutes," Esther mused. "My mother sure had some questions when I told her about Michael."

"My father wasn't all that thrilled about August," Betsy murmured.

As their words sank in, Lilly stopped pacing and propped her hands on her hips. "You all have been through this too."

After exchanging glances with one another, her girlfriends started to laugh. "I was wondering when you were finally going to catch on!" Betsy exclaimed. "Sure, each of our situations was different, but we all had to overcome some roadblocks and questions from our families."

"We persevered, though," Mary said.

She heard what they were saying, but Lilly still felt as if they were making light of her situation. "I'm not playing a game, you know. I'm really having second thoughts."

"I know," Betsy said. "But it's going to be okay."

"We don't know that, though."

"You're right. We don't know that for sure, but everything is still going to work out," Mary said.

"You three are making this sound so easy. It's not." Not wanting to cry in front of them, she turned her head and blinked several times.

Esther jumped to her feet and pulled her to the couch. "Lilly, you've gotten yourself into quite the state."

"I know."

"Try to calm down, okay?"

Dabbing at her eyes, she nodded. "Okay."

Handing Lilly a tissue, Mary spoke. "Lilly, if we seem amused, it's because you're usually so contained and cautious."

Betsy nodded. "I'm usually the one who acts impulsively. You have to admit that we all can't help but be a little surprised by the way you're pacing and fretting."

Trying to see her actions from their points of view, she mumbled, "I guess it is out of sorts."

"Almost as much as deciding to move back to Ohio so you can live with November," Esther said. She smiled. "But just because you're doing something out of the ordinary doesn't mean that I think you're doing something wrong. Not at all."

"But don't you think I'm doing a lot without thinking things through?"

"Maybe. But it's no worse than me falling in love with Michael," Esther said. "That was something I sure didn't expect to happen."

"But you two are a perfect match."

"Jah, I think so too. But I met him on the beach, he's younger than me, and when I decided to marry him, neither of us were in what anyone would call a great financial situation." She softened her voice. "But I didn't care. All I knew was that if I didn't spend the rest of my life with him, I would regret it."

"You haven't regretted it for a moment, have you?" Mary asked.

Smiling, she shook her head. "I love him and he loves me. When I'm with him, I feel like anything is possible. Nee, when I'm with Michael I sometimes don't even think about dreams and wishes. All I want to do is be grateful to God for bringing the two of us together."

"We could all share our stories of falling in love and making changes," Betsy said, "but we don't need to, because you already know them. And you supported us even when we doubted ourselves."

"We're going to miss you," Mary said. "But do we want you

to be happy with cleaning rooms at the Marigold Inn and seeing us from time to time instead of taking a chance on being with Eddie and his family?" Mary shook her head. "No way."

As their words sank in and reached her heart, she slumped back against the soft cushions of the couch. "You all are right. I need to calm down and concentrate on what I want most."

"Which is?"

"Which is being happy. Doing something for myself. Letting my heart guide me instead of a handful of emotions that don't really matter much in the light of day." She lifted her chin. "Even if I get there and regret it, I still want to go."

Betsy clapped. "Gut girl. I'm proud of you."

"I'm scared, though. Even though I feel as if the Lord is in charge and guiding me to do this, I'm still a nervous wreck."

Mary turned even more serious. "Lilly, you can change your mind, you know."

"Really?"

"What's the worst that can happen?"

"Well . . ."

Betsy said, "I reckon the very worst is that you realize that Eddie and life on his family's farm aren't the right future for you, so you take another bus trip back to Pinecraft."

"That's right," Mary added. "You come back, stay with one of us until you get your feet back under you, and then do what you're doing now."

Making such a big mistake sounded awful, but maybe they were right. "You all won't think less of me?"

"Lilly Kurtz, we became friends in the middle of an ice storm. We were strangers but still poured our hearts out to each other," Mary said.

"When I came down here, my only intention was to apologize

to Mary Margaret and get a break from all my so-called friends," Esther said. "Instead, I became close to all of you."

"See?" Betsy added. "The four of us are the definition of being steadfast friends. Don't ever think that we won't be here for you. No matter what."

Next thing Lilly knew, the four of them were each putting out a hand and clasping it with the others, just like they were teammates on a soccer team. She was not the only one who was holding back tears, either.

"No matter what," Betsy said.

"No matter what," she, Mary, and Esther echoed, just as the front door opened.

Michael gaped at the four of them. "What in the world is happening? I walk out to get more ice and return to find you four looking like you're in the middle of a funeral. Is everything all right?"

"Oh, sure," Esther said softly.

"I find that hard to believe. Every one of you is crying."

"I promise, they're good tears, Michael," Mary said.

He nodded at Mary but only had eyes for his wife. Walking to her side, he pressed his lips to her brow. "I hate to see you cry, Esther."

"Nothing to worry about. We're just being wallflowers."

After studying each of them, his expression cleared as he headed to the kitchen. "Jah. Okay. I'll leave you to it, then."

When he walked to the kitchen, Lilly giggled. Her friends were right. Everything was going to be just fine. And if it wasn't, she'd figure out a way to make it so.

31

It was five o'clock, everything at the inn was pretty quiet, and Penelope was manning the front desk. Nancy knew there was no reason to stick around, but she couldn't seem to help herself. Everything felt too quiet.

After wandering around the living room and straightening pictures that didn't need to be straightened and plumping pillows that didn't need to be plumped, she headed toward the kitchen.

She might as well face the truth: she wanted to be with Phillip. She wanted his company. No one could make her smile or put all her problems into perspective like he did.

Peeking into the kitchen, she prepared herself to be disappointed. Phillip usually got to work before the sun rose. Because of that, he was usually finishing up his day by four.

But there he was, covering a tray with plastic wrap, when she stepped inside.

Obviously hearing her footsteps, he looked up. And then smiled. "Hey, you. I thought you were long gone."

"I thought that you were too," she replied as she wandered in. "Are you busy?"

"Only busy trying to get out of this kitchen," he joked.

"Oh." She pasted a smile on her face. "Yeah, I bet."

He gave her a puzzled frown. "Nancy, did you need something?"

"I don't need anything important."

"You sure about that?"

Walking closer, she shook her head. "No."

"Nance, what's going on?"

Stopping in front of him, she slumped. "The truth is that I was kind of hoping we could talk for a few minutes. Are you in a hurry to get home?"

He stared at her for a long moment. "I'm not in that big of a hurry. Do you want to go to your office?"

She shook her head. "No way. I've been there all day."

"That's how I'm feeling about this place."

She took a chance. "You know, I live just a couple of blocks away. Would you like to come over? I could put out some cheese and crackers. Um, I think I have a bottle of wine too."

"You know what? I'd like that. We both need to get out of here."

"We really do," she agreed with a smile. "I can give you my address, and you can come over as soon as you're ready."

"I could do that. Or you could give me about five minutes and then we can drive over together in my Jeep."

"I'll wait." Suddenly, she felt flustered. "I'll go get my purse and then I'll meet you . . ."

"At my vehicle in five minutes."

"Yes. I'll see you then." She turned back around and hustled out of there.

Her wish had come true. Phillip hadn't left. All she had to figure out now was how not to make a complete fool of herself when they were sitting in her living room.

She should've known that Phillip would make it easy. He met her at his Jeep, helped her into the passenger seat, and then drove the short distance to her small cottage a couple of blocks away.

When they went in her front door, he didn't comment on her pile of sandals next to the door, the stack of magazines on her coffee table, or the fact that the bedroom door was wide open and she hadn't made her bed.

Instead, he nodded when she asked if he'd like a glass of wine. As she sliced an apple and arranged a portion of gouda cheese and some crackers on a dinner plate, he asked her questions about her fifty-year-old cottage and seemed entertained when she told him stories about the renovations she'd done on her limited budget.

When they finally sat down, she felt far more relaxed than she'd been in two days.

"I should've asked you over days ago. I finally feel like I can breathe again."

"Have things really been that bad?"

Though it was tempting to shrug, she nodded. "Yeah. Every conversation I've had with Lilly since she told me she was leaving has felt awkward."

"I'm sorry."

She sighed. "That's what I wanted to talk to you about, Phillip. I feel terrible that she's leaving." Focusing on the candle flickering in front of her instead of his gorgeous eyes, she whispered, "I thought I was a better boss than I am. Lilly's such a sweetheart. I think I ran her off because I didn't believe in her right away."

"I think you're being too hard on yourself, Nancy. I've talked to her quite a bit about Sweatergate, and she seems to have gotten over it."

"She's indicated as much to me too. But I can't help but feel that if I had thought more about her feelings instead of just reacting, she might not want to leave."

He took a sip of wine before putting his glass down. "Nancy, as much I would like to believe differently, I might have done the same thing you did. When you're in the service industry like we are, we're taught to cater to the customer. Let's face it. Lilly wasn't a longtime employee; she'd only been here a couple of weeks. I love the girl too, but you had to face reality, and that reality was that you felt like you had to take the Martins' side."

"But I was wrong."

"Everyone makes mistakes, Nancy." Looking torn, he added, "I shouldn't have gotten so upset with you, but I did. I think you need to stop beating yourself up. You're human." He looked at her intently. "Understand?"

"Yes."

Looking pleased, he leaned toward her, resting his elbows on his thighs. "Here's the last bit of my two cents. Sorry, but I don't think Lilly's motivation has as much to do with wanting to leave her job as it does with hoping to stay near Eddie."

"Maybe."

"Certainly."

She couldn't help but think Phillip was making Lilly's departure seem awfully convenient. "But, ah, doesn't her sudden decision feel kind of out of the ordinary?"

"Do you want my honest opinion?"

"Yes."

"Her deciding to leave so quickly does seem like it's sudden, but maybe that's a good thing."

"How so?"

"Because I think there's something else going on—and his name is Eddie Byler."

She blinked. "You think they're that serious?"

"I absolutely do. Haven't you noticed the sparks flying between the two of them?"

"Yes, but I told myself that I was imagining things."

"You weren't."

She searched his face. "When did you see them?"

"I noticed that they seemed to be drawn together quite a while ago. But I really noticed something was up when Lilly was so upset about Sweatergate. She really leaned on him."

"I still regret the way I handled that."

His expression softened. "I know. But as bad as the situation was, maybe something good did come out of it. Lilly and Eddie got a lot closer. That young man looked ready to take on the world for her."

Thinking back, Nancy had to admit that she had noticed more than a few sparks between Lilly and Eddie. "I guess that's one way of looking at it."

"I never thought I would say this, but watching that young couple fall in love was kind of fun to see."

"I agree."

"One time, I spied Eddie, Lilly, and November sitting together in the living room. Eddie and Lilly could hardly take their eyes off each other." He chuckled. "Even in front of his grandmother! That says something."

Her insides warmed. She liked the idea of Phillip noticing things like that. He always came off as kind of full of himself, but she was starting to realize that underneath that confident exterior was a very observant man. "I noticed that they seemed to get on really well, but I'm still surprised that she's going to move to his family's farm. That's a huge step."

"It is, but . . ."

Phillip's cheeks were stained red. He was blushing! "But what?" she prodded. When he still hesitated, she said, "Come on. Don't be circumspect now. I want to know what you're thinking."

He looked away. "I could be wrong, but the thing is . . . I can see how none of what they were doing makes perfect sense . . . but it doesn't need to."

She was still at sea. "Why is that?"

He leaned closer. "I think it's pretty obvious, don't you?"

She shook her head.

"They were falling in love."

Her insides felt like they were doing somersaults. "Phillip Shaw, you are a romantic."

He lifted one shoulder, like that was a flaw that couldn't be helped. "I might be, I don't know." Reaching for her hands, he linked their fingers together. "But I have to admit that there have been moments when I've felt something pretty electric when we've been alone."

His words were so cheesy, she couldn't help but smile. "Is that right?"

"Oh yes."

"But what does that mean?" she murmured to herself.

"This." Phillip glanced down at their linked hands, seemed to come to a conclusion, and then tugged them up to standing.

Next thing she knew, her hands were on his shoulders and his were curved around her waist. They were standing so close that nearly every bit of their bodies were brushing against each other.

"Phillip," she whispered.

His answer was a kiss. Nothing sweet. Nothing tentative. His lips felt like a brand, and the intensity took her breath away.

240

And because she was a grown woman and it had been so very long since she'd felt so cared for or desired, Nancy found herself kissing him right back. She pressed closer, enjoying the way he held her in his arms. The way he smelled faintly of coffee and sugar and cologne and Phillip. It was practically intoxicating.

Or maybe it was simply everything he'd just referred to. Sometimes love couldn't be helped.

Sometimes the only thing that was needed was an acceptance of what was already there.

And when that happened?

It was a beautiful thing.

32

It had taken Lilly, his grandmother, and Eddie three days to get to Middlefield. After shipping three boxes full of Lilly's belongings and some of her friends' gifts and their purchases to the farm, they'd then boarded the Pioneer Trails bus in Sarasota.

That sixteen-hour bus trip to Berlin had been exhausting for all of them, his grandmother most of all. Instead of hiring a driver to take them to Middlefield, they'd elected to spend two nights in a rental house there.

The house had three bedrooms, a cozy living room with a fireplace, and a decent kitchen. After napping for a few hours, he and Lilly had walked to a nearby market and picked up some ready-made food. That evening, they'd sat in the living room and eaten supper together.

Maybe it was just exhaustion, but Lilly hadn't seemed herself. She'd been quieter than usual, which was saying a lot since she already was on the quiet side. There also seemed to be shadows under her eyes, as if she wasn't sleeping well or was maybe even deeply troubled.

Of course he wanted to fix everything for her. But when his

grandmother noticed that he was about to question Lilly and press her to tell him what was troubling her so much, Mommi cautioned him to hold his tongue.

"Give her some time to adjust, Edward," she said. "This is a big step for her."

"I understand, but she seemed so excited about it when she made the decision. Now it seems like she feels the complete opposite."

"I think that's normal."

"For what?"

"Oh, child. Haven't you ever experienced buyer's remorse?"

"Feeling upset about spending money on something I wasn't sure I should have? Of course. But this isn't that. This is different, right? We're not worried about presents. We're talking about her life."

"Which is all the more reason to give her space. Just because she's experiencing mixed emotions about something doesn't mean she wants to change her mind. She just needs a moment. A little time," she added gently.

"I suppose."

"I know, child. Listen to me."

Eddie knew his grandmother was a wise woman, so he didn't argue anymore. But he soon realized that even if Mommi was right, it didn't make his concern about Lilly diminish. He wanted her to feel like she had made the right decision. He couldn't push her to feel that way, however.

The next day the three of them went out to lunch, explored a bit, and then returned to the rental. They spent the evening doing a puzzle together and eating pizza that they had delivered. By the time they went to sleep that night, Lilly seemed to be more herself.

He was simply eager to get home.

His parents had arranged for a driver to pick them up at the rental and drive them to the farm.

What he hadn't known was that his parents had decided to come with the driver.

Although their intentions were good, he hadn't been happy about their surprise. Neither had November. They'd kept exchanging annoyed looks when his parents didn't even attempt to pretend to do anything but question Lilly while they were on the road to Middlefield.

"Lilly, I believe you are twenty-four?" Mamm asked.

"I am."

"And you are the youngest of three children?"

"Yes. My brother John is a carpenter. He's ten years older than me and married to a really nice woman named Samantha. My older sister's name is Katie and she's nine years older. She's married to Anson and they have five children."

"Five!" his mother exclaimed.

"She and Anson wanted a big family. They're really happy."

"Tell me about your parents," Daed said.

"My parents? Well, my father manages a store and mei mamm sells baked goods and helps him out in a dozen ways. They are good people."

"What do they think about you moving here?" Mamm asked.

Lilly looked like she'd just stepped on a stage naked. "Um, well . . . I haven't told them yet."

"Why not?" Mamm asked.

"Mamm, stop," Eddie said.

"Nee, Eddie, it's okay," Lilly said. "I . . . I mean, I don't mind talking about myself." She took a deep breath. "The truth is that I wasn't sure what to say to my parents. The decision to move to your farm was made rather suddenly. I knew they'd have a lot of questions."

His father cleared his throat. "I'm glad you brought that up. Why did you decide to move? It does seem like a sudden decision."

"It was."

Just as his father looked ready to begin another barrage of questioning, Mommi stepped in.

"Hank, you haven't even asked about how I'm feeling. Don't you care?"

And just like that, the conversation was redirected, at least for a moment.

"Are you okay?" Eddie whispered to Lilly.

Lilly's light blue eyes warmed. "Jah."

"I'm so sorry about this." Eddie was embarrassed with how nosey they were acting. But short of starting an argument in front of their driver, he didn't know how to make them stop.

He settled for covering Lilly's hand with his own. The last thing he wanted was for her to think she didn't have any support.

Tilting up her chin, she smiled softly. Letting him know that she was going to be all right.

"Eddie?" Mamm asked. "Is everything okay?"

"Jah." He squeezed Lilly's hand one more time before he released it. "I was just making sure that you two haven't upset Lilly with all these questions."

His father looked hurt. "We don't want to upset anyone. We're just curious . . . and concerned."

He'd had enough. "Mommi and I invited her to stay with us, Daed," he bit out. "I told you that when I called. And Mamm, when we were on the phone, you said that her coming to stay with Mommi was a good idea."

"I haven't forgotten," Mamm said. "But I still don't understand why everything happened so suddenly."

"Yes, why did you choose to come here?" Daed asked. "Is it really to help out mei mamm?"

"Daed, enough!" Eddie called out. "You're being rude."

"Eddie, stop," Lilly said in a gentle tone. Pressing her palm to his chest, she smiled up at him as she continued in a soft voice. "I appreciate you intervening, but your father is right. Nothing he is asking should be too difficult to answer." Turning to his father, she said, "Hank, I guess my reasons for coming here are complicated. I don't have a specific motivation. There were a lot of reasons."

His father's lips thinned. "I see."

Eddie had had enough. "Mamm, Daed, Lilly discovered she didn't enjoy working at the hotel in Pinecraft as much as she thought she would. Mommi and I enjoy her company and thought it would be nice if she could help out some around the house."

"And keep me company and help with some basic things," Mommi added.

His mother interrupted again. "But, what about—"

"But nothing," Mommi said. "Beth, I love you, but you and Hank need to stop twisting and turning what's obvious into something that ain't. All you need to know is that everything is going to be just fine."

There was steel in her voice. His mother looked taken aback and his father, while it appeared he didn't agree completely, seemed to know better than to add more questions.

"We're glad you are here, Lilly," Daed finally said. "I apologize for the awkward welcome."

"There's no reason to apologize. Thank you for allowing me to stay for a while."

For a while? Though Eddie knew that it was going to take some time for all of them to find their place in the household, he didn't have a bit of buyer's remorse. Instead, all he could think about was that Lilly was really special and he would have missed her terribly if she wasn't in his life every day.

They were meant to be together. He could feel it in his bones and in the way he felt protective about her. He wanted to be her champion. He wanted to help her fight her battles. He wanted to be the person she could lean on.

Just like the way she'd become the person he searched for in a room. With her, everything was better.

33

She'd been a wimp. Instead of simply stopping by, she'd left her parents a message to tell them that she'd left Pinecraft and was going to live in Middlefield with the Byler family. *Then* she'd asked if she could stop by.

Her mother had replied with a very terse message, saying that they would like to see her as soon as possible. When she'd shared that with November, November had encouraged her to go that very morning and had even gone so far as to hire her a driver, a Mrs. Gritton.

She'd just put on a cloak when Eddie knocked on the dawdi haus door. When he saw that she was already dressed and ready for her visit, he frowned.

"What's wrong?"

"What's wrong is that I had to find out from my father, who found out from his mother that my girlfriend is going to visit her parents today."

There were so many startling things in that statement, she'd hardly known where to start. "You think of me as your girl-friend?"

248

"Well, yes. Don't you think of me as your boyfriend?"

She did, but not publicly. "Kind of."

"Kind of!"

"Eddie, calm down. I've got enough going on. Do we have to talk about this right now?"

He sighed. "We probably should, but I reckon we are in a time crunch. When do we leave?"

"Eddie, are you sure you want to go?"

"I'm absolutely sure. I'm going with you to see your parents."

"My siblings might be there too."

"That's even better. I can meet them all at the same time."

She was already a nervous wreck. Now she felt rather ill. "There's no need for that."

"There's every need. I know you're worried about their reactions."

"I am worried, but they'll be all right. Once they got over the shock, they sounded okay when they left their message on the phone."

"I think that's all the more reason for me to be by your side, then. They're going to have questions."

She exhaled. "Okay, but, um, don't expect them to be like your family, okay?"

"Lilly, let's not pretend that the first conversation we had all together was that easy. My parents had a lot of questions."

"They did, though your grandmother helped a lot. After all, she kept answering before we could."

"She was really good about that." He looked back at the dawdi haus. "Maybe we should take her with us."

She knew he was joking, but part of her kind of wished that November actually was going with them to her house. Eddie's grandmother would be the perfect buffer between her timidity and her parents' rather forceful nature. And with Eddie in the mix? Well, it was enough to make her want to wish she'd never left Pinecraft. At least everyone had wrapped their heads around that.

He put an arm around her shoulders. "Hey, you know I was kidding, right? No way would I do anything to make things worse for you."

"I know." Looking up into his eyes, she attempted to smile. "I'm just a little worried about what they're going to say."

All traces of amusement faded from his expression. "I know. But Lilly, you're a grown woman and you haven't done anything wrong. You have every right to choose where you're going to live and what you want to do."

"I think they're going to wonder why I didn't involve them in the decision making."

"Is your job their decision?"

"Of course not. But I can see their point."

He gazed at her for a long moment then said, "I want to come with you. Please let me."

She raised an eyebrow. "Would you really stay back if I asked you to?"

"Jah. I wouldn't like it, though. And it's not because I don't trust your opinion. It's because I care about you. I don't want you to ever feel like you're alone."

Since that was exactly how she'd been feeling, Lilly realized he had a point. She exhaled. "Okay, then. Eddie, would you please come with me to visit my parents? I'd love for you to meet them."

"Danke. I'd be happy to."

A few moments later the driver pulled up the drive. Running to her room, Lilly grabbed the souvenirs she'd picked up from Pinecraft for her family and joined Eddie in the car.

And then they were on their way. For better or worse, it was time to honestly speak to her parents about her wishes . . . and introduce them to the man who had become so important to her.

The man who she felt was about to be the love of her life.

34

Eddie knew that Lilly had a confusing relationship with her parents. He also thought he understood some of the reasons for the strain. What he wasn't prepared to see was just how tentative she was around them.

Lilly acted as if she was afraid to do something wrong around them. She continually watched her parents for cues about what they wanted and then followed their lead. It was exhausting to watch, especially when he realized that her parents seemed to be oblivious to the whole dance.

He couldn't help but compare Lilly's timidness to the way he'd seen her at the inn. There'd been a quiet confidence to her movements there. She'd been efficient yet serene. Eddie had listened to more than one person compliment her efforts, whether it was the way she'd cleaned a room or the way she'd gone above and beyond when asked for something.

To see her be so uncomfortable in the home she grew up in broke his heart. It also made him even more determined to show Lilly how much he admired and appreciated her. Even when they disagreed, Eddie wanted to be sure she never doubted his love for her.

Yep. He had big plans for them.

If they somehow managed to survive the next hour.

Her parents, who'd introduced themselves as Fran and Gabe, were currently staring at him as if he were an interloper. If Eddie hadn't been so determined to stay by Lilly's side, he had a feeling that they would have politely shown him the door. That was the key word, he thought. *Politely*. Fran and Gabe Kurtz were extremely polite.

Still standing in the entryway of the house, with its gleaming hickory floors and spotless white walls, Eddie was struck with how beautiful the lines of the two-story entryway were. Wide, dark-stained beams crisscrossed overhead, encouraging one's eye to look up. Beautifully hand-woven rugs in shades of brown muted their steps. His father would have admired it all.

He would also have felt the same way Eddie did—that the immaculate surroundings were pleasing but far too chilly to be relaxing.

Lilly had donned a dark gray dress, thick black stockings, and serviceable black tennis shoes for the visit. The somber color made her skin appear luminescent and pale. And though she always arranged her dark blond hair neatly under a crisp white kapp, today it looked as if it had been pulled back with force. Almost like no strand of hair dared to slip out of place.

Again, he couldn't help but compare this version of her with the Lilly at her going-away party. That woman had been dressed in bright yellow, had looked delightfully mussed after being hugged by everyone, and had glowed with happiness.

This transformation made him sad—and made him want to kiss Lilly so intensely that some color would appear in her face and a few of those gorgeous locks would escape their confines.

Just imagining how it would feel to do such a thing made

him swallow hard. He'd thought about kissing Lilly before but not like that.

He flushed. What was wrong with him? He needed to be thinking about her heart and her happiness—not how attracted he was to her. He should be thinking of comfort, not kisses. And especially not while meeting her parents!

"Eddie?" Lilly whispered. "Are you all right?"

He blinked. "Pardon?"

"You seem to be in a daze."

"I guess I was." He gazed into her eyes and smiled softly. "I'm sorry."

Her father cleared his throat.

When Eddie turned his attention back to her father, one of Gabe's gray eyebrows rose.

"I'm sorry. Did you say something, Gabe?"

The man's manner turned arctic. "Mei frau asked if you would like a cup of kaffi."

His parents would have expected him to apologize profusely for his rudeness. His grandmother, however, would have glared at Gabe and lifted her chin. She never did have patience for bossy folk. Deciding to follow November's lead, he nodded. "Jah, danke."

Gabe's lips thinned.

Lilly tensed even more beside him . . . which made Eddie ashamed. He should be trying to make her more comfortable, not the opposite.

"I'll help you, Mamm," she blurted.

Her mother, who seemed to be studying Lilly as intently as he had, shook her head. "Nee. You sit down with your . . . friend and your father. Getting coffee is no trouble. It's a blessing that we have enough for our guest."

It was a gentle but firm reminder that they'd expected Lilly to come there alone.

Eddie bit his lip to keep from muttering something snarky. Boy, they weren't happy that he was staying by Lilly's side. Not by a long shot.

"We can put my cloak and your coat on the hooks by the door," Lilly said.

He reached for her black cloak and hung his coat and the cloak on two hooks, then followed Gabe and Lilly into a living room. A large stone fireplace anchored the space. The fire in it was rather tepid and didn't give off much heat or light, which was kind of a shame since it was November and the wind was rather strong outside.

In front of the fireplace were a pair of couches and a dark gray chair with matching ottoman. A large square coffee table rested exactly in the middle of it all. Only the stream of pale sunlight from the large windows on either side of the fireplace warmed the area.

"Please sit down," Gabe said. "Eddie, you may have the chair."

"Danke, but I don't mind the couch. I'll sit next to Lilly."

Lilly shot him a perplexed look, but Eddie pretended not to notice. Now that he understood what her life was like here, he was on a mission to make her comfortable. Or, at the very least, to make her see that he'd always put her needs first. He wanted Lilly to understand that there was nothing he wouldn't do in order to make her happy.

Which was what he was attempting to do at that very moment. Though Lilly hadn't indicated that she needed him to stay by her side, a sixth sense was telling him to stay close.

Fran appeared with a metal tray holding four cups and a plate of cookies. After setting it in the center of the table, she passed each of them their drinks as well as one cookie and a napkin.

Everyone's coffee was black, and there was no offer of milk or sugar. That was how he preferred his, but he knew Lilly usually drank hers with cream and sugar. With quite a bit of cream and sugar. She took a small sip of her drink and grimaced slightly. It was on the tip of his tongue to offer to fetch her a little of each, but he refrained.

None of them tasted their cookie.

"Lilly, perhaps you could now tell us why you left Pinecraft," Fran said. "All you talked about for the last year was moving there."

"Yes. Tell us what happened." Gabe's eyebrows lowered. "And how you ended up living at this man's house."

Eddie stiffened. Her father was acting as if they were living in sin. He resented the implication. Just as he opened his mouth to correct Gabe, Lilly spoke.

"I'm not living with Eddie, Daed. I'm living in the dawdi haus with his grandmother." She set her coffee cup on the table. "There are two bedrooms there, a small living room, and a kitchenette."

"What are you doing there, exactly?"

"I asked Lilly to come live with my grandmother. She's still spry but needs an extra hand from time to time. Lilly is amazing at helping her with Mommi hardly being aware that she's doing so. We're all very impressed with her. My grandmother can be a handful at times."

At last Lilly's cheeks bloomed with color. "Danke, Eddie, but you know I enjoy November's company."

Fran took another sip of her coffee and set it down. "Lilly,

I'm still confused. You've never shown any interest in caregiving. I always thought you enjoyed cleaning motel rooms."

"I enjoyed working at the Marigold Inn, but it wasn't the best fit. There were some problems."

"So, instead of working through them, you quit," her daed said.

She looked down at her hands, which were clenched in her lap. "Jah."

Lilly wasn't going to defend herself. She was going to let her parents think the worst about her. He hated that.

Unable to *not* defend his girl, Eddie jumped in before he could stop himself. "There was a problem. A married couple pulled Lilly into their unhappy marriage and blamed her for something she didn't do. It wasn't right."

"What did they think you did?"

"They accused me of stealing."

Fran inhaled sharply while Gabe visibly tensed. "I assume you did no such thing?"

Hurt flashed in Lilly's eyes before she hid it. "You are right. I did not steal anything."

"Gut." Gabe turned to Eddie. "Though Lilly is not ours by blood, we raised her with good values."

"I'm sorry?" They knew their daughter had been falsely accused and was visibly shaken by the experience. But that was all Gabe had to say?

"Did Lilly not tell you that she was adopted? We adopted her when she was almost two years old. Her mother was very ill." He waved a hand. "I suppose she couldn't be blamed, since Lilly's father was in prison, you see."

"My mother had kidney disease," Lilly corrected quietly.

"Whatever the reason, they took you to the children's home. I'm so glad we found you, child," Fran said.

Pure sympathy coated her mother's voice. However, instead of encouraging one to feel for Lilly, it was twisted slightly, like her mother wanted to make sure the attention fell on their good deeds and not Lilly's honor.

A knot formed in Eddie's stomach as another wave of shame coursed through him. He'd been so sanctimonious when he'd lectured Lilly about being open and honest. Why hadn't he tried harder to learn more about her home and family? Now that he was seeing things for himself, he wanted to wrap her in his arms and never let her go. It was no wonder she'd wanted to escape this home.

And keep so many of her feelings to herself.

Worried, he glanced at Lilly again. She was sitting straight and tall. Her expression was a mask. After that first tentative sip, she hadn't touched her coffee.

He loved Lilly. Loved her completely. Oh, not because of her history or because the cool, rather condescending way they were treating her was so awful but because of the way she was holding herself together. Lilly was strong.

Lilly Kurtz was one of the strongest people he'd ever met in his life.

He couldn't change her past and he couldn't change the way her parents treated her. However, he could certainly change her future and the present.

And, if he had his way, he was also going to change the way they treated her.

There was no time like the present. Leaning over, he picked up her coffee cup. "I know this coffee isn't to your liking. Would you like me to find some cream and sugar for ya?"

While Lilly's eyes widened, her father inhaled sharply. As if Eddie had been asking for someone to bring over a cow and milk it too.

With a wary look at her father, Lilly finally answered. "Eddie, there's no need."

As far as he was concerned, there was every need. He'd watched her serve breakfast to dozens of people at the Marigold Inn. He'd watched her cater to his grandmother's wishes all day long. He'd admired Lilly's giving nature. It was something that had drawn him to her from the very beginning.

But that didn't mean she didn't ever have any wants or needs of her own. And one of those was her fondness for coffee so sweet it practically made his teeth curl.

Getting to his feet, he spoke gently. "You know it's no trouble." Before she could answer, he turned to Fran. "Do you mind if I go to the kitchen to take care of Lilly's coffee? She prefers it with milk and sugar."

Her mother frowned. "We've always served coffee black."

Why that mattered was a mystery to him, but at the moment he didn't care. Eddie suddenly felt like they were in a battle of wills—and maybe it wasn't his imagination. He was now determined not only for Lilly to be catered to, but for her parents to see that she now had a champion and he wasn't going to let even the smallest problem in her life go ignored.

"That may be the case, but I know she likes the brew a bit sweeter. I'd like to see her happy."

Fran stood up. "I'll go get the sugar bowl and milk."

"Thank you."

While they waited, he noticed that Lilly's skin was flushed. Whether it was embarrassment from his request or her parents' behavior, he didn't know. "I'm sorry," he murmured.

"Here is your milk and sugar, Lilly," Fran said.

"Danke."

He noticed her hand was trembling. "I'll take care of it for you."

"Eddie."

Her voice held a warning, and he supposed it might have been justified. He had turned into someone he didn't recognize. He was usually easygoing and didn't get ruffled easily. But he now knew that she was the exception. Where Lilly was concerned, he was as protective as a guard dog.

With her parents looking on, he added two spoonfuls of sugar and a liberal dose of cream and stirred the additions in. "Here you go," he murmured as he returned the cup to her hands.

When she immediately took a sip and smiled, he felt like he'd just accomplished a huge feat.

Turning to Fran and Gabe, he said, "My parents are looking forward to meeting you both. My grandmother too. You'll have to come to our farm one day soon. Perhaps for an early supper."

"Lilly, does this mean you have made up your mind?" her father asked. "You are really going to live with this man's family?"

She put down her cup, which was now only half full. "I am."

"Are you sure? You barely know them."

When Eddie was about to rush to her defense, she rested a hand on his arm.

"That's not true," she said. "I actually know Eddie and November better than some people I've lived near my whole life. We spent a lot of time together at the Marigold Inn."

Gabe was staring at her hand on Eddie's arm. But instead of seeming to be upset by their connection, her father looked thoughtful. "I see," he murmured. "I think I'm beginning to see a lot of things at long last."

Eddie didn't have any idea what Lilly's father was suddenly seeing. All he cared about was that Lilly felt supported. He covered her slim hand with his own, hoping the connection would help her feel assured. "Your daughter was so kind to my grandmother and such a hard worker. But she's more than that. She's special. From practically the first moment we met, I couldn't take my eyes off her."

"She surely is special," Gabe said. "We've always thought so. I'm glad you noticed that too."

Noticing that Lilly was turning bright red, Eddie chuckled. "I know I'm embarrassing you, but I'm speaking the truth. From practically the first day we met, I wanted to get to know you better. I was so desperate for a few moments of your time, I was willing to do whatever it took—even help you with your job."

She smiled at him. "It's probably good that you didn't act on that."

"Maybe, but at least at the farm I can help you now."

"Eddie, you sound like a suitor," Fran murmured. "Is that what you are?"

"Mamm, nee," Lilly said.

He turned to face Lilly. "It's okay," he said. "I've got nothing to hide. Besides, you know how I feel about you, right?"

She swallowed. "I think so."

"I guess I need to be more clear, then. I love you and one day I hope to earn your love."

Lilly released a ragged sigh. "Eddie, you already have it."

No longer caring about their audience, he moved to grasp both of her hands. "When you are ready, I'll propose to you then."

She laughed. "Is that a warning?"

"Not at all. It's a promise."

Lilly's eyes, always so luminescent because of their pale blue color, were shining. They looked so bright, Eddie was tempted to kiss her right then and there. It was a blessing that he hadn't completely lost all sense of what was right and proper.

"Lilly?" her mother asked.

Looking startled, Lilly pulled her hands from his and turned back to face her parents. Two seconds passed as her face became a mask yet again. "Jah, Mamm?"

Fran smiled. "I am happy for you. So happy. You've found a man who is worthy of you."

Eddie was stunned. Here he'd thought they were about to throw him out of their house . . . but instead her mother was giving Lilly her approval.

By his side, Lilly appeared to be just as puzzled. "Mamm? What are you saying?"

"She means that you are a special woman, child," her father said. "We're glad you've found a man who realizes that."

Her mother continued. "I've never been too good at speaking from my heart, but that doesn't mean we don't want the best for you. After all, the day we met you proved that dreams do come true."

Tears were falling down Lilly's cheeks. Just as Eddie was about to wipe the worst offender with the side of a finger, she stood up and hugged her parents.

They both hugged her back. Each of her parents looked like they were holding a precious gift. The transformation that had taken place in front of his eyes was almost shocking.

Or perhaps not.

Eddie had always believed that the Lord performed miracles

all the time. He'd also believed that no problem was beneath His attention.

Perhaps they'd all needed this reminder that He also helped people's hearts heal, as well.

When at last the three of them broke apart, Lilly turned to him with a smile. "I'm so glad we came back."

When she stepped toward him, he reached for her hands again. "I am too." There were so many other things he yearned to say, but it wasn't the right time.

That was okay, though. For now, it was enough.

35

After paying the driver and waving her away, Lilly turned to walk toward the dawdi haus.

"Wait, Lilly," Eddie called out. "Can we talk?"

"You'd like to talk some more?" she teased. "I would have thought that you covered everything in front of my parents."

"Don't be mad. I know I said too much too soon, but I couldn't help myself. I wanted them to know that you're cared for. That I appreciate you."

"I think they know that now," she joked.

Looking slightly embarrassed, Eddie chuckled. "Jah. I guess they do. But there's nothing wrong with that."

"I don't think so, either."

"Honestly, as long as no one mistreats you, I don't care what people say. All that matters to me is that you know my feelings for you are sincere."

"I never doubted that."

"Lilly, I love so many things about you. I love how caring you are with everyone you meet. I love how hard you work. I love the way you can read a book in a day and always look so pretty. I love how you seem timid but you're strong enough to move to another state by yourself . . . and brave enough to come here too."

Those words! Her heart felt as if it were beating a mile a minute. She swallowed, trying to pull herself together so she didn't start crying. "You, ah, certainly love a lot of things about me."

"You're right. I do." He stepped closer. "That's because I love you. You know that, right?"

Feeling like she was in a daze, she nodded. His words were so sweet and tender. They matched the heat that was shining in his eyes. And the feelings in her heart. "I know you love me. Just like you know I love you too."

He released a ragged sigh. "I think this means I can take you in my arms."

"And?" she prompted.

He laughed. "And kiss you too."

At last. At last she was going to have her first kiss. She looked up at him, waiting for his cues.

He didn't disappoint. He reached for her hands and linked their fingers. But after the briefest of squeezes, he ran his hands up her arms. Though she had on both her cloak and her long-sleeved dress, she felt the motion as if they were touching bare skin.

When his hands reached her shoulders, Eddie paused. She inhaled, wondering if he'd now pull her into his arms.

Instead, he ran his hands up her neck, stopping only when he was cupping her cheeks.

Her lips parted.

"I love you, Lilly," he whispered as his lips brushed against hers. Kissing her for the very first time.

When he raised his head, his gorgeous, bright blue eyes searched hers. A myriad of emotions shone in their depths.

Hope. Worry. Love. So much love. He was also looking for a signal from her.

She wasn't going to make him wait another second. "I love you too. So much." She raised her hands to his neck and pulled up on her tiptoes. Just so there was no misunderstanding.

Eddie murmured something under his breath before claiming her lips again.

This time there was no tentativeness. No hesitation. Nothing but everything she wanted. Their kiss was filled with longing and love. Passion and desire.

Everything that she'd ever dreamed of having.

No, everything that she'd ever secretly hoped for.

Eddie Byler loved her. He loved her and had fought for her and protected her. Just the way she wanted to do for him. It seemed only natural to want to show each other how much they cared through fierce kisses.

When he finally lifted his head, Lilly was breathless. Like she'd run a mile in bare feet. Everything felt tingly and electrified. She had to force herself to drop her hands and press them against her sides.

A little shocked by it all, she met his gaze. Eddie looked a lot like she did. Stunned. On fire.

He swallowed. "Okay, then."

She had to smile at that. "Am I supposed to know what that means?"

Still looking a bit shell-shocked, he ran a hand through his hair. "I'd like us to marry soon. The sooner the better." He took another step backward, almost like he didn't trust himself not to hold her close and kiss her again.

To be honest, she wouldn't mind that at all. "Is this your proposal?"

He ran a hand over his face again and chuckled under his breath. "Yeah, I guess it is. Lilly, you know I love you. You know I want to spend all my time with you. And from what we've just experienced, I think it's obvious that there's passion between us too. I didn't know I was waiting for you, but one day, in the middle of a vacation, there you were. It's like you were an answer to every secret hope and dream I've ever had. I don't want to let you go." He exhaled. "Will you marry me?"

"Yes."

"Soon?"

It turned out that Eddie had a way with words.

Or maybe it was simply a way with her.

At the moment, since her mind felt a bit like mush, she decided to let him have whatever he wanted . . . since she wanted the same things.

"Yes," she said again. "We can marry as soon as you want."

His lips curved into the sweetest smile. "That's good."

She couldn't help but laugh. "I think so too."

Epilogue

The Marigold Inn was in fine form. It was decorated for Christmas and practically everything that didn't move was covered with pine boughs or palm fronds and white lights.

A giant white flocked tree decorated the entryway. Whimsical ornaments with birds and fish and palm trees and sailboats decorated nearly every branch. Lilly had loved the unusual tree at first sight.

Honestly, she thought that everything about the inn on December twentieth was perfect.

Especially since it was her wedding day.

Standing in the back hallway, she watched Amber and Penelope direct all the guests to the white chairs set up outside. It was a small wedding, as far as Amish ones went. Only about fifty people were there. But since she had all her friends, their spouses, and both her and Eddie's families, Lilly knew she didn't need anything—or anyone—else.

"You were right, Daughter," her mother said. "This place is a beautiful spot for a wedding."

Lilly looked at her mother, whom she no longer thought of as her adopted one. Only as Mamm. "Thank you."

A lot had happened between them in the weeks since she and Eddie had agreed to marry. Not only had she and Eddie made plans for their future—they were going to take over the dawdi haus and November was going to move back into the main one—but they'd visited her parents every week.

Maybe it was Eddie's way—or maybe it was simply that both she and her parents were determined to have a closer relationship. But whatever the reason, they'd finally become closer. The way she'd always hoped they would be. As they talked more, she'd opened her heart to them and shared so many of her worries.

And to her surprise, her father had revealed many of his secret fears too. She hadn't been the only one to feel as if she wasn't quite good enough.

Even though all those things had involved a lot of prayer and worry, deciding the details of her wedding had not. From the first, she'd wanted to marry in Pinecraft.

When Nancy had offered to host the wedding free of charge, Lilly had jumped at the chance.

"Fran, it's time for you to sit down," Nancy urged. "Your family is looking for you. It's time to start."

Though her mother nodded, she didn't move. "Lilly, are you ready? Are you sure you'll be okay?"

She knew her mother was asking about far more than just a short walk down the aisle. She was asking about her future happiness. "I'm going to be just fine," she replied. "I promise, I'll be right behind you."

After giving her a tight hug, her mother walked through the French doors and joined the other gathered guests.

"So, how are you doing?" Nancy asked. "Are you ready to get this show on the road?"

"I am." She smiled at her former boss. "Everything looks so beautiful. And that cake! It's a work of art!"

"Phillip said he wanted to make a cake worthy of you."

She bit her bottom lip in an effort to keep from dissolving into tears. "Thanks for everything. You've helped to make this day the best one of my life."

Nancy looked like she was barely holding back the tears herself. "That's as it should be. You're marrying a good man and are surrounded by all your family and friends. I'm delighted to be a part of it." Her voice thickened with emotion. "Lilly, I'm so glad we met."

"Me too."

Nancy reached for her hand. "Are you ready?"

Looking at the plain gold band that now decorated Nancy's left hand, Lilly smiled. "I am. I'm glad we fell in love at the same time."

"Phillip gave me everything I never knew I needed but had secretly hoped for. I am blessed."

"I feel the same way about Eddie."

"Then let's get you outside so you can get married. The preacher is starting to look nervous."

"That's Elias. He's our preacher from home."

"Well, he looks like a very proper gentleman." Looking a little worried, Nancy added, "I hope he's not thinking everything here is too fancy?"

"Not at all. Honestly, I think Elias is anxious to get this wedding over so he can go to the beach."

Nancy winked. "He might not be the only one."

Lilly chuckled as she walked by Nancy's side outside. The

chairs were set up for a typical Amish wedding. Two sets of chairs faced each other, with the men on one side and the women on the other.

As the bright sun and scent of fresh flowers surrounded them, everyone assembled got to their feet and turned. There, on the first row of the women's side, sat Mary Margaret, Betsy, and Esther, her three matrons of honor. They were all in blue like she was and eagerly waiting for her to take the empty seat in between them. Her mother and sister and sister-in-law, as well as November and Eddie's mother Beth, were beaming.

Across the aisle sat Eddie. Surrounding him were her brother, her best friends' husbands, and all of Eddie's friends and family. She barely noticed them, though. She only had eyes for her future husband.

He had on a crisp white short-sleeved shirt, a dark blue vest, and an intent look. She shivered. She loved the way he looked at her.

After giving her one more reassuring smile, Nancy took her seat while Lilly at last took her own.

And then Preacher Elias walked to the center of the aisle. "Since our bride and groom were anxious to have this wedding, and we all traveled here to Pinecraft to attend it, I think it's time we got down to business. Ain't so?"

Laughter followed his comment.

When he began to speak about marriage and devotion and love and honor, Lilly allowed the words to float around her. Her only focus was on the man whose love changed her life. Eddie was hers. They loved each other and would soon be man and wife. Before God and all their friends. Everyone.

An hour later, she stood in front of Edward Byler, and the two of them spoke their vows. Their voices were solemn and clear.

Lilly knew that one day their children would probably ask her and Eddie all about their courtship and wedding.

One day, she might even be able to spin them a story filled with romance and honor.

But at the moment, all she felt was love. Love for her husband, love for their families, and love for her girlfriends, especially Mary and Betsy, who had been the first people to show her that true love came without expectations or rules or boundaries.

Instead, it came by itself. In its purest form, love was simply love.

She was blessed to now know that.

Eddie took her hand. "Are you ready to start our life?"

"Oh yes," she whispered.

Of course, she had a secret. As far as she was concerned, her life had already started the moment she'd stepped on a Pioneer Trails bus and headed down south to Pinecraft.

From that moment, there was no going back.

Acknowledgments

Boy, time sure does fly! It seems like just a couple of weeks ago I was chatting with my agent, Nicole, about a proposal for these three books. Now it's already time to wrap up another series. It's been such a privilege and an honor to write this trilogy for Revell, and I'm so grateful for the many people who made this dream a reality.

First, I owe a great deal of thanks to the editorial team. Both Andrea Doering and Kristin Kornoelje worked so hard to help me make these novels something to be proud of. From brainstorming ideas to providing feedback, to checking facts and dates and characters, both of these ladies were incredibly helpful and patient.

I'm also so very grateful to art director Laura Klynstra, for designing such gorgeous covers for the entire series. They're eye-catching and beautiful and portray my wallflower heroines perfectly.

I'm also indebted to Brianne Dekker and Karen Steele for all their hard work with marketing, promotion, and a hundred other things they did to make sure these books reach readers' hands. Brianne and Karen, thank you for championing this series and providing so much enthusiasm and support for these books.

A big thank you also goes out to the many ladies of the Buggy Bunch who've helped review and promote these books, to Jean Volk who manages so much behind the scenes, and to Jeane Wynn—an amazing publicist and angel on earth. Of course, I'm also thankful to dear friend Lynne Stroup for providing valuable feedback for all of the first drafts.

In addition, I want to give a big shout-out to all the amazing librarians who have invited me to their libraries, hosted reader groups, purchased my novels for their collections, and placed my novels in readers' hands over the years. I'm so grateful to all of you!

Finally, thank you to all my readers. Your steadfast support has enabled me to spend my days doing what I absolutely love—writing books for you.

Dear Reader,

Back when I was in elementary school, I was painfully shy. I'd cry if I had to give a book report, stutter if I got too excited or nervous, and often missed out on opportunities because I was too embarrassed to ask questions. Over time, I developed skills to cope with my shyness, but I still remember wishing that I was different or, at the very least, viewed differently. Going away to college was an exhilarating experience for me. Yes, I was still quiet and shy, but I finally had the chance to make a fresh start with people who had no idea how awkward I used to be.

I guess those memories are a big part of the reason I wanted to write the Season in Pinecraft series. I knew I wasn't the only person who longed for a chance to "start over." I figured even Amish girls might also long for a big change every now and then.

I hope you enjoyed getting to know Mary Margaret, Betsy, and Lilly and connected with their journeys. I must admit that I'm fond of all three of them. Each in her own way was stronger than she looked and inspired many other characters in their books. I thought they were terrific heroines.

For those of you who've never had the opportunity to visit Pinecraft, Florida, I hope you will get the chance to visit one day. I promise, it really is a wonderful place! If you happen to go, don't forget to spend an hour or two out on the beach at Siesta Key. Take off your shoes, relax on the sugary-soft sand, watch the pelicans fish in the distance, and feel the warm sun on your face. It's a lovely spot full of hope, sunshine, and fresh air.

Wishing you many blessings—whether you're in Siesta Key or in your own backyard.

Shelley Shepard Gray

Turn the page for a sneak peek at
the first trip to Pinecraft in

Her Heart's Desire

1

MARCH

There were only two beds in the motel room. Two beds for the three of them to share. Looking at the somewhat shabby space, Mary Margaret Miller felt her insides knot. When the Pioneer Trails bus driver had announced they'd needed to make an emergency stop in Georgia because the storm was too fierce to drive through, it had almost sounded like a grand adventure. Mary had never traveled much farther than Sugarcreek or Berlin, Ohio. And though she did know quite a few Englischers, most everyone she knew was Amish, just like her.

She'd been so excited to see new things and meet new people, she hadn't even been too concerned when the bus pulled into the parking lot of a small, rather run-down motel just off the highway. But now, as she stood next to two girls she barely knew and studied the forlorn pair of beds, Mary realized that her spur-of-the-moment decision to travel to Pinecraft, Florida, by herself hadn't been the greatest idea.

Not at all.

Or perhaps her earlier prayers on the bus were to blame.

After all, she had suggested to the Lord that surely anything would be better than being on a large bus in the middle of an ice storm. Maybe He had decided to take her at her word.

Lilly broke the silence first. "Do either of you want to guess what that stain on the wall is from?"

All three of them turned to stare at the dark blob seeping down from the ceiling to rest near the light switch. "I-I've been trying to pretend it wasn't there," Betsy said. "Obviously, that plan isn't going too well."

"I would say that I've been trying to not think about the bedspreads, but I canna seem to think about anything besides who all has touched them previously," Lilly murmured.

Betsy wrinkled her nose. "M-maybe we should put them on the floor, jah? They m-might be infested."

"That would surely be best," Lilly said.

Straightening her slim shoulders, Betsy glanced Mary's way. "Are you all right?"

"Hmm? Oh, jah." Finding her voice at last, Mary attempted to sound optimistic. "Do you girls have any thoughts about how we should decide who gets to sleep alone tonight?"

"I don't mind sharing a bed with either of you," Betsy said. "I doubt I'll s-sleep much anyway."

"It doesn't matter to me either," Lilly said. "Betsy might be wide awake, but I'm exhausted. I've been so nervous about this trip, I haven't slept much for the last week. I could almost sleep on the floor." As they all looked at the threadbare carpet under their feet, Lilly wrinkled her nose. "Scratch that. I'm not going to put my head anywhere near that carpet."

Mary smiled at her. "I wouldn't let you even if you wanted to do such a thing. You'd likely get a skin rash or something."

After carefully pulling off the comforter and tossing it in the corner of the room, Betsy sat down on one of the beds. "That settles it, then. I'll share this bed with Lilly, and you may have the other one all to yourself, Mary."

Now Mary was embarrassed. Why had she even brought up their sleeping arrangements in the first place? No doubt the other girls thought she was the type of person who always needed her way, even at the expense of others. Tentatively, she said, "Sorry if I sounded pushy. I . . . well, I sometimes say all the wrong things."

Betsy shook her head. "There's nothing to forgive. If we're being honest, I-I'm so happy to be out of my little Kentucky town and doing something different, even staying in this motel feels exciting."

"I feel the same way," Lilly added as she carefully pulled the straight pins from her kapp, then set them on the dresser. "I can't even remember if I've ever had a sleepover with two friends."

"M-me neither," Betsy said with a smile before she seemed to realize what she'd just insinuated. "I mean, not that you two are my friends or anything."

Mary gaped at the other two women. All three of them were in their early twenties. Betsy, with her dark hair and matching eyes, was a true beauty, and Lilly looked like everyone's best friend. She was so chatty and smiley. How could they, too, have trouble making friends? It didn't seem possible.

Worried there was a private joke between them that she was unaware of, she frowned.

As soon as she did, Betsy said, "Did I offend you, Mary?"

"Nee."

"Are y-you sure?"

Seconds sped by as she debated what to say. It had been so

long since she'd felt like she could be completely honest. No, that wasn't right. It had been a long time since she'd been able to allow herself to be vulnerable. People could be cruel, and she'd learned that from personal experience. She'd been bullied and teased by so many kids when she was in school.

Almost everything inside her was protesting letting even the smallest bit of her guard down. Her heart wasn't eager to be bruised, especially not now, with these two new girls. If she said the wrong thing, it could ruin her whole vacation.

On the heels of that was the memory of her evening prayers a few weeks ago. She'd knelt at the side of her bed, praying and crying and asking the Lord to help her make a new start. And He had. In just a few weeks, she'd sold enough of her greeting cards to buy a bus ticket to Pinecraft for a long, much-needed vacation.

Her parents, well aware of how miserable she'd been for years, had been supportive. They'd even chipped in a little so she could stay at the Marigold Inn for two weeks. And her father refused to let her pay him back. All he asked was that she try to be positive while she was on vacation. Try to let other people see the *real* Mary Margaret that he and her mamm knew and loved.

Even Preacher Marlin had stopped by their house to offer encouragement. He'd brought over some of his favorite postcards from Pinecraft and told her about each one. While sipping his lukewarm coffee liberally laced with cream and sugar, Preacher Marlin even confided that he'd had one or two adventures on the beach in Siesta Key.

She'd giggled, thinking about their gentle, seventy-year-old preacher kicking up his heels in the sand and surf.

But most importantly, Mary's favorite preacher had reminded her that she was a person worth knowing. They'd prayed together about that too. By the time he'd left, her resolve had grown even stronger to experience as much as she possibly could on her vacation.

Now, sitting in the motel room, all those good feelings settled in her heart. She'd promised people who cared about her to try to come out of her shell. Was she really going to throw all those promises away and go back to the person she'd been in Trail, Ohio?

No. No, she was not.

After taking off her kapp and shoes, she sat down on the bed too. "Betsy, you didn't offend me at all. To tell you the truth, I was just thinking that both of you seemed like the type of women who have lots of friends and beaus. I was surprised." Realizing that neither had said a word about boyfriends, she cleared her throat. "Or do you have boyfriends?"

Betsy chuckled as if the question was mighty humorous. "N-nee."

"I don't either," Lilly said without even a flash of a smile. "What about you?"

Mary realized then that she could either keep all her bad experiences and disappointments to herself . . . or she could be completely honest. The decision was easy to make. She didn't want to lie and had the feeling that her lies wouldn't sound believable anyway.

Taking a deep, fortifying breath, she said, "The truth is . . . back in my hometown of Trail, I didn't really take."

Lilly's eyes widened. "What do you mean?"

"I wasn't popular," she replied, inwardly wincing because "not popular" was a big understatement. "I wasn't popular at all with the boys in my church district." Deciding she might as well admit the whole truth, she added, "Nor with the girls."

Comforted by Betsy's and Lilly's sympathetic looks, she added, "I've always kind of been on my own."

"Me too," Betsy said. "I have bad asthma and it's kept me from doing a lot of activities everyone else does. Plus, I used to stutter even more than I do now, so it was hard to even speak to the other kids." She shuddered. "E-every time I get upset or really excited, my mouth seems to freeze. I was teased a lot."

Teasing someone for stuttering was especially cruel. "I'm sorry."

"I am too, b-but I've learned to accept how things are." She smiled at Mary. "I only shared that so you'd know I mean it when I say I've spent a lot of time by myself as well."

Lilly joined them on the bed, leaning up against the fake wood headboard. "I've been a loner too. My parents adopted me and made sure everyone knew it."

When both Mary and Betsy gasped, Lilly chuckled softly. "Sorry, I guess that came out kind of bad. Was it too much to hear from a relative stranger?"

"Not at all," Mary said quickly. When Lilly gave her a knowing look, she smiled. "But it was a lot to hear so boldly."

After they shared another smile, Lilly looked down at her lap. "I don't usually confide so much. Actually, I never do. I guess I feel comfortable with the two of you. So comfortable I don't even think about how my words might sound. I'll try to be better."

"Don't," Betsy said. "I like that you're being so honest. B-be as honest as you want."

"Okay, then." Lilly took a deep breath. "I love my adoptive parents—I really do—but there's been times when I wish I wasn't a symbol of their good works. It's been hard to live down."

She rolled her eyes. "Here we are, all Amish. All in communities where living simply and being part of the group is valued. But instead of feeling like I was just one of the crowd, I was always known as 'poor Lilly, whose parents adopted her.'" She lowered her voice. "Or poor Lilly; there must have been something wrong with her because her real parents gave her up."

"Ouch," Betsy said.

"The label has stung. I'm not gonna lie."

The three of them regarded each other, and a new calm seemed to fill the air.

"You two are wallflowers like me," Mary blurted.

Betsy raised an eyebrow. "What's that?"

"It's, um, an old-fashioned term. It's a girl who kind of stands on the sidelines and watches while everyone else does things." Trying to think of a better example, she said, "Once, I checked a romance novel out at the library that was about wallflowers. See, in this book, all the girls were asked to dance except a pair of women. They were essentially ignored and had to spend most of the evening sitting in chairs and wishing for boys to ask them to dance."

"While everyone else lives, you mean," Lilly said. "If being a wallflower is the correct term for it, then that fits me perfectly. That's what I've been doing for years now—standing off to the side and waiting to be noticed."

Betsy nodded. "While everyone else just walks by."

Mary felt a lump form in her throat. The girls' comments were so close to how she often privately felt, it was stunning.

Betsy and Lilly seemed really nice. It was too bad that they also felt like they'd been overlooked.

Mary felt a little depressed . . . and maybe a little angry too. She wasn't perfect, but she wasn't a bad person.

It wasn't right. There was more to her than that. She was nice, was reasonably attractive, and had a really good heart. There was no reason every other girl in her hometown had a better chance than she did of finding a beau or making good friends. It was time people started seeing the person she always wished they'd see.

It was time to start anew.

"I don't know how you two feel, but I'm sick of being a wall-flower," she blurted.

Betsy's eyes widened. "Well, of course you are. B-being a wallflower stinks."

Lilly giggled. "Indeed."

"Okay, no pun intended. However—"

Mary interrupted. "What I'm trying to say is that I don't want to just stand around and hope someone notices me or invites me to do things anymore."

"I don't either, but what can you do?" Lilly asked. "It's like our futures were determined when we were little girls."

"I can't do much at home, but I can be different in Pine-craft, right?" Though she was doing her best to sound confident, Mary realized she was really looking to them for guidance and support.

Betsy slowly nodded. "You're right. I can't exactly hide my stuttering, but no one here has to know that I'm an asthmatic with an overprotective mamm."

"No one is going to know I'm an adopted foster child except for you two," Lilly said. "What about you, Mary?"

"No one is going to bring up any embarrassing situations from my past because I'm not going to say a word about them. From this point on, all I'm going to be is Mary Margaret from Trail, Ohio."

Feeling cleansed by their confessions and almost buoyant, she added, "And you know what? I don't care if we make a ton of other friends anyway. If the three of us stick together, we can have our own fun, right?"

"Right." Betsy grinned. "Starting this minute, we are wallflowers no more."

A knock on the door interrupted their conversation. After peeking through the peephole and seeing Anna, their English guide, and her husband Jerry, the bus driver, Mary opened the door. "Yes?"

Jerry held out a pizza box. "Here you go, girls. One pepperoni pizza and three sodas. Do you need anything else?"

Mary looked at the other two girls, then shook her head. "Danke, but nee. We have everything we need right here."

Anna smiled at the three of them. "I knew it. I told Jerry here that if there were three people on our bus who were going to take this setback in stride, it was you three pretty girls. I bet none of you has ever met a stranger."

Mary just smiled, but as she closed the door, she felt a surge of satisfaction. She might be in a run-down motel room in the middle of an ice storm . . . but already her future was looking a whole lot brighter.

Shelley Shepard Gray is the *New York Times* and *USA Today* bestselling author of more than 100 books, including *Her Heart's Desire* and *Her Only Wish*. Two-time winner of the HOLT Medallion and a Carol Award finalist, Gray lives in Ohio, where she writes full-time, bakes too much, and can often be found walking her dachshunds on her town's bike trail. Learn more at www.ShelleyShepardGray.com.

TRAVEL TO PINECRAFT
WITH THE FIRST IN THE SERIES,
Her Heart's Desire

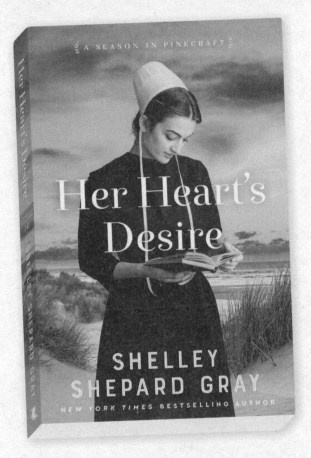

RETURN TO PINECRAFT WITH
Her Only Wish

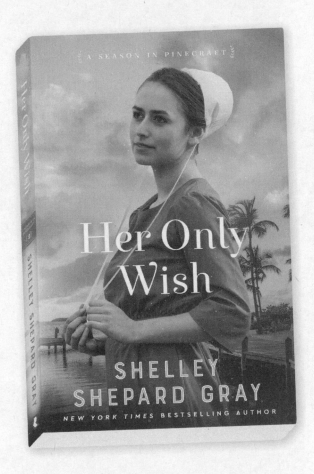

"*Her Only Wish* features Betsy in an uplifting story of
friendship and the power of a renewed perspective.
A noteworthy elevation of an enjoyable series."

—*Booklist*

If You Want More Sweet Amish Romance, Pick Up *Lost and Found* by Suzanne Woods Fisher

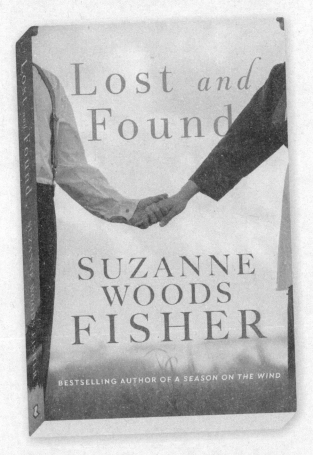

Trudy Yoder shares a passion for birding with Micah Weaver—and she has an even greater passion for Micah. Her romantic hopes fizzle when Micah volunteers to scout a church relocation. Trudy doesn't know that he's searching for her estranged sister who once broke his heart. And Micah doesn't realize that what you're looking for isn't always what you find.

Meet Shelley

Find her at **ShelleyShepardGray.com**

AND ON SOCIAL MEDIA AT

ShelleyShepardGray   ShelleySGray   Shelley.S.Gray